MURDER AT HARBOR VILLAGE

Barry tried to follow me onto the porch and set up a little howl when I closed the door with him still inside.

"My grandson," I said to the chief.

He nodded. "I understand you'll be working here, Ms. Mack, and I wonder if you can help us. We need to identify this woman."

"Dolly Webb didn't know her?"

"She didn't look. Some people are squeamish."

"I'd be glad to help." I didn't want to be considered squeamish. "But I haven't met many people here yet."

"Just come take a look."

I agreed. "Let me tell Stephanie where I'm going."

Chief Boozer talked while we walked. "I'm thinking she's too young to live here. Might be a staff member. Or somebody's daughter."

That gave me a jolt. Having a daughter of my own, I'd have to try to help.

"Or maybe she lives nearby," the chief went on. "The office staff isn't here yet and people in that back building are busy with dressing and breakfast. All their residents are accounted for, they say."

We crossed the parking lot, sand and gravel crunching with our steps. There was yellow crime scene tape around the pool now.

I was imagining what a body would look like after a drowning...

Books by G.P. Gardner

Murder at Harbor Village

Published by Kensington Publishing Corporation

Murder at Harbor Village

GP Gardner

LYRICAL UNDERGROUND
Kensington Publishing Corp.
www.kensingtonbooks.com

Mys
Gardn

LYRICAL UNDERGROUND BOOKS are published by
Kensington Publishing Corp.
119 West 40th Street

New York, NY 10018

All Kensington titles, imprints, and distributed lines are available at special quantity discounts for bulk purchases for sales promotion, premiums, fund-raising, educational, or institutional use.

Special book excerpts or customized printings can also be created to fit specific needs. For details, write or phone the office of the Kensington Sales Manager: Kensington Publishing Corp., 119 West 40th Street, New York, NY 10018. Attn. Sales Department. Phone: 1-800-221-2647.

Lyrical Underground and Lyrical Underground logo Reg. US Pat. & TM Off.

First Electronic Edition: November 2018
eISBN-13: 978-1-5161-0899-2
eISBN-10: 1-5161-0899-X

First Print Edition: November 2018
ISBN-13: 978-1-5161-0900-5
ISBN-10: 1-5161-0900-7

Printed in the United States of America

Acknowledgments

Thanks to the Thursday lunch group—Bud, Jon, and Diane—who provided ideas and answers and constant encouragement. And thanks to my wonderful agent, Dawn Dowdle, and to editor John Scognamiglio and the staff at Kensington.

Chapter 1

Sucker punched. That was the way I described my first few hours in Fairhope.

I drove down from Atlanta on a Wednesday, planning to stay three nights and get some serious thinking done. It was late June, hot and sunny. School was out and the Fourth of July was coming up, so there was a line of traffic on the interstate near the beach exits, but the old highway from Bay Minette to Spanish Fort was wide open.

I found the motel right away, a Holiday Express out on the four-lane. By the time I'd unloaded the car and made multiple trips across the asphalt parking lot, I was drenched with perspiration, so I showered and changed into cropped white pants and a striped pullover. Just like that, I was transformed from wrinkled, apprehensive college professor to relaxed tourist.

"Where do you recommend for dinner?" I asked at the desk.

"What do you like to eat? Seafood?" The clerk was college age with a flop of dark hair and tiny gold ear studs. He pulled out a list of restaurants and highlighted a couple of choices then marked locations on a map of town and handed it to me with a copy of the weekly newspaper.

"I see I asked the right person." I stacked the items he'd given me.

"There's an art walk Friday night and a concert and fireworks on the Fourth, if it doesn't rain."

I thanked him and walked out to the car, where I sat with the door open, fanning myself with the newspaper while I studied the map.

I thought of Fairhope as a village, although technically it was too large for the word, but it had a village vibe—a schizophrenic variety of shops, old and new, mixed up with scads of people. There were flowers everywhere, even hanging from the lampposts, and benches tucked in wherever there was room. People of all ages sat on the benches or jogged with baby strollers or walked little dogs fresh from the groomer.

I whipped into a just-vacated parking space in front of a deli, plunked myself down on one of the benches and called my daughter, Stephanie, in Birmingham.

"You have got to see this place, honey. It's St. Mary Mead come to life. Without the stone walls."

"Mom," she whined, meaning I should get a grip and hurry on up to Birmingham. "I'll bet it's hot. How's the bay? I heard it's so full of duck poop you can't swim."

"Haven't seen it yet. And you know I don't swim. But the town...you are going to love the town."

As anyone could have guessed from that conversation, she didn't want me moving to Fairhope. Not that I'd even considered it before she got all huffy on the subject.

I set out on a quick tour of downtown, walking off the day's fatigue. I found a bookstore, a coffee shop, a couple of breakfast places, a couple of banks, clothing boutiques, a town clock, art galleries, consignment shops and candy stores and at least a dozen people who smiled and spoke as if they knew me.

I found my car again and was smiling even before I rounded a curve and saw Mobile Bay, with the sun suspended low in the cloud-filled sky, reflecting off the water. I probably gasped, but there was no one else in the car to hear.

And I wasn't the only one who appreciated the scenery. At the rose garden beside the water, pedestrians zigzagged in all directions, ignoring crosswalks. I parked again and headed for the pier, following the sidewalk that circled the fountain. A gust of wind hit the tower of water and gave me and a few shrieking kids an unexpected misting. A few feet farther and I stopped to lean over low boxwood hedges for a close-up sniff of a few perfect rose blooms. Talk about clichés!

The wind picked up at the pier, a quarter-mile long concrete span stretching out into the bay. Halfway out, the seafood restaurant provided a brief windbreak, and I rearranged my windblown hair while I admired the sailboats tied up in the little marina.

"Here, let me make room for you." A tiny, white-haired woman slid to the middle of her bench.

I thanked her and sat down.

"Looks like the sailboats are going in." She pointed to a flock of small boats half a mile away. "Are you a regular?"

I gave her a blank look.

"I don't think I've seen you here before."

"My first visit. I read about it in an article on retirement hot spots." She held out a delicate, bony hand. "I'm Nita Bergen."

"Cleo Mack."

"And have you found a house yet, Cleo?"

I laughed at this. And then I said the strangest thing: "Not yet."

I wound up telling Nita Bergen my life story...the condensed version ending with the topic I had come to Fairhope to consider. "I'm not even fifty yet and they've just offered me early retirement."

She was so sympathetic. "Oh, my dear. That's such a big decision. And you didn't expect it?"

"The problem is, I have to decide right away. Before the fall semester begins. And there's a nice cash bonus if I accept, but it's a one-time-only offer. No pressure there."

"Oh, my dear!" She was an excellent listener, picking up every nuance and asking frequent questions.

Eventually I apologized for talking so much. "How rude of me. I haven't learned anything about you. Have you always lived here?"

She shook her head, every silver hair in place, in spite of the wind. "I was born in Virginia, lived there all my life, and retired from the government. But my husband had connections here and he always talked about coming back. I would say 'Al-a-*bam*-a?' and turn up my nose. But one summer we drove here from South Florida, and as soon as I saw those big oaks, with ferns growing on their branches, and the Spanish moss and flowers and the nicest people anywhere..." She threw her hands up. "What could I say?"

I nodded, having just experienced almost the same reaction. "And was it the right decision?"

She nodded emphatically. "I love Fairhope. And you will, too."

I laughed and tried, too late, to apply the brakes a little. "I haven't really made the decision yet."

"I know a good realtor."

We sat on the bench while the sun sank in the western sky. Nita introduced me to half a dozen people walking on the pier and, when it was just the two of us, we talked. At last the molten, glowing mass reached the horizon and people stopped all around us to watch. After the briefest interval, no more than a couple of minutes, the sun dropped out of sight. And the crowd actually applauded!

"Wait," Nita said softly, patting my hand to keep me in place on the bench. Her gaze had shifted upward, to the sky above us. "Just watch now."

Almost immediately, the sky lit up, the clouds turning coral and pink and gold, with a few streaks of purple. Gradually, the glow swelled and expanded to fill half the sky. I'd never seen anything like it, and tears filled my eyes.

Nita seemed pleased with the sky and with my reaction. "I thought it might be good today. The clouds have to be just right. And it won't last long. Keep watching."

Sure enough, after about a minute, the colors began to fade. Dark crept up around us, and even the air changed, cooling perceptibly as the breeze became more persistent.

"Doesn't it make you think of a cathedral? A sky cathedral."

The big show was over and the flow of pedestrians ebbed toward shore. Nita removed her sweater from her shoulders, draped it over one arm and picked up her handbag, ready to depart.

I dropped my sunglasses into my bag. "How is this restaurant?"

"Oh, you haven't eaten? And it's so late already!" She was silent a moment. "We come here sometimes, but always at lunch. I can stay if you want company, but I'll have to call Jim."

The restaurant was crowded and cold. Nita worried that I didn't have a sweater, but I lied that I was warm enough. I ordered shrimp and grits, served with Conecuh sausage and sweet peppers. It arrived quickly, considering the crowd, with a cup of hot tea and tiramisu for Nita. She cut the dessert into halves and then sliced one half into two parts.

"You'll want to try this, and I'll take some home for Jim." She pushed one of the small pieces onto the edge of my plate and took a bite of the other one. "How can you retire at such a young age? You won't be eligible for Social Security for years."

We talked while I ate, and she shared my focus on practical things like income, housing and insurance.

"Are you married? Do you have family there?"

I shook my head. "No husband, and my only daughter's in Birmingham. She thinks I should move there, but I'm not so sure. I don't want to be too close, if you know what I mean."

She nodded knowingly. "Too bad we sold our home last year. You could've stayed with us until you found a house. But there's no guest room in the apartment."

"I don't know that I want a house." I noted her inexplicable generosity to someone she'd just met. "I'm already envying my friends who don't have to deal with lawns and leaks but just call the manager when an appliance quits."

"A condo? There aren't many good apartments, but there are some condos on the bay. Let me call my realtor friend."

We swapped phone numbers, and I paid for our food, over her protests, then we walked to the parking lot together. Even with the breeze, the night air felt warm after the air-conditioning of the restaurant.

I held her Buick's door open, while she buckled up, then handed her the takeout box with Jim's dessert. "Thanks for staying with me."

"I'm here most evenings. Unless it's raining. But we'll talk tomorrow, I'm sure."

I drove back through the enchanting little downtown to my motel, walked by the desk to tell the nice young clerk how much I'd enjoyed my dinner on the pier and went to my room. After brushing my teeth and changing into pajamas, I got out a book of Sudoku puzzles, swiveled the television toward the lounge chair with ottoman and fell sound asleep. Even Stephanie's phone calls didn't rouse me.

Thursday morning I called her back.

"Mom!" She was fired up. "I called you twice last night!"

"I was in a noisy restaurant. Didn't see your message until late. What's up?"

"I was calling to tell you to come here tomorrow. I can arrange to be off so we can look at houses and apartments all afternoon."

It was what I had expected, more of the same push she had started a week ago.

"I don't think so, honey. You'll be tired at the end of the week, and you and Boyd need some time for the baby. Anyway, I get a special rate on the room if I stay three nights."

She sniffed. "Someone wants to pay you to quit working. How hard can the decision be?"

I shifted to my professor voice. "As you know, it's not just a matter of leaving my job, which I usually like. I have to figure out whether I'll have enough money. Should I get a job, where will I live, how will I spend my time? It's not always easy to make new friends at my age." But I already had one here, didn't I?

"Well, I had another reason for calling. There's a quilt show at the Fairhope Art Center and some of our Guild members have entries. I was hoping you could take photos of the display and send them to me." She gave me the names of three individuals and I scribbled them down. "Susan has two entries, so be sure you get both of hers. And get all the prizewinners.

If you'll send the photos today, I can post them in the shop before tonight's class. And you'll be here Saturday? You promise?"

"Early afternoon." I added the numeral 2 beside Susan's name.

I had breakfast at the oldest restaurant in town, according to its window sign. While I ate, the men at the next table talked about poetry. I tried to focus on my financial materials, but it was hard to ignore two old men talking about *internal rhyme* and Billy Collins, so I didn't accomplish much.

I was eager to get out and see more of the town. The restaurant manager invited me to come in again and gave me directions to the art center. I got there as it opened for the day. A chatty volunteer named CJ was working the front desk, and I told her about the errand Stephanie had given me.

"She'll want this listing of the entries." CJ handed me a slick, colorful flyer. "It tells you if the item is for sale and what the price is. Do you quilt?"

"No. But Stephanie co-owns a shop in Birmingham and has tried to get me interested. She thinks I need a retirement hobby."

CJ wanted to know all about Stephanie's shop—where it was located, what type of sewing machines and sergers did it carry, was it participating in the row-by-row project, whatever that was.

I shook my head. "I really don't know much about it, but I can give you a card. Do you often have quilts on display here?" I searched in my shoulder bag for my wallet, where I kept a few of Stephanie's business cards.

"Once a year." CJ gave a little pout. "It's usually the three Ps. Painting, pottery, photography. We have classes." She gave me a copy of the class schedule and a membership application. "And we can always use volunteers, if you're interested."

I handed over Stephanie's card and got out a ten-dollar bill to push into the Plexiglas donation box on the desk. Then I spent a pleasant hour looking at colorful quilts in intricate designs, ranging from king-sized to micro. I took a lot of photographs, including shots of the ribbons Susan had won, and e-mailed all of them to Stephanie.

It was almost noon when I finally got to the bay. I parked on the bluff above the rose garden, where tall, skinny pines framed a military memorial and a gorgeous view of Mobile Bay. I walked across the grass and selected one of several benches with a panoramic view. The temperature was already pushing toward ninety, I guessed, and I could just make out a large ship, maybe a tanker, against the opposite shore. Closer by, a persistent movement in one of the trees kept drawing my attention, but I could see nothing there. A squirrel, I thought, but a squirrel should move around. Finally, I got up and walked closer, expecting to find an injured bird or a trapped butterfly.

At first I didn't know what I was seeing, then I realized that what I'd thought was a knot on the tree was actually a camera, encased in a plastic cover. A webcam. I looked where it was aimed, at the rose garden in the park down below. The camera emitted faint clicks as it panned right to left, slowly and erratically.

I walked back to my bench and got there in time to hear my phone ringing.

Nita was calling. "I'm just letting you know my friend Vickie is making a list of homes and condos for you to see. You can stop at her office this afternoon and pick it up, or she can drop it off here and you can get it tonight. I hope you'll come play dominoes with us. We have a little group that gets together every week and one of us can't be here tonight. And we always send out for sandwiches."

I said I'd love to come, and got directions. And then I switched the phone to voice mail and spent the next ninety minutes sitting on a too-low, too-hard wooden bench, brushing off an occasional ant and completing a retirement planning form the HR office had given me.

When I finished, I was happy but hungry. The webcam was moving around again as I walked past it, heading back to the car. It made me think of a lizard's eye, and I wondered if it followed me as I walked.

As I approached the car, I noticed a sign for a restaurant, a block down the street. I dropped my folder in the car, clicked the doors locked again and kept walking.

The restaurant was in an old house, with a street-side wooden deck that held eight or ten tables, separated by arrangements of potted shrubs and herbs. Inside, there were more tables, all occupied, and a line of people waiting at a takeout counter. I was about to get in line when a woman, sitting alone at a table for four, waved in my direction and motioned me over.

"Are you waiting for someone?" she asked when I was close enough to hear her. "If not, you can join me."

"Cleo Mack." I pulled out the chair across from her and stuck out my hand. "You're so kind. I'm beginning to think this is the nicest town in the world."

"Jamie Barnes." She had a killer grip and an impersonal smile. She was thirty-something, I guessed, sporty looking, with shockingly white teeth and straight, shoulder-length hair streaked in shades of gold. Her sleeveless white shirt exposed well-muscled, suntanned arms. "I take it you're a visitor."

"My second day in town. Do you live here?"

The server, in a rush, dropped off a basket of breadsticks and chanted the day's specials. Jamie was eating a salad with a piece of fish and drinking red wine. I decided on the quinoa salad the server recommended, with iced tea.

"I moved here from New Orleans, and before that, Pensacola, and before that, Tampa. I've moved around some, but I seem to be stuck on the Gulf Coast." Jamie tucked a strand of hair behind one ear and took a sip of wine. "I'm an RN, but I work in administration mostly. What about you?"

"Social work. I teach and chair my university department, in Atlanta."

Her eyes narrowed. "Tell me more. You have friends here?"

"No. I drove down to do some thinking. Seems I've unexpectedly become eligible to retire, and it's thrown me for a loop."

"Why does nothing like that ever happen to me? Are you going to do it?"

Moment of truth. I hesitated and then nodded, answering my own question, as much as hers. "Yes, I think I will."

As soon as I said it, a smile ignited in my chest and blossomed all the way to my cheeks; I was going to retire! I laughed and felt almost giddy. "I may need a part-time job, but I should be able to dig something up. Teach a course or two, maybe, or consult."

The server brought my lunch and refilled my glass. The salad had a tangy, citrusy dressing that was quite tasty, or maybe I was just hungry; after all, it was three hours past my usual lunchtime. I ate quickly, listening to Jamie or answering the questions she posed.

"And you'll move to Fairhope?"

"I think so. I like what I've seen, and I need a bit of an adventure."

"You're not looking for a husband, I hope. It's a buyer's market here. You want a husband, you buy one."

I shook my head. "I'm out of the marriage market. I had a bad one and a good one and quit while I was winning."

"Same here. Now I'm in a relationship that's outlasted the marriages."

Um-hum, my urban self said, *want to bet that partner's female?*

Jamie was smiling, looking toward the water. "That's Mobile across the bay. I guess you know that."

I looked, but the far horizon was a featureless, lavender haze, not unlike my future.

Jamie had shifted to telling me about her work. "Ever hear of Harbor Health Service? Based in Houston. We own nursing homes and independent or assisted living facilities all over the South. The facility here is Harbor Village. I'm sure you've seen it."

I didn't think so.

"You should stop by. We're out on the four-lane. We have apartments and condos for independent living, and we just expanded our Assisted Living unit. No nursing home, but you'd be surprised how many people get by with assisted living if the services are enhanced and personalized. And every little enhancement increases revenue." She arched her eyebrows and laughed, apparently sharing an insider joke with me.

I needed to pay closer attention. "And how do you decide to transfer a resident to a skilled nursing facility?" It was a question such places wrestled with, I knew.

She shrugged. "Our policy is pretty flexible. Officially, it's when the activities of daily living require more than one aide. I see you know the issues. Is your specialization with seniors?"

"I have to stay up to date. I supervise interns at some facilities like yours."

"Really? How long are you going to be in town?"

"Just one more day. I'm going to look at housing tomorrow and drive to Birmingham Saturday."

A few minutes later we paid our checks and left. Jamie got into a BMW two-seat convertible parked beside the deck, and I walked back to my car on the bluff. I wasn't sure I liked Jamie Barnes much, but it didn't seem important, since I never expected to see her again.

With the financial planning done, I was feeling more like a tourist. Or a prospective resident. I picked up a box of chocolates made at one of the little candy shops and then drove slowly through some residential neighborhoods. Houses on the north bluff were large and imposing. South of the pier, the elevation dropped, the streets were shadier and the houses more modest and charming, surrounded by live oaks, palm trees, big-leafed fatsia and elephant ears and chaste trees in shades of white and blue and purple. Near the water, streamers of gray Spanish moss swung from the trees.

There were only a few houses with "For Sale" signs, but when I saw one, I pulled over and checked the size and interior photos and price, using the real estate app on my phone. Nothing was cheap, certainly not the little blue cottage with a picket fence and screened front porch, and not even the plain-Jane red brick ranch house with jalousie windows, straight out of the sixties. I began to wonder where ordinary people lived in this town.

I crisscrossed the area, angling gradually back toward my motel. When I got there, I showered and dressed for dominoes with Nita and friends. I put on a peach-colored linen shirt with black pants and ballet flats, checked my reflection in the mirror, picked up the box of chocolates and went to the lobby.

The same gangly clerk was on duty again, and I noticed his nametag said Hunter. He was chatting with a family with three little kids. When they moved away from the desk, he greeted me. "Hi there. Enjoying your visit?"

I nodded. "I wonder about people who grow up here. Wasn't the rest of the world a letdown for you?"

He laughed. "I didn't grow up here. And I don't live here now. Robertsdale is twelve miles away and a different world. And the other side of the bay—I go to the University of South Alabama now—is a different universe."

I showed him the directions Nita had given me and he pointed north. "Go past the shopping center and it'll be on your left. There's a big display at the entrance, wooden pilings and ropes and carved pelicans. Harbor Village, the sign says. It's for old people."

"Oh. I've heard of Harbor Village, but I didn't realize my friend lived there."

He was blushing and stammering, waving his hands like he was under attack by bees. "I didn't mean to say old people. I meant seniors. Retirees! It's a nice place, really. Lots of their family members stay here. Don't tell anybody I said old people. I'll be fired."

I grinned at him and went out to the car.

I had no trouble finding Harbor Village. There was a carved wood sign, with pelicans and posts, and a banner beneath saying *It Takes a Village*. The place made a good first impression, with a wide street, a grassy median with flowers and palm trees, and an abundance of parking. Residential buildings were painted pastel beach colors—yellow and green and pink—while the large, central building looked like something from a fairy tale, three stories tall with a thatch-like black roof, dormers, red shutters, hanging ferns and a wrap-around porch. I spotted a beauty shop, a restaurant and a swimming pool. No sign of Mickey and Minnie, and no children, but there was definitely an air of fantasy about the place.

Nita's building was at the corner, beside a row of garages. I parked under a five-globe lamppost and picked up my handbag and the box of candy.

"Hello there! I'm Jim," a man boomed, sweeping the apartment door open. "You must be Cleo. Come in, come in." Jim was a confident, erect, take-charge kind of guy, well over six feet, with thick, wavy, snow-white hair. He shook my hand vigorously. "I've heard a lot about you."

Nita came out of the kitchen, drying her hands and looking even tinier beside her husband. She gave me a hug and began to introduce two people watching us from the couch.

Jim interrupted. "Do you know Dolly Webb, Cleo? And this is Riley Meddors. Now, they're not a couple. They're both single and on the make. Right, Dolly?"

Nita looked embarrassed. "Jim, are you serving the wine?" She gave me a slight eye roll and I handed her the box of chocolates. "Oh, my dear, you didn't need to—"

"Red or white?" Jim noticed the candy and took the box from Nita's hands. "Cleo, you have discovered my weakness! Look, Nita. Dark chocolate. I'll just put it here beside my chair."

Nita and Jim were opposites, physically, and the same was true for Dolly and Riley, but Dolly was the taller, more athletic of that pair. A turquoise shirt and silver necklace set off her short white hair.

Riley was cheerful and low-key, with an easy smile and hair still more reddish-brown than gray. "Nice to meet you." He shook my hand and then returned to the couch.

"We don't know any social workers or college professors," Nita said, "but we invited the smartest people we know. Dolly is a mathematician and Riley is a banker."

"*Was* a banker." Riley gave me a boyish grin. "Now I'm a lazy bum."

"My husband was a mathematician," I said to Dolly. "Did you teach?"

She waved the question away. "No. I worked forty years in a basement with no windows. Who was your husband?"

I told her Robert's name and she gave a little start and looked at me more closely. "Oh, yes, of course, Robert Mack. A great guy, everybody knew him. I forget, did he die about a year ago?"

"Hard to believe it's been almost four years." I felt a special little bond with Dolly.

I knew the moment I saw the Bergens' apartment that a decorator had been in charge. Furnishings weren't lined up with the walls but clustered to create functional areas. A thick carpet, in muted shades of red and gold and acid green, was angled under the couches. At the back of the room, a fig tree reached for the skylight, tiny white lights winding through its leafy branches.

"What a beautiful apartment, Nita." I turned in a circle, taking in artwork, track lights and luxurious fabrics. "It looks like the cover of *Architectural Digest*."

Dolly agreed. "That's exactly what I tell her."

"Thank you, dears. I can't take credit for the décor. We had someone do it. Otherwise we'd still be in the house, quibbling over what we should keep."

"My mother taught me the rules of decorating," Jim said. "Something dark and something light, something dull and something bright. That's just what we got. Plus, I wanted nice firm arms to push up with, not those low, squishy things. Would you like a tour, Cleo?" He handed me a glass of wine. "Just be careful with that drink and come this way. I'll let Nita show you the kitchen later."

"I want to come, too." Dolly struggled to her feet.

"You've seen it lots of times," Jim said.

"Yes, I know. But I want to see it again. With all this decorating going on, I may decide to do something to my place."

I caught Riley's glance and we traded smiles.

The private side of the apartment was just two bedrooms and two baths, with a utility room separating them. Jim had taken the larger bedroom for an office, furnishing it with an executive-sized desk plus a worktable, a wall of bookcases, a recliner, a TV and a daybed. "If one of us isn't feeling well, I sleep back here."

He had also taken the master closet and filled it with neatly arranged clothing, color-coded containers in a variety of sizes and an army of shoes on slanted shelves. The adjoining bathroom had a large, tiled shower. "If I'm ever in a wheelchair, I can roll right in and hose down. And here's the panic cord. Pull it and security will be here in a couple of minutes, day or night. There's one in every room."

Dolly was examining the various shaving, dental, and skin care products and devices arrayed on shelves between the twin sinks. "You'd have to get up awfully early to use all this stuff. And don't be too sure about security. My neighbor pulled the cord at midnight and nobody came."

Jim herded us toward the second bedroom. "This is where we sleep, and Nita gets the bathroom in here." He pushed the door open. Nita's bathroom was half the size of his. "There's a tub in here. She likes that."

"Very nice," I said.

Whatever toiletries Nita used must be confined to the vanity drawers; the glistening countertop held a box of tissues and a blooming peace lily.

It was a luxurious apartment, with a garage in the building next door, round-the-clock security and certainly a maintenance crew at the ready. It was located next to a shopping center and only a mile or so from the bay, and it was exactly what I wanted. The question was, could I afford it?

Jim led us back to the main room, where Nita and Riley had prepared the table for dominoes. "Want me to call in the sandwich order?"

"I've already done it." Nita took the chair Riley held for her. "They'll be here at six thirty."

"Well, I've got work to do. Call me when they get here." Jim headed for his office.

We played a game called Mexican Trains. Riley and Dolly were quick and competitive players, but I had to ask a lot of questions about the rules, and the first hour slipped by quickly.

When the doorbell rang, Jim popped out of his office to answer it and returned to the table with bags of sandwiches and potato chips. "It was forty-five dollars, including the tip. Which comes to what, Riley?"

"Nine dollars each." He was pushing the game tiles to the center of the table, making room around the perimeter for dining.

"Like a human calculator," Jim told me.

Dolly and I prepared and served drinks, while Nita cut the sandwiches into smaller pieces and arranged them on a pair of apple-patterned platters. Jim passed around plates and then filled his with several big sections of Philly cheesesteak. I took turkey with greens and cheese and another filled with a still warm, aromatic mixture of sautéed zucchini, red peppers and onions.

"That's my favorite." Nita took a similar piece.

"Listen, Cleo," Jim said. "The clock is chiming. That's the Westminster melody, you know."

It was a familiar campus sound. I asked Dolly and Riley, "Do you live here, too?"

"Yes," they answered and set about explaining Harbor Village to me.

"There're six apartment buildings. This is one of two doughnuts," Dolly said. "I have a one-bedroom around back, but it's nothing like this."

I didn't understand. "Two doughnuts?"

She nodded. "A square doughnut, of course."

Riley elaborated. "We call it that because of the shape of the building. You'll see it in an aerial photo Harbor Village uses in promotional materials. There's an open courtyard in the middle."

"Oh." An interior courtyard was a nice touch and had the additional advantage of reducing the number of close neighbors.

"And across the street is another building just like this one," Dolly said. "Both of them green."

Jim was eating, apparently ignoring the conversation.

"And next door…" Nita prompted.

"The next building is L-shaped, one on either side of the Boulevard," Dolly said. "Riley lives there."

"The pink buildings," Riley said. "And next to them are yellow, U-shaped buildings. The two-story buildings have elevators, of course."

"Don't forget the condos," Nita said.

Jim suddenly tuned into the conversation but must have misunderstood. "No, honey, the condos don't have elevators. They're all one level."

Dolly ignored him. "You saw the condos when you came in, and there's another set at the back of the complex."

"And an Assisted Living building." Jim tapped his temple. "Thinking ahead."

"Something we hope we'll never need." Nita smiled.

"Hope for the best, plan for the worst." Jim took another section of sandwich.

Dolly continued, "And then there's the wedding cake."

"The what?" I was puzzled again, which amused them. "I'm detecting a bakery theme."

Riley shook his head, smiling and chewing.

"Some people think the main building looks like a wedding cake," Nita explained.

"Three tiers," Dolly said.

I nodded, recalling the huge white building with the imposing black roof and red shutters. "I might've said a house from a fairy tale. It needs round-faced children hanging out of the top windows."

"Most of us call it the big house," Jim said. "You know, like a prison."

"Well, I don't like that connotation." Nita frowned.

"Tell me about living here. Is there a waiting list?"

There was a burst of laughter.

"Oh, I was hoping you'd consider it," Nita said. "But can you get in? There's supposed to be an age limit, but I don't know how strictly it's enforced. It would be so nice to have some young people here."

"Not too young," Jim cautioned. "You don't have children, do you?"

"I wonder about vacancies," Riley said. "The upstairs units in my building are usually empty, but I see people going up there all the time lately. Some of them look pretty young."

"Age fifty-five and up," Jim said firmly. "Says so on the sign out front. Now, Dolly, what were you saying about security not coming when somebody pulled the cord? What night was that?"

"Oh, I don't remember. A week ago."

"Last Thursday? I'll see who was on duty. Might need to say something to management."

Nita steered us back to the apartment question. "Do you think you might move here, Cleo?"

I nodded. "But I should go slow and see how the idea wears. I'll have a house to sell, and I haven't moved in fifteen years."

"One step at a time," Riley said.

"Hire it done," Dolly said. "That's what I did."

"People say Fairhope is an ordinary little California coastal town," Jim said, "that just happens to be located in Alabama."

When we finished eating, we cleared the table and the four of us played dominoes until the clock chimed 8:30. Riley won.

"Riley always wins." Nita smiled sweetly.

"How does he do it?" Dolly wondered. "I tried to watch tonight, to see what strategy you use, but I didn't see anything out of the ordinary."

Riley smiled and got out his wallet. "Nine dollars, everybody, for the sandwiches. I'll treat you, Cleo, since it's your first time."

I protested, but it did no good.

And Nita waved away my offer of assistance with the cleanup. "No, honey. It's just loading the dishwasher now. And I'm so happy you might be moving here. It's given me a burst of energy."

"Get a unit with a garage." Jim had come out of his lair to see us off. "That'll be this building or the one across the street. Garages are in the next building but that's better than not having one."

"Upstairs units are the bargain," Riley said. "Cheaper and less noise."

"And you can sleep with the windows open," Dolly said.

"No, you don't." Jim shook his head.

"I didn't say I did. I said you could if you lived upstairs. Anyway, how do you know I don't?"

Jim reddened and chuckled. "I pay attention, Dolly. Security, you know. I've never seen your windows open."

"That sounds like an excuse to snoop around. Somebody may shoot you."

We lingered at the table until Dolly looked at her watch and stood up abruptly. "Nine o'clock. Bedtime."

"Dolly swims at six every morning," Jim said.

"Just weekdays." She picked up her glass and set it on the ledge of the pass-through to the kitchen. "Would you like to join me tomorrow, Cleo?"

I shook my head. "Maybe next time."

"I'll walk you out as I go," Riley said to me. "That is, if you're ready to leave. We keep early hours here."

"No, no." Jim ignored a sharp look from Nita. "I'll see Cleo to her car. Almost time for my nightly patrol, anyway."

"I hope you find a house or condo tomorrow, dear. Don't forget the materials Vickie left for you. Did you make an appointment with her?"

I told her we were meeting at ten the next morning and verified that I knew where to find Vickie's office, while Jim let the others out.

He waited beside the door for me, holding his cane, a flashlight and an overstuffed envelope from the realtor. "Looks like you've got homework to do, Cleo. If I were you, I'd think about housing from an investment standpoint. Harbor Village isn't cheap but it's good value for the money."

Nita gave me a hug.

Jim and I walked across the porch and down the sidewalk.

"Did you say you do a patrol every night?"

"Oh yes. Just keeping an eye on things. Part of the military training."

"You were in the military?"

"Thirty years. But that was then, and this is now. Where are you staying?"

I clicked the car unlocked and named the motel, and he nodded.

"Nice place. They have a little Continental breakfast every morning. Lots of fruit. Get yourself a banana for later in the day." He closed the car door with a slam and gave me a salute.

Chapter 2

I called Stephanie when I got back to the motel. She sounded a little grim and asked immediately, suspiciously, "You haven't made a decision, have you?"

"I think I may do it, honey, but I don't want to worry about money. Everything okay with you?"

"Dad called. He's getting married again."

"Good for him." I hadn't seen Travis in years and wasn't even sure where he lived now, but it seemed he and Stephanie were trying to get to know each other. I suddenly wondered if he had other children, but it wasn't the right moment to ask. "You know what they say, third time's the charm."

"Yeah, but this is the fourth time. That I know of."

"Oh. Well. Anyone you know?"

"Some woman from Louisiana. I met her once and she was rude to both of us. Mom, are you sure you don't want to drive up here tomorrow? I can cancel the sitter and we'll stay home and visit."

I hated to let her down when she was clearly feeling a little insecure, but I was pretty sure I was dodging a bullet on this moving-to-Birmingham proposal. "I've still got a few things to do here, but I'll see you Saturday."

Vickie, the real estate agent, had two houses and one condo lined up to show me Friday morning.

The houses looked good from the street but inside we found small, dark rooms, low ceilings and musty odors. And the prices were well above my absolute maximum.

"Don't worry too much about list price," Vickie told me as I sputtered over the first one. "Agents are always hoping some fool will come along.

And you'd be surprised how often it happens. But I don't waste my time if a place is really off the chart."

The final place we saw, a condo, was affordable and nicely customized with oak cabinets and granite counters in the kitchen and bath and built-in bookcases surrounding the sliding doors to the patio. A hall closet had been converted to a mini-office, but there was no room for Stephanie to stay over occasionally. The location was ideal, right on the bay and a short walk to restaurants and shops, but the only view was of the next building, and it was on the ground floor.

"I don't think I'd like people looking in the windows." I looked out at a woman walking past.

She waved, and I waved back.

"But there are no steps," Vickie said. "Maybe you're not old enough to appreciate that."

"I'm old enough to be thinking about Harbor Village. What do you think of it? Can I get in if I'm not fifty-five?"

"Probably. If they've got vacancies. Ask Jim Bergen. He's got some favors to call in, I'm sure."

She turned off the lights and locked the doors and we walked back to her car. "I've got a nice place I'm about to list in the fruits and nuts, but I can't show it until Monday. When are you leaving?"

"Tomorrow. What are the fruits and nuts?"

She laughed. "The streets in the old part of town are named for local fruits and nuts. Pecan, Pomelo, Satsuma. So when we say fruits and nuts, we mean near the bay and pricey. And maybe a little weird."

I invited her to join me for lunch.

"I wish I could, but I've got a closing in Daphne in an hour. To be honest, I never have time for lunch."

Her emaciated appearance suggested that time was pretty scarce for the other meals, too.

"Business must be good."

She rolled her eyes. "It's cutthroat. Most people can't take it. I hope you aren't thinking of trying."

I rode to Vickie's office with her, got my car, drove back into town and lunched at Andree's, a cute deli that had caught my eye earlier. About twenty tables were crowded together on a black-and-red checkerboard floor. The food was good, the staff friendly and the prices reasonable. And while I ate, I planned my afternoon.

My first job involved a little shopping. I left the car where it was and walked a block to de la Mare Street, where I got another box of chocolates.

Then I spent some time browsing through Fairhope Soap Company, making up a gift basket for Stephanie. After that, I had to rush in the bookstore, where a knowledgeable clerk helped me choose a couple of books for Barry, my grandson who was almost two.

The next stop was the motel, to leave the chocolates in a cool place. While I was there, I returned some phone calls, including one from my dean. I caught him still in the office.

"I was wondering if you've made a decision. Looks like everybody else will take the money and run."

"I've got a month to decide," I reminded him.

"You do, but I don't. I've got a new semester looming."

"Do you know anything about Fairhope?"

He groaned. "Is that our competition? I'll just activate your retirement now."

I laughed. "I'll see you Tuesday."

And then I was off on my final errand of the afternoon, a visit to the rental office at Harbor Village.

The administrative offices of the retirement community were located in the wedding cake building—the big house, as Jim called it—so I parked in the same lot I had used the night before. Automatic doors opened with a gush of cold air, and I walked into a two-story lobby with a giant chandelier and a soaring wood ceiling. A sign gave two possible destinations. "Dining Room" was written on an arrow pointing right; "Administration" had an arrow to the left.

The lobby was furnished in natural rattan with colorful, tropical-print fabrics and glass-topped tables. An end table between the couches held a tall metal lamp shaped like a parrot, with a square, red lampshade. I took my phone out and snapped photos for Stephanie, moving from the chandelier to the seating area then the fountain and fern bed visible through the back window wall.

There was a wide archway to the office area, where a young woman wearing round red glasses was smiling at me. I walked toward her and we exchanged greetings.

"I'd like to talk with someone about an apartment."

She hopped up, tall and slender with a happy smile, a cute little nose and brown curls that bounced when she moved rapidly. "I'm Patti." She stuck out her hand.

"Cleo Mack. And are you—what would it be—the rental agent?"

"Oh! Cleo!" She looked startled and bobbed her head, setting her curls aquiver. "Jamie's expecting you." She sat down again and reached for the desk phone.

Now I was startled. "What?"

She held up one finger, stalling me while she punched in a number. "She told me to call as soon as you got here. If you'll just have a seat in the lobby..." She pointed while speaking softly into the phone.

I was stumped but followed directions and sat on one of the colorful couches. Had I possibly told someone I was coming here? *Jamie*, the receptionist had said; wasn't that the woman whose table I shared at lunch yesterday? I tried to remember making an appointment with her but knew I had not.

When Patti finished her phone call, she walked out to join me. "Let me be sure I understand." She smiled nervously and raised one finger to count. Bright green nail polish with cherry red dots. "You're Cleo Mack?"

I nodded and a second finger went up.

"And you asked about a job?"

"Cleo Mack, yes. A job? No. I don't know anything about a job."

Patti rolled not just her eyes but her entire head in exaggerated relief. "Okay, I thought so. You asked about rentals, right? But Jamie doesn't handle rentals, and she's expecting you."

"About a job? That's news to me."

"Yes, it's all very curious." She plopped down on the second couch and leaned toward me, her manner suddenly conspiratorial. "But I know that's what she said. I even wrote it down. See?"

She showed me a sticky note with my name written on it and an abbreviation I didn't understand—*RES SERV.*

"We couldn't believe it either, not after all the lectures about cutting costs, but you know Jamie. She can pull strings when she wants to." She pursed her lips and gave a shrug. "I got her on the phone, but she's at the bank. She'll be back in a minute. Why don't I get us something to drink and then I'll tell you all about Harbor Village. Water?"

"Great." I used her absence to reflect on Jamie Barnes. I'd told her about the early retirement offer and that I might need a part-time job, but nothing about renting an apartment at Harbor Village, because the idea hadn't occurred to me until last night. And she had said nothing about finding me a job. I was sure of that.

Patti fetched bottled water for us and sat on the second couch, folding one leg under her. Her name was Patti Snyder, and she appeared to be about twenty-five, going on fifteen—which made her the exact same age as my daughter and gave me an immediate sense of intimacy.

"What do you do here?"

"Transportation," she answered promptly. "The residents call me Patti Wagon, because I drive them everywhere. To doctors' offices, mostly. And when I don't have a passenger, I work at the reception desk or take photographs for the newsletter. Just whatever."

"And this job you mentioned—what is it?"

"Resident Services. See?" She showed me the note again. *RES SERV*, it said. "We had somebody but she left at least a year ago."

"What sort of things did she do?" I had told Jamie I was a social worker, so maybe this would be an appropriate job for me.

"Everything. We all do everything, to be honest. I help out in the dining room sometimes, delivering food to people who are sick or just want to eat in their apartments."

"Who handles rentals?"

She grinned. "I forgot you asked about that. That would be *Cyn-thee-ah*." She stretched her mouth dramatically and emphasized the first syllable: *sin*-thee-ah. "We're almost full, and there's a waiting list. That's what she tells everybody, but I don't really believe it. I don't really believe anything Cynthia says, if you know what I mean." Another eye roll. A swig of water. "The dragon lady says we need more residents. How can that be if we're almost full?"

"How many people live here?"

She shrugged. "A bunch. Cynthia might know."

"Who's the dragon lady?"

She shook her head and her curls bounced. "Our boss, but she's never here. Just stops by occasionally to fire somebody." She giggled. "Not that it's funny. We all live in fear." She giggled again.

"If I took a job here, do you think I could get an apartment too?"

She grinned and shrugged. Her curls shook. "Don't ask Cynthia, ask Jamie. If she wants you to take this job, she might bump somebody off."

My eyebrows shot up and she rushed to correct herself. "Oh no, no! I didn't mean that. Bump somebody *off the list*, I mean. That sounded bad, didn't it?" She turned and looked toward the door. "Oh, here she comes. Thank goodness." She raised a hand and waved vigorously, bangles clinking down her arm.

Jamie Barnes was walking toward us, looking like she'd just come from an exercise class, rather than the bank. Her leggings were black, with dangling ties that wrapped around the calf, and with them she wore a tank top and a gauzy, floating shirt.

"Good luck," Patti Wagon whispered and scurried around me, taking her bottle of water with her.

* * * *

"So, you got my message." Jamie gave me another of her power handshakes. "I should've gotten your phone number yesterday, but I had no way of knowing this job approval would come through so fast. Never happened before. You know how I found you? Had my assistant call every motel in town and leave a message for you."

I didn't admit that I hadn't received any message. "Did you? Every one? Well, I'm here now. Tell me about this job."

She frowned, distracted momentarily, and reached out one finger to wipe a layer of dust off the parrot-shaped lamp between us. "I can't remember how much I told you yesterday. It's part-time, a resident services position. Are you interested?" She lifted her hair up off her neck and fanned herself with it. She had damp circles under her arms.

"Jamie, I'm not entirely clear about the organization here. I thought you were an RN."

"I am, but I fill in for the administrator, too, since she's only here a day or two a month. If you want my opinion, that's not working too well."

"And your job title is…"

"Director of Assisted Living. My office is in the Assisted Living building." She pointed toward the back of the complex. "Did you see our new pool? It'll be open tomorrow or the next day. By the Fourth, for sure."

I nodded. "And what are the duties of Resident Services?"

She glanced at her watch. "Oh, the usual. I think a social worker would be ideal." She rattled off references to hospitals and home health care, broken eyeglasses and laundered hearing aids, "…and coordination with maintenance. Lots of computer problems, but we usually can't help with those—do you know anything about computers? And families are always wanting something—is dad getting confused, why isn't mom answering her phone, why does she cry every time we talk."

"This is beginning to sound like a big job."

Jamie shook her head. "Half-time, four hours a day. I'm not saying you can't put in more hours occasionally, but you take off comp time to make up for it. What I'm saying is, you don't get paid for more than twenty hours. Which reminds me. What kind of salary do you expect?"

I wanted enough to pay my insurance and help with the rent on a luxurious apartment like Nita's, but I wasn't eager to give her a figure. "What did you pay the last person?"

"Hmm, I'll have to check." She looked at her watch again and stood. "Look, I'm trying to get away a little early today. Why don't I show you around while we talk?"

We did a fast lap around the central core of Harbor Village. I didn't mention what I'd heard last night about the buildings being donuts and L-shapes and U-shapes, but I found those descriptions quite helpful to my orientation.

Jamie ticked off the organizational chart. "The rental desk, housekeeping, assisted living, maintenance—what am I forgetting? Oh, yes, the dining room. Five departments."

"Who answers the emergency calls? Is there an RN on duty all the time?"

She was surprised. "Oh, no. Definitely not. Too much liability. We never do that."

She pointed out the maintenance building, garage-size with a wide roll-up door closed up tight. "I'm never sure if they're out on a job or just sneaking away early. Want to see an apartment?"

She opened an unlocked door into a living room painted a dark, depressing terra cotta color. "It hasn't been cleaned yet. We let people buy their own paint if they want a special color like this. Sometimes I think that's a bad idea."

We walked quickly through the rooms, which were nothing like Nita's. I guessed from the smell that a dog had lived there.

"Pets are allowed?"

Jamie wrinkled her nose. "That's another bad idea, but yeah, inside only, nothing over thirty pounds."

I loved dogs but I knew they'd make problems for residential services. And be a rich source of complaints from other residents.

"You asked about emergencies," she said, as we turned the corner beside the big house. "They're not always medical, you know. People lose their phone or step on their glasses and expect you to do something about it in the middle of the night. The Assisted Living office takes calls at night—sometimes they go and sometimes they send the security guard. And if it's medical, we call an ambulance, notify family and make sure the apartment gets locked up." She waved dismissively. "Let's look in here."

Assisted living was a sprawling, yellow building with white gingerbread trim, located behind the swimming pool. Jamie introduced a few residents sitting on the shady porch then led the way through the automatic door. "This dining room is just for this building, and our residents get three meals a day."

"And the other residents don't?"

She shook her head. "Just lunch for independent living, and there's an extra charge for that."

She led the way to a scruffy little office on a back hallway, where a buxom woman, wearing bright blue scrubs and a frown, sat at a scarred and battered old desk. She stacked some papers together and slid them into a folder when we appeared in the doorway.

"This is Michelle, my assistant. Cleo's going to be handling Resident Services." Jamie grinned at me. "Right? Have I persuaded you yet?"

"I thought you were leaving early," Michelle said.

"Oh, dang!" Jamie looked at her watch and spun around, heading for the door. "I'll walk you back to the main building."

We passed a pink building with sliding glass doors on three sides. I could see straight through it.

"The indoor pool," Jamie said. "Heated in winter. We get lots of rec club memberships because of that pool."

The adjacent outdoor pool, enclosed in a six-foot high, wrought iron fence, still had piles of sand and construction debris strewn around it. I was walking faster to keep up with Jamie and barely had time to look.

"Physical therapy rents space in this end of the building. The Goldenrod Grille and the hair salon are rentals, too." She pointed them out as we rushed past the main dining room.

"Not much to see here. We have a cook and a helper, and the housekeepers have a little office down this hall."

I got a quick glimpse of a dark dining room with a few tables and booths.

"It's just one meal a day, at noon, and most people don't want it. To be honest, it's not very good. Corporate thinks we should work on that, but we haven't gotten to it. Maybe you will." She gave me a quick glance over her shoulder. "You know, that's not a bad idea."

We reached the lobby and she stopped. "I won't bother showing you the offices. You'll have your own, because of privacy issues, but right now I don't know which one it will be." She glanced at her watch. "Look, I've got to run. I hope you'll take the job. If you think of any questions, call me next week. And send a copy of your resume. I'll be out Monday."

"What about an apartment? I'd like to live here. Any chance of getting one soon, so I don't have to move twice?"

She squinted. "You'd be right on the premises. Might help with night calls occasionally. I think that could be worked out. You'd have to pay for it, of course."

"Of course. And I'd want a garage."

Jamie grimaced but nodded. "We'll talk next week. I'll see what I can do."

* * * *

I went to the pier that night and found Nita sitting on a different bench, out beyond the restaurant. The sun was low in the sky, the breeze just perceptible and there were twice as many people.

"I've been thinking about you all day." She patted the bench beside her. "Did you find a house?"

I sat and told her my news.

"A job and an apartment! Oh, my dear!"

I agreed; it was more than I could've hoped for, and there was still more. I was getting excited about the work to be done. I was feeling engaged in a way that had eluded me since Robert died.

A red-haired young woman smiled and waved at Nita, and Nita motioned her back and took her hand. "This is Emily, Cleo—one of your soon-to-be colleagues. Emily, I'm not sure what your job title is."

"Oh, are you Cleo?" Emily gave a little squeal of excitement. "Patti told me all about you, and I'm so glad to meet you. Patti will be so jealous! When do you start? Monday, I hope."

It was another case of trying to apply the brakes. "We're still in the negotiating stage. I don't even have a firm offer yet."

"Shoot for the stars." Emily waved a skinny, freckled arm then bent closer. "I'm the bookkeeper and I know there are some big salaries available. Unfortunately, I don't get one of them." She threw her head back and laughed.

The sunset was pretty, but no cathedral sky.

* * * *

My visit to Birmingham was pleasant, except for a little dread about telling Stephanie I wasn't moving there. I loved seeing the hills after the flatlands of the coast, and Barry was at that adorable stage where he walked and talked and was easily entertained.

I told Stephanie my plans and she insisted on showing me a couple of apartment complexes anyway, both of them located on high-traffic roadways.

"Why isn't there something for seniors," I asked, "in walking distance of restaurants and shops?"

"It's a zoning thing, Mom. Nobody wants apartments in their neighborhood. It lowers property values." She changed the subject. "Dad's wedding is next weekend. He wants us to come, but I hate to miss three days of work."

"Make it a vacation. Visit Fairhope on the way."

"Why? You won't be there."

"No, but you could see the quilt exhibit at the art center." That idea scored some major points with her.

* * * *

The campus, when I got home, felt like a visit to the distant past. I went to the dean's office and told him I was accepting the retirement offer, and he came around the desk to give me a hug. "Oh, I never doubted it, Cleo. Not with Robert gone and Fairhope in the picture. We're going to miss you."

Later in the day, he called my office, where I was sorting through my accumulation of professional books.

"Forgive me if this is presumptuous, Cleo, but I've got a new history guy coming in, a young man with kids who need to be in this school district. He's looked but hasn't found anything they can afford. So I'm wondering, what are you going to do about your house?"

And that was how my house came to be sold in a few days, without ever officially being on the market. I got a good price, but not the bonanza I had fantasized about, and there was now some pressure about when I would move.

I talked with Nita in Fairhope every few days, and she suggested I look for an estate sale specialist to help with the downsizing. "We have several good ones here, so I'm sure you'll find one in Atlanta."

And I did find a nice woman with a whole crew of helpers, who worked me into her tight schedule, took some bigger items to consignment shops and held a three-day sale at the house then donated everything that was left and presented me with a nice check. She was a lifesaver.

I talked with Jamie Barnes in Fairhope a couple of times. When I first called to tell her the salary I wanted, she was in a bit of a huff. "Corporate wants to handle it." She gave me a name and phone number.

"What about the apartment?"

"Don't say a word to corporate about an apartment! I'm taking care of that. What color do you want it painted?"

Kimberly, at corporate, said she'd been with the company for thirteen years and knew I'd love it. Then she offered me a salary and benefits to love.

A few days before my move, Jamie called to say everything was ready for me, the apartment painted, the office selected and keys waiting at the reception desk. "Lee's going to be here your first day."

"And who is Lee?"

"Our Executive Director. Just between us, she's a real PITA."

"A what?"

"A pain in the ass. She's not here often, and we never know when she's coming. She likes to surprise us. She also manages a couple of Villages in South Carolina and a Harbor House in Myrtle Beach—Harbor House is the name for our skilled nursing facilities. But Lee spends most of her time in Houston."

"What's her last name?" I was jotting notes as we talked.

"Lee Ferrell."

"Sounds familiar. Is she a social worker?"

Jamie laughed. "No. I told you what she is. But you've probably seen her name if you watch public TV. She's a big donor, along with her late husband, and I won't even say what he was."

* * * *

Stephanie and Boyd and little Barry did go to Travis' wedding in New Orleans. And then they visited Fairhope. They sent me photographs of Barry on the pier, terror and delight mixing on his face as he threw pieces of bread to a flock of gulls circling overhead and diving down to snatch the bread. He also dug holes in a sandy beach I hadn't seen and ran through a splash pad I had missed.

Looking good, Mom, Stephanie texted. *We approve.*

She also sent a photograph of her father and the wedding party. Stephanie and the other attendants wore emerald green sheaths with one shoulder bared, and Stephanie's cryptic caption—*Dresses off the rack! Even the bride!*—suggested that the happy new family hadn't quite happened yet.

At first glance, the new bride looked too young for Travis, but there were certain things makeup and lighting couldn't conceal. The expression in her eyes hinted at something else, too—like maybe he'd met his match this time. But I wished them all well. Travis was still a handsome devil, and a little gray hair added distinction. Why didn't it work that way for women?

* * * *

Six weeks after my first visit to Fairhope, I left Atlanta a day ahead of the moving van and spent the night at the Fairhope motel. My favorite desk clerk wasn't on duty, but there was a pleasant woman in his place. Thursday morning I dressed in jeans and a T-shirt and had breakfast in town. The moving van was due mid-afternoon.

"See, everything did work out," Patti Wagon told me, rushing around the desk to give me a hug. She handed over my keys, strung together on a pink paperclip. "And we're so glad to have you here. You can't even imagine." She fluttered her eyes and looked heavenward.

"Oh, I need to write you a rent check. Is there paperwork for the apartment? A lease, or any resident procedures?"

"Jamie said hands off. She's handling it. Give me a check and I'll see that she gets it, but I don't have anything for you to sign."

"How do I make out my check? To Harbor Village?"

She pursed her lips and held up a finger. The nail polish was blue this time, with white stars. "Wait a minute. I'm remembering some stink about that. I'd better ask." She grabbed her phone and repeated my question then signaled to me. "Jamie wants to talk to you."

"Are you getting settled?" Jamie asked, brightly.

"I'm just picking up the key and waiting for the moving van."

"Make out two checks to Ferrell & Associates, one for rent and one for the deposit. Tell Patti to put them in my mailbox and I'll get them next time I'm there."

My apartment wasn't in Nita's building but at the rear of the donut building on the opposite side of the boulevard. The most direct access was via a wide sidewalk running along a waist-high patchwork of wood and wrought-iron fencing that enclosed the rear yards of garden homes on the next street. My unit was number eight and had a screened porch at the corner of the building.

I did a walk-through of the empty space, freshly painted in a grayish white. The air-conditioning was set on subarctic, but the movers would be here soon. I left it as it was. There was new carpeting—light gray and low-pile—in the main room, where the ceiling was high and sloping, with recessed lighting. The all-white kitchen was small, but a full-length window looked out to the interior courtyard. I ignored old appliances and imagined glass shelves with pots of orchids.

There were two bedrooms and two baths, one with an oversized tile shower. Thinking ahead, Jim would say. The small laundry room had a washer and dryer already in place and what looked like a pet flap grafted into the door. And in the dining area, a single garden door opened to the walkway that circled the courtyard. It felt clean and spacious, and I liked it.

I took the remote control from the kitchen counter and went to check the garage, which was more than large enough for my car, with shelves and a walkout door at the back. I tested my apartment key on the door then moved my car into the stall and began unpacking things I'd brought with me.

Apparently there was a Harbor Village tradition that all residents visited new arrivals as soon as possible, so people stopped by all morning. I met everyone who lived in my building, including Ann from next door, who brought a plate of cookies.

Nita and Jim drove over on their way to an early lunch.

"Come with us," Nita said from the passenger seat.

"I'd love to." It was early, but I was accustomed to Eastern Time. "Do you want to see the apartment first?"

She smiled sheepishly. "I already saw it. I hope you don't mind. Dolly and I came to see which one it was, and the painter let us look around. Are you pleased with it?"

I nodded. "I love it."

"You ladies can talk while we eat," Jim said. "We're going to Ruby Tuesday and we want to get there early."

I went inside for my purse and shopping list and met them at the restaurant. We sat in the sunroom and I ordered baked pasta.

Jim and Nita were disagreeing about something when I arrived. "This place is dependable," Jim said. "Generous servings."

"But I should have prepared something at our apartment," Nita insisted.

She asked about the estate sale and I gave them a quick rundown.

"She did all the organizing and pricing and advertising, brought a big staff, sold almost everything and donated what was left. I wound up with an empty house and a check for three thousand dollars. Plus a nice tax deduction for the donations."

Jim perked up. "A check, you said? She didn't deal in all cash?"

"She took checks and credit cards at the sale, but she wrote one check to me."

"Ah." He nodded. "Now *she* has to deal with the bad checks and bogus cards. That's good thinking, Cleo. And how much did she charge you?"

"Jim!"

"Forty percent. And I gave her a discount on a couple of items she wanted for a rental house. That seemed fair after she worked me into her schedule on short notice."

I had swilled my first glass of tea and the server brought another one.

"There's something I want to ask you about." Nita looked and sounded unusually serious. "Do you like cats? You're not allergic or phobic or anything, are you?"

I laughed. "I like cats fine. I had one for years. But why?"

"This is the problem." She patted my wrist a few times, as if she were stalling while she decided just how to phrase something. "I barely knew the woman who lived in your apartment. She wasn't here long and moved back to New Jersey, I understand. But I'm very much afraid she abandoned her cat. She's a pretty little calico, with a white chest and feet, and I saw her hiding under the shrubs at the back."

"How could somebody do that?" I had a little catch in my throat.

She nodded. "I hoped you'd feel that way. And I have a confession. I propped your screen door open so she could get back in, and Jim has been putting a little food out every day."

"I haven't seen any cat," he said, "but the food disappears. Could be anything. A cat, a dog, even a raccoon."

"I hope we haven't attracted raccoons to your porch," Nita said. "But we have coyotes, too."

"Not in the summer, Nita. They come in cold weather."

"Yes, I know that, but they come after cats. And I just can't bear to think about that pretty little thing, accustomed to a safe apartment, and now she's out there with dogs and coyotes and traffic. How a person can be so cruel…"

"I'll be on the lookout," I promised. "Now that I think of it, I noticed a pet flap in the door to the laundry room."

Nita's eyes widened. "The litter box! I'll bet the litter box was in there. Is there room for it?"

I nodded. "Probably. In the corner."

I fished in the pocket of my purse for the list of supplies I needed to pick up and added cat food, litter box and litter. "I suppose I should be prepared. If she doesn't show up, I'm sure there's an animal shelter that accepts donations."

"Bless your heart." Nita beamed.

Jim shook his head. "Another animal lover."

"Haven't you been feeding her?"

"Just on the porch. Can't have her starving."

We finished lunch and I set off for the grocery store, where I bought paper products, Diet 7 Up, bottled water, a bottle of merlot, cheese, bread, crackers, fruit, almonds covered in dark chocolate, plus cat supplies and a couple of frozen dinners. Then I rushed back to Harbor Village. As I lugged bags up the sidewalk between the garages and apartments, I met a nice-looking young man wearing khakis and a tool belt that clinked when he walked.

"Ms. Mack? I'm Stewart, from maintenance. You need a TV hooked up for the weekend?"

He helped me get my bags into the kitchen. "I'm afraid I scared your cat off. She'll come back, won't she?"

"She was on the porch?"

"Yeah. You probably don't know, but they don't allow outdoor pets here. I won't tell them, but somebody will."

"Thanks." Now I had to figure out how to lure her inside and hope we'd be compatible.

Stewart connected the cable to the TV I'd brought in the car and left it sitting on the floor. He gave me a card with a phone number to call about Wi-Fi. "Call me when you get ready to hang pictures. Fridge working okay?"

"It's cold." I put the cheese and soft drinks on the center shelf.

After Stewart left, I wiped out cabinets and put away the dishes and glasses I'd moved in the car, set up both bathrooms with tissues and towels and new shower curtains and was just putting the new litter box into the laundry room when someone knocked at the door. The moving van, I assumed, and rushed out.

"Mom?" Stephanie yelled. "Are you here?"

"Stephanie! I had no idea you were coming!"

I shot across the room, threw the door wide open and gave her a hug. She had a sleepy, tousle-haired Barry in her arms.

"Barry, honey. Do I get a hug?"

No, I did not. He scowled at me and then buried his face against Stephanie's neck.

"Talk to your grandmother," Stephanie coaxed, to no avail.

On the porch sat a laptop bag, a small suitcase on wheels and a gigantic shoulder bag overflowing with baby gear. How had she carried all this stuff? And where were they going to sleep? Where had I packed the extra sheets and pillows?

"There's no furniture yet." I pointed out the obvious. "But let me bring your things in." I put everything in the bathroom. "The movers won't need to be in here and we can close the door."

"I've got his quilt in the bag," Stephanie said. "If you'll get it out and fold it a couple of times, he'll go right back to sleep. There was a moving van behind us."

I folded Barry's quilt into a pallet before walking out to the parking lot, where I found the truck and three men, just backing into position at the end of the sidewalk. One of them asked, "You want to show me the apartment?" The other two lowered the ramp, threw open the furniture compartment and began trundling my possessions out.

The movers set up my bedroom first. When that was done, Stephanie found two boxes labeled "bed linens" and dragged them back, then grabbed a corner of Barry's pallet and slid it to the bedroom, too, while he slept soundly. "I'll work back here." She closed the door.

The movers shifted to the dining area. The china cabinet required all three of them working in synchrony and, without asking, they put it right where I'd imagined it.

I got them bottled water, not very cold, from the refrigerator, and they drained the bottles before going to work on the second bedroom. Finally they brought the chairs and couch and tables for the living room and then took a rest and stood under the AC vents, arguing whether it was the heat or the humidity.

"We've got some bookcases," the boss said, and I pointed to the long wall.

I moved the TV out of the way until one of the low bookcases was in place and then positioned it on top. My computer desk and chair went under the front windows.

The boss brought a form for me to sign and popped out a pink copy for me. I had generous tips ready and walked out to the screen porch to deliver them personally. The few pieces of patio furniture I had were already arranged, cushions in place. And the cat food dish, I noticed, was right where it had been, still full.

"Less than an hour!" I said, in disbelief. "And you did a great job."

The movers grinned. "Unloading is the easy part."

I gave them more bottles of water and encouraged them to drive down to see Mobile Bay before they headed back to Atlanta. And then they were gone and the relocation was a done deed. I looked around, not quite believing my eyes. Except for unpacking about thirty boxes, I was moved in.

Stephanie came out of the bedroom and draped an arm around my shoulders. "All done? That was fast. And look how perfect everything looks. You didn't need me at all."

I hugged her. "Oh, you know that's not true. You made my day. And look at all these boxes to be emptied."

She had my bedroom looking perfect already, right down to the new dust ruffle for the bed and glowing lamps on the night tables.

"Amazing. This would have taken me the rest of the day."

"I think there's room for a little table on this wall." Stephanie looked around with a critical eye. "You've got some art or photographs or something, right?"

We started on the guest room, spacious enough for the guest bed plus Barry's old crib from my house, modified now with a lowered mattress and only a partial rail on the front. We weren't actually hammering but there was a little tapping. He woke up and came to help.

Stephanie offered him a snack but he shook his head. "You like your bed?"

He climbed aboard and sat for a couple of seconds.

"He'll still wake up before I do, but at least he won't fall over the high rail."

As if demonstrating, Barry flipped to his stomach and slid off to the floor, giggling. Stephanie and I laughed with him.

It was time for another break. We got cold drinks and moved to the living room couch and chair or, in Barry's case, the maze of boxes.

I looked around. "I think this is just about perfect. Will the kitchen window be too bright for orchids? I'm thinking maybe glass shelves. And I've already met Stewart the handyman, who'll put them up."

Chapter 3

While Stephanie showered, I decided Barry and I would go for a little walk. "Want to go outside?"

He pointed to the door.

The office staff should've been around still, and it seemed like a perfect opportunity to show off my grandson. "Want me to carry you, Barry? Are you getting tired?"

"No!"

He did allow me to steer him toward the big house and through the automatic door.

A woman wearing tall, platform shoes with a bright green dress in about a size two was walking across the lobby, looking like an ad from a fashion magazine. She watched us and suddenly veered our way. I was sure I'd met her and tried to jog my memory for her name, but no luck. Maybe she was a TV personality.

"Cleo? I'm Lee. Nice to meet you, and nice to have you joining us at Harbor Village."

"Lee," I repeated, still drawing a blank. And then—*Eureka!* "Lee from corporate?"

"Right." She drew the word out and gave me a little cough of a laugh, like I'd said something stupid.

So naturally, like an idiot, I started babbling. "Sorry I didn't recognize you. Jamie told me you'd be here, but I thought she meant Monday, when I start working."

Lee shot me another glance. "People are always trying to figure out when I'm coming. It's like a cottage industry here. But I'm never predictable. Remember that." She put on a forced smile. "And we may as well get this out of the way now. I *hate* working with family. It always causes problems. So don't expect any favors." She glanced at Barry and sniffed slightly, then swept her gaze across the lobby. "Oh crap, where is that Stewart?"

And then, with long, fashion-model strides, she stalked off toward the dining room.

I reminded myself to breathe and, without asking him, swung Barry up and scurried off in the opposite direction, toward the office.

Patti Wagon, still watching the departing Lee, came quickly to meet us.

"Who is *this*, Cleo?" She tickled Barry's leg and reached for him and, before I could say he was shy of strangers, he practically flew out of my arms and into hers. My knees were a little shaky, and not just from carrying Barry.

"Oh, aren't you adorable. Let's see if I have something in the candy jar." She carried him to her desk and found a few M&Ms in a glass jar. I nodded approval and Patti gave them to Barry.

I was willing myself back to normal when Stewart walked in, his tool belt clanking.

"Who have we got here?" he asked loudly.

Barry pushed away from Patti and darted to him.

"Oh, you like pliers?" He squatted so Barry could get a close look. "Don't pinch your finger, kid."

Patti spoke softly. "I see you met our dragon lady."

"Yes. She warned me not to expect any favors."

Patti rolled her eyes and bounced her curls. "Nothing surprises me where she's concerned. Just remember, she's not here much. And she just approved hiring you, so you're safe for now. I don't suppose she told you what her name is?"

"You don't know her name?"

"She remarried recently. We have a bet going about whether she'll change her name or keep it the same as the money. The Ferrell fortune, I mean." She giggled nervously and kept watch on the lobby.

"She's looking for Stewart," I said.

"Uh-oh." She looked at him and repeated, "She's looking for you."

"Uh-oh." He stood up with a clank of tools. "Which way did she go?"

"Dining room," Patti said, and Stewart headed off in that direction.

I said to Barry, "We'd better go, sweetie."

"Why don't you use this door?" Patti walked us away from the lobby, down a hallway between offices and changed the subject to something more normal. "Would you like for Stewart to come hang pictures and things?"

"How about Friday?" I asked.

"You know that's tomorrow, right? He's probably booked already but I can check."

"I've lost a day. Next week is fine. Better, probably, since Stephanie and Barry will be here in the morning." I took Barry's hand and more or less fled.

The fresh air cleared my head and silenced the OMG chorus that had been crooning in my head. As we approached the apartment, I saw a note stuck in the screen door. I assumed it would say that Stephanie had finished her shower and gone for a walk, but I was wrong.

"Back at 6 to take you to dinner," the note said. It was signed "Riley." I stuck it in my jeans pocket.

Stephanie was in the hall bath with the door open, drying her hair. "Hey, guys." She switched the dryer off and picked up a hairbrush. "Have a nice walk?"

"Barry had three M&Ms and decided to be a handyman when he grows up. He likes Stewart's tool belt. And I had a strange encounter." I told her about the woman from corporate and what she had said about working with family. "She looks like a million bucks and is a member of the donor class."

"Everybody here is like family." Stephanie frowned. "Why would she work here if she doesn't like that? And why would she work at all, if she's rich."

"Good question. She looked familiar. I think she might be a social worker." Stephanie snorted. "A rich social worker? That's an oxymoron."

"Maybe I offended her sometime. We might've served together on a committee."

She shook her head. "Oh, Mom." She gave me a hug and back pat. "Don't let it bother you. Now, what are we doing for dinner?"

"I found this stuck in the door." I gave her Riley's note and she scanned it.

"Riley? Who is Riley? And why haven't I heard anything about him?"

I shrugged. "Just a nice man who lives here. We don't have to go if you'd rather not."

"Oh, definitely, let's go."

"Now, don't start anything. Where's my suitcase?"

I showered, dried my hair, put on white pants and a sapphire blue cotton sweater. A little moisturizer, a little lipstick and mascara, and I looked more presentable than I felt.

Stephanie had given Barry a bath and was stuffing him into a striped yellow-and-orange T-shirt and short blue overalls.

"You look adorable," I told him.

"No!" he shouted and kicked while his mom tried to wedge his feet into blue canvas shoes.

Riley appeared promptly at six. I introduced Stephanie and Barry and offered to let him off the hook. "You'll get three of us tonight, I'm afraid. More than you bargained for."

"And one of us is tired and cranky," Stephanie said.

Riley gave me a look and shrugged. "She doesn't seem any crankier than usual."

Stephanie laughed like that was really funny, and Riley grinned. "The more, the merrier, I always say."

Bonding with Stephanie, check.

"I'm sure you're tired. Let's go someplace nearby. I'll bet you'd like an early night," Riley proposed.

And now I was the one who appreciated him.

"Why don't I drive," Stephanie said. "The car seat is difficult to move."

"Oh, I forget about car seats," Riley said. "Didn't have them when mine were little. Shall we go to the pier restaurant? Ought to be a good sunset."

"How many children do you have, Riley," I asked as we walked past the garages and across the street to Stephanie's car. I held Barry's hand, and Stephanie had gone ahead of us to reorganize the car.

"Two boys. What about you?"

"Stephanie is my one and only."

"She's still a kid. My boys are forty-something now. Both in Washington, both attorneys."

"And you lost your wife?" I didn't know whether from death or divorce.

"Yeah, she wandered off a long time ago and I didn't look for her." He grinned. "Truthfully, she's in Washington, too. In fact, she and Nita worked together, many years ago. And Nita is the reason I found Fairhope." He chuckled, revealing tight wrinkles at the corners of dark blue eyes. "And now you know my entire life story."

Stephanie and I were grateful just to sit in the restaurant, but Barry was interested in the boats in the marina and especially the ducks beginning to gather for the night. He was quite happy to go outside with Riley for a closer look. I watched through the windows and saw Barry talking with great animation.

"Riley isn't understanding a word of that, is he?"

Barry put both hands up and covered his head, still talking and pointing to the sky occasionally.

"Oh, how cute." Stephanie whipped out her phone and began filming. "He's telling Riley about feeding the gulls."

We had a good dinner, and there was a pretty sunset, although not a cathedral sky. We paid at the register and walked back to the car. I hadn't seen Nita, but she could be anywhere on the pier.

"Riley, I assumed you live at Harbor Village, too." Stephanie gave a signal and slowed to turn in at the entrance. "Want me to drop you somewhere?"

He was in the front seat, beside her. "No. I took my car around to Cleo's, thinking I'd be driving."

Barry pointed at the pelican sculpture as we went by and said something, I wasn't sure what.

"He's going to know exactly how to find grandma's apartment," Riley said.

At the big house, the chandelier and all the recessed lights were on in the lobby, illuminating it in the twilight, like a stage waiting for actors. Stephanie turned left and, as we turned into the parking area, I saw Lee from corporate sitting on the couch with her head tipped back, looking at the chandelier. Probably Stewart was there somewhere, working on switches or something. Poor guy. I hoped she wouldn't fire him.

We parked across the drive from my garage. There were only a few cars in the lot at this hour, just two SUVs parked side by side, and what I assumed was Riley's car near the street, plus a couple more in the distance.

"Let's walk this way," I proposed as we got out of the car. "There's someone I want you to see in the lobby."

Stephanie came around to extract Barry from the car seat. "That rude woman?"

"Yes. Did you see her?"

"I noticed all the lights on," Riley said. "That's unusual."

I shrugged and laughed. "I wouldn't know. This is my first night here."

But when we rounded the corner of the building, the lobby was totally dark. The windows reflected the five-globe street lamps around the intersection.

"Ha!" Riley said. "That was quick. Well, ladies and Barry, I'll say good night now. Nice to meet you, Stephanie. How long are you going to be here?"

"We'll leave in the morning. Then Mom can rearrange everything."

"Maybe you can meet Nita before you go," Riley suggested. "If she'd known this little fellow was here, she'd have come with us tonight." He offered his hand to Barry, who reached out with a laugh to slap it.

Ah-ha! Nita had sent Riley to take me to dinner. I hoped she wasn't planning to do any matchmaking.

Riley patted Barry's shoulder and raised his eyebrows at me. "Mexican Trains tomorrow night? Five thirty at the Bergens'."

"I thought it was Thursday nights."

He grinned and shrugged. "It was, once."

Uh-oh. They'd changed dominoes to include me? Affirmative on the matchmaking.

Stephanie gave him an air kiss and said she'd be back frequently and he gave a little wave and sauntered off toward his car.

I saw the cat as we neared the screen porch. Stephanie was carrying Barry and neither of them noticed the mostly dark shape hovering over the food dish. The cat stopped eating and watched as I closed the porch's screen door behind me and went around Stephanie to unlock the apartment.

"We're going to brush our teeth and get ready for bed."

"I think I'll sit out here a minute."

"Don't let that woman worry you, Mom. You'll win her over in no time."

"Thanks, honey. I'm over it already."

I closed the door to keep the cool air inside and sat on the wicker love seat. I wondered if the cat would be afraid of me, but that wasn't the case. She came over right away and examined my ankles.

"Hello, pretty." I gave her back a slow stroke. Soft, like feathers.

She blinked big yellow eyes, meowed a soft, raspy meow and sniffed my ankles and hems thoroughly before going back to her dish. When I went inside a few minutes later, she oozed past me and stopped just inside the door. Then she set off on a feline inspection tour, sniffing furniture and boxes, rubbing her cheeks against corners and pausing frequently to look around, as though she were expecting someone. All the while, her plume of a tail waved back and forth. When she disappeared among the boxes, I looked around, taking inventory and planning the rest of the unpacking. I expected Stephanie to come back for a chat, but the only sound I heard was the cat, checking out the litter box. Eventually I gave up and began turning off lights, heading for bed and, at that point, Stephanie appeared in the hallway, dressed in shorty PJs.

"Mom, I think I forgot to lock the car. Will it be okay, do you think?"

It was my first night at Harbor Village, and my own car was in a garage. I stuck out my hand. "Let's not risk it. Give me your keys and I'll check."

She showed me her remote. "You don't have to walk all the way out. Just click this when you get halfway there. The horn will beep to tell you it's locked."

I walked to the end of the sidewalk, past mostly dark apartments in my building. Lights were still on in about half the houses across the fence, and the five-globe lamps cast a pleasant wash across the sidewalks.

At the corner of the garages I looked across at the still-dark lobby of the big house. There was no person in sight, anywhere. I aimed and pressed Stephanie's lock button.

Her horn beeped and the car lights blinked twice and, at almost the same instant, the headlights flashed on both of the SUVs parked in the center of the lot. An engine started, and the car facing away from me began to move in a big loop, circling back toward my position. I turned and walked behind the garage to see that the walkout door was locked, and then I headed for my new apartment and bed. It had been a long, long day.

* * * *

Friday morning I woke at the usual Atlanta time. A calico cat was curled up against my shins.

"Good morning," I greeted her, and she stood and stretched, all four feet close together, and soaked up a little petting. "Wonder what your name is. And how could anybody abandon you?"

She purred and twisted about in tight little circles of ecstasy. Loose hairs floated in the air.

"I'll get you a brush today," I promised.

After a few minutes, I got out of bed and went to my suitcase, lying open on the floor in front of the closet. I got the jeans I'd worn yesterday and pulled on a stretchy bra and a clean black tee. The cat watched every move then hopped off the bed and shot out to the kitchen as soon as I headed that way.

"Okay," I told her, speaking quietly, "we'll move your dish inside."

But when I went out to the porch to get it, I was distracted by odd noises coming from somewhere beyond the garage. I heard voices and throbbing engines, gravel crunching and, slicing through the other sounds, the harsh static of a two-way radio. A fire truck, I imagined, but I hadn't heard any sirens.

"I'll be right back," I told the cat. And I walked down the sidewalk to see what was going on so early.

Stephanie's car was parked just where we'd left it, and one of the SUVs— now I saw it was silver—was a few spaces beyond, near the center of the lot and not far from the side door of the big house. Maybe it belonged to the night security man, based on the fact it was there both early and late.

The big house was dark and silent, but the other parking lot, in front of Nita's garage building, was a hive of activity, with half a dozen police cars, a fire truck and two ambulances, all of them with lights pulsing.

Another police car sprayed gravel as it went through the intersection without stopping.

I walked closer, keeping near the garages, then stopped when I reached Harbor Boulevard. The excitement, whatever it was, seemed to be at either the indoor pool or the new outdoor pool, which had been under construction on my previous visit.

Someone wearing what appeared to be a white bathrobe walked in a wide arc around the emergency vehicles. It might be Dolly, since she claimed to swim early in the mornings. She was looking over her shoulder toward the pool, making slow progress, and didn't see me wave. A police officer trailed her at a distance, shouting something I couldn't make out.

"Okay, okay!" the woman yelled back, and the officer pointed in my direction.

"Dolly? Dolly," I called. "Is that you?"

She looked toward me vacantly. "Yes. Who is it?"

"Cleo," I said. "Nita's friend. I moved in yesterday."

Dolly came closer. "You're who? Nita?"

I walked toward her. "Remember me? I'm Cleo Mack. We played dominoes a few weeks ago."

She came closer, peering at me inquisitively. The policeman was still following her.

"Oh, yes, Cleo. I remember you. Robert Mack's wife. It's getting to where I can't see anything." She lifted a corner of the towel draped over her arm and patted short, slicked-back hair. "I don't usually greet friends looking like this. You'll have to excuse me. You got here just in time for the excitement, didn't you?"

She sounded casual and social, considering the time of day and circumstances, whatever they were. The policeman was still walking in our direction.

"What's going on?" I gestured toward the vehicles.

She was dismissive. "Oh, some fool in the pool. Drowned, I suppose. I called nine-one-one and went inside to swim, and now they're acting like I'm trespassing."

"I think he wants to talk to you." I pointed to the policeman who was now right behind her.

"What now?" Dolly shouted to him. "I'm going, I'm going!" To me, she said, "Can they really tell us we can't be here? I pay rent, and they won't even let me swim."

She set off, stamping her way to the middle of the intersection before the officer got her attention.

"Ladies," the cop called, motioning for Dolly to come back. He was a big, hefty clone of the actor Samuel L. Jackson, with a shiny brown head, black-framed glasses and a black uniform covered with patches and pockets and flaps and leather pouches. "I'm going to need your names since you're the only people around. Just a formality." His voice was deep and reassuring, like a radio announcer.

I asked, "What happened?"

"I told you, someone drowned." She looked at the cop. "Who was it?"

"Your name is?" He was looking at me, pen poised over a notepad. His name, Chief Boozer, was printed on a patch above his pocket.

I gave him my name and apartment number and told him I needed to get back there, since no one knew where I was.

He nodded, and I told Dolly I'd see her later.

I told Stephanie what was going on outside while we prepared toast and fruit. We didn't have a lot of breakfast foods to choose from, so the meal didn't take long. As I cleared the table the drowning victim was on my mind. *Probably an Assisted Living resident who had wandered away during the night.*

Stephanie called Boyd and summarized the accident in a few words before discussing her plans for the day. Meanwhile, Barry was making truck noises as he marched a path through the maze of moving boxes.

There was a knock at the porch door and I saw Chief Boozer waiting.

Barry tried to follow me onto the porch and set up a little howl when I closed the door with him still inside.

"My grandson," I said to the chief.

He nodded. "I understand you'll be working here, Ms. Mack, and I wonder if you can help us. We need to identify this woman."

"Dolly Webb didn't know her?"

"She didn't look. Some people are squeamish."

"I'd be glad to help," I didn't want to be considered squeamish, "but I haven't met many people here yet."

"Just come take a look."

I agreed. "Let me tell Stephanie where I'm going."

Chief Boozer talked while we walked. "I'm thinking she's too young to live here. Might be a staff member. Or somebody's daughter."

That gave me a jolt. Having a daughter of my own, I'd have to try to help.

"Or maybe she lives nearby," the chief went on. "The office staff isn't here yet and people in that back building are busy with dressing and breakfast. All their residents are accounted for, they say."

We crossed the parking lot, sand and gravel crunching with our steps. There was yellow crime scene tape around the pool now. I was imagining what a body would look like after a drowning. How long had it been submerged? Or had it floated? Would gulls have gotten to it?

"Surely someone here will know her." Someone other than me.

Boozer shrugged. "Some of the people who live here aren't exactly playing with a full deck, you know."

Did he mean Dolly?

The fire truck and a couple of police vehicles were positioned around the ambulance, blocking the gaze of onlookers now beginning to trickle out of the apartments to stand in clusters around the parking lot or on the porch of the big house. We went between vehicles, into the circle of officials, and I saw Jim Bergen with the group of responders. He gave a little nod and inched forward. All eyes turned toward me.

The body was under a white cover, on a gurney behind the ambulance. Probably some senile lady who wandered away from her apartment, I imagined, or one of Jamie's assisted living residents who hadn't been missed yet. Why hadn't they summoned Jamie for the identification? Or anybody other than me.

A medical attendant stood by the gurney, waiting for the Chief to give a signal.

He nodded and took my elbow. In case I fainted, I supposed.

I knew who it was as soon as I saw a bit of the water-soaked green dress, but I made myself look at the blotchy face. There were remnants of bright lipstick, the skin was puffy and wrinkled, eyes closed, and the hair dark and wet and crudely pushed back from her face.

I turned away from the gurney and nodded to Chief Boozer.

Chapter 4

The chief gave a signal and I heard the clank of the gurney as the attendant rolled it into the ambulance.

The doors slammed, and I cleared my throat. "Her name is Lee—Lee something. She's in charge of this facility but works out of Houston and is here only occasionally. The residents may not even know her."

A couple of people made notes while I talked.

"How do you spell Lee?" one asked.

I shook my head. "I've never seen it written. Oh—the last name's Ferrell. She's a big donor to public television."

One of the cops let out a soft whistle.

"How sure are you?"

I looked up at Chief Boozer. "I met her for the first time yesterday and she was wearing the same green dress. The staff members here can tell you more than I can." I imagined him talking to Patti. "Try Jamie Barnes in the Assisted Living Building. She fills in when Lee isn't here."

He offered to have one of his people walk me back to the apartment, but I told him I was fine. And I wasn't alone. Stephanie was here, and Jim Bergen was waiting to walk back with me. He tried quizzing me about details but I was distracted, saddened that someone so young and strong could die so suddenly. There was a sense of personal loss, too. Fairhope had been a new start, a place untainted by loss. Now I was reminded; bad things happened everywhere.

"Is your daughter still here?" Jim asked.

I snapped out of my reverie and invited him to come in and meet Stephanie and Barry.

He was quite taken with Stephanie, who always looks pretty and feminine and flirts with old men, but he had no rapport with Barry.

"Stephanie will be leaving soon," I told him. "Can she stop by and meet Nita?"

"Cleo, that's an excellent idea." He consulted his watch. "Nita's not an early riser, but nobody could sleep through this noise today. Let me go back now and bring her up to date. Then you come over whenever you get ready, and I'll get out and see what I can hear. Good plan. Bye, little fellow." He reached to pat Barry's head but backed off when Barry glared at him.

Stephanie had been busy while I was out, unpacking glassware and dishes and arranging things in the china cabinet, along with table linens and decorative stuff I should have gotten rid of. She had a pile of boxes waiting to be cut down for recycling. When that was done, the three of us went out through the courtyard and the lobby of my building.

"So this is where you'll get mail." Stephanie went to the bank of boxes to look for number eight.

There were a few people outside, standing and talking or walking. I saw two police cars parked near the swimming pool, but the yellow tape was gone.

Nita must have been watching for us. She opened the door before we got to it.

"Oh, Cleo! How terrible! I just can't believe this." Then she saw Barry and lit up.

Stephanie got a hug. Barry got a double handshake, with Nita down on his level as she addressed him.

He hid behind his mother at first and grinned coyly at Nita. He'd probably never seen such a tiny adult. But he warmed up quickly and gave her his cutest smile.

When we were leaving, Nita lagged behind and asked quietly, "How do you suppose she managed to drown?"

I told her my theory about the shoes. "I didn't see her feet this morning, but the shoes must've tripped her."

"Or maybe she turned an ankle and fell," Nita said. "I heard the shoes were Jimmy Choos."

She certainly didn't seem to be troubled by a drowning. I let the professional side of me take over. "At least she didn't work directly with residents, so they won't feel a personal loss. And I hate to say it, but the people who did know her didn't like her very much. Maybe this won't be a big trauma for the community."

"But such a terrible beginning for your new job. I hate that."

I smiled and nodded my thanks and Nita patted my shoulder. She seemed to have a direct line to my thoughts.

"Remember to come at five thirty for dominoes. We'll have a lot to talk about tonight, but we won't let it spoil the evening."

Stephanie and Barry were waiting at the edge of the porch.

I said to Nita, "Thank you for sending Riley to take us out last night."

"Oh, did he? How nice." She wasn't admitting anything. "Riley is a special person."

"We went to the restaurant on the pier," Stephanie said.

Hearing that, Barry sprang into action, rising up and down on tiptoes and speaking directly to Nita. I got the message when he pointed skyward.

"He fed the gulls at the pier," Stephanie translated. "Not last night, but on an earlier visit."

"How smart you are, Barry." Nita turned to me. "And speaking of animals, any progress with our feline friend?"

"She's in the apartment and seems right at home. I woke up with her sleeping on the foot of the bed."

Nita broke into a big smile. "Oh, that's a relief! And do you like her? Is she friendly?"

"Mom?" Stephanie's eyes were wide. "A cat?"

"I'll tell you all about it. She came last night after you went to bed. Nita, I've had an idea about her. What was the name of the woman who lived in my apartment? I thought I'd call the vets and see if I can learn the cat's name."

She liked the idea. "I'm no good with names, but Jim will know. Or he can look her up in the directory. There's a vet in the shopping center around the corner. Maybe she went there."

We walked back across the street to my apartment. Stephanie took Barry to my bedroom and introduced him to the cat, but they were wary of one another. Then she packed up her bags and a box of lead crystal I had saved for her and began taking things to the car. Barry and the cat moved to the living room, where they inspected an empty box.

Stephanie returned and stood watching them. "Maybe he's old enough for a pet. I'm hoping he'll sleep through the drive. Got anything for snacks?"

I was already washing grapes and had zip bags filled with sliced cheese and crackers.

Stephanie grabbed a grape and looked around the apartment. "I hate leaving you with all this work."

"Don't talk with your mouth full. Didn't your mother teach you anything?" I added some chocolate covered almonds and put all the snacks into a plastic bag from the grocery store.

She went out and returned after a couple of minutes, arms full of bed linens. "Any idea where the detergent is?"

"I bought some yesterday. But just leave everything on the washer."

I kept busy after they left, trying to avoid thinking about poor, soggy Lee. She seemed to have been living a charmed life. So why had she been at the swimming pool last night, still dressed for the office? Even a good swimmer might be in trouble if she took an unexpected plunge while wearing a tight dress.

Soon I had worked myself into a snare of imagination and speculation. But the energy went to good use. I unpacked books and arranged them in the bookcases. Then I emptied the last of the kitchen boxes and arranged the small appliances on the counter. While I was putting the iron on the shelf in the laundry room, I put Stephanie's sheets in to wash and kept watch as the machine filled with water and began to churn. No leaks, and everything seemed to work properly.

The Wi-Fi man showed up and had to knock loudly to get my attention. "The modem can go anywhere."

"I don't want blinking lights in my bedroom. And I don't think my guests would like that either."

We settled on a shelf in the living room bookcase and chatted while he worked.

"Heard you had some excitement here this morning. Looks like they'd keep the pool locked at night."

I cut open more empty boxes and stacked them flat, ready for recycling. At one point I made a trip to the bedroom and found the cat curled up in her spot on the bed, yellow eyes narrowed sleepily but watching the door. I made up the bed without disturbing her and gave her a few rubs. *Got to get that brush today.*

I was seeing the Wi-Fi guy off when I spotted Chief Boozer and a female officer trudging up the sidewalk.

I waved and called out, "Are you looking for me?"

The chief was frowning. "Maybe we'd better go inside." He introduced his officer, Mary Montgomery, a large woman who didn't smile but gave me a tough-guy nod.

The apartment was looking good, if you ignored the flattened boxes stacked beside the dining table. Boozer sat on the couch, and Officer Montgomery and I took chairs.

He didn't waste time with pleasantries. "Where is your husband, Ms. Mack?"

I hadn't expected that. "He died four years ago. Why?"

"Let me rephrase that. I mean Travis McKenzie, your daughter's father."

I gasped and popped out of my chair. My hands flew to my mouth. "Is Stephanie all right? What happened?"

"Your daughter's not here?"

I glanced at Montgomery then sat down again, heart racing. "She left for Birmingham this morning. Chief, what is this about?"

"Did you know Travis McKenzie and Lee Ferrell were married?"

I stared at him. When I tried to speak, I could only stammer. "Travis … Lee…I…" I closed my eyes and at last got another word out. "Ohmygod."

Mary Montgomery sounded bored. "You okay? Need some water or something?"

I drew a deep breath, suppressing the comment I'd almost blurted out.

"I'm okay. Of course I didn't know. But it does explain a couple of things." I told them about Lee Ferrell's comment when we met in the lobby yesterday. "She knew about our connection, but I didn't. I thought she was just rude."

"And? What was the other thing?"

I needed a moment to dredge up my second thought. "Oh, yes. It explains why she looked familiar to me."

"You met her before." Officer Montgomery sounded accusing.

"No. But I saw a photo. Let me get my phone."

I had to scroll through several weeks of messages from Stephanie.

While I looked, the Chief asked, "When did you last see Mr. McKenzie?"

I shook my head. "It's been a while. Years. I'm not even sure where he lives now. New Orleans, I guess. Stephanie went there for the wedding."

"He's here," the Chief said.

I dropped the phone in my lap and looked at him to be sure I'd heard right. "Here? In Fairhope?"

"Did your daughter see him while she was here?"

"You don't mean he lives here!"

"No, staying in a motel. Came to the station this morning, looking for his wife. He drove through Harbor Village and found her car."

I slouched against the back of my chair and my earlier, repressed thought came back with a vengeance. This time I didn't bother to suppress it. "I wonder if they had a prenup."

Mary Montgomery let out a snort.

"I don't mean to suggest anything," I backpedaled, embarrassed. I picked up the phone again and scrolled for the photo. "Just an impulsive thought. Here it is." I looked at the photo before I handed the phone to Chief Boozer.

He took it and was looking at the wedding photo when the phone rang. He passed it back to me.

It was Stephanie calling, saying she was at Prattville, almost home. "Dad called." She sounded agitated. "You're not going to believe this, Mom. I don't really believe it myself—"

I cut her off. "Chief Boozer is here now, honey. He just told me."

"I can't come back, Mom. I don't have any more clean clothes for Barry. I've already changed him twice today." Her voice was close to a wail and I couldn't help smiling at the way she could focus on the trivial details. Just like her mother.

"Are you driving now?"

"I'm stopped at Cracker Barrel."

"Let me see if Chief Boozer wants to talk with you."

He nodded and I put the phone on speaker and held it so all three of us could hear.

He asked Stephanie for her last name and phone number and Officer Montgomery made notes.

"When did you last see your father?"

"At his wedding in New Orleans. In July," she answered.

"What about his new wife—did you know her well?"

Stephanie was still talking when Chief Boozer reached for his own buzzing phone and passed it to Officer Montgomery, who went out to the porch to answer.

"If we'd just been a little faster last night," Stephanie said, "I would've recognized her, and this might not've happened. Oh, I just can't believe it!"

Boozer was staring at me. He told Stephanie he would talk with her later and disconnected the call.

Officer Montgomery returned and spoke quietly to the chief. I couldn't hear most of what she said, but one phrase came through and claimed my attention—*inconsistent with drowning.*

Boozer nodded and his gaze slid back to me. "Want to tell me about last night?"

It seemed insignificant, but I couldn't avoid feeling guilty, as though I'd concealed something. "The three of us—Stephanie, Barry and I—went out to dinner with a friend who lives here. When we got back about eight, all the lights were on in the lobby. And Lee was sitting on the couch."

"About eight?"

"I can check the time on my charge slip to be sure, but it was close to eight."

"Who was with Ms. Ferrell?"

I shrugged. "I didn't see anyone. I wanted Stephanie to see her—I'd told her how rude Lee had been earlier—so we got out of the car and walked around the corner. And in just that couple of minutes, the lights had been turned off and the lobby was totally dark."

He was silent for a few seconds. "Who was with you, besides your daughter?"

I gave him Riley Meddors's name. "He lives in the next building." I pointed toward the two-story building next door.

"You didn't go into the lobby?"

"No. We said good night to Riley in the parking lot and came home. When I saw Lee earlier in the afternoon, she was looking for Stewart, the handyman. So when I saw the lights on and Lee looking at them, I just assumed Stewart was in the building somewhere, working on them." I felt terrible about pointing a finger at Stewart. "He seems like a nice guy."

All at once, Boozer was in a hurry to depart. He stood. "That receipt from last night—is it handy?"

I got my purse and found the receipt in the outside pocket. "Seven fifty-six. We were at the restaurant on the pier. I signed this at the counter and we walked out and back to the car—not rapidly, we had a two-year-old—and we drove straight here, so...what? Another twenty minutes, maybe, until I saw her in the lobby? That makes it about eight twenty. Do you want this?" I held the receipt out to him.

"Not now, but hang on to it."

* * * *

A couple of hours passed before Stephanie called to say she and Barry were at the quilt shop and she would talk with me again at bedtime.

I asked her, "How's your father?"

"Okay. More angry than grieving so far. He doesn't like the way the police are treating him."

"I suppose that's natural. He didn't have anything to do with it, did he?"

"Oh, Mom. Don't be silly."

I went back to unpacking the printer and hooking it up, and another visitor arrived.

"They ran us out." Patti Wagon's eyes were wide, her curls shaking. "Nobody knows what's going on! The police have been in and out all afternoon. What do you think it's about?"

Another young woman was with her, and I invited both of them inside before I recognized the friend.

"Emily's our bookkeeper," Patti said.

"Oh, yes. We met at the pier a couple of month ago. Nita Bergen introduced us."

"Of course. And it's part-time bookkeeper." Emily had gotten a summer haircut, short on top but reaching to her shoulders in back, with stray bits standing out to give her a fuzzy red aura.

"I was about to get something to drink," I said. "I have Diet 7 Up and bottled water."

We all chose 7 Up and I opened three cans and poured them into short glasses with a few ice cubes, while the girls examined the apartment.

"Very sophisticated, and it looks so comfortable already." Patti strolled around looking at everything.

"Have you heard the news?" Emily asked.

"I've heard nothing but news since I arrived. I expected life here would be simple and peaceful."

"Jamie's leaving," Patti announced.

I stared at her. "Well, no, I haven't heard that. It's a shock, actually." I set out a basket of napkins, plus coasters for cans and glasses, and sat on the couch.

Patti and Emily took the chairs.

"She's going to Charleston, promoted to Executive Director." Emily clapped her hands.

Patti said, "Lee finally does something good for someone and immediately drops dead."

"Don't say that." Emily giggled.

"No, I shouldn't. That was ugly of me. I'm really sorry she's gone. I'm sorry anybody has to die, especially like that. But why did they put us out of the building? We've been there all day. If they were afraid we were going to destroy evidence, why did they leave us in there for hours?"

"They put you out?"

"Yes! The cops came in, told us to take our purses and anything else we needed and wait on the porch. We've been out there an hour already."

"I don't get it," Emily said. "The pool is its own little fenced-off area. They could seal it off without disrupting our entire operation. I've got work to do."

"And the phone is ringing constantly. Did you see the body?" Patti asked me.

"Yes."

"Was it all—you know. How did it look?"

"Wet." I left it at that. "Don't some residents live in the main building? Did the police put them out, too?"

"They wanted to," Emily said, "but we told them it wasn't possible. Right at naptime, with wheelchairs and walkers? No. No way."

Patti added 7 Up to her glass. "They're down there right now, putting up yellow tape that says crime scene, posting official notices on the doors and telling people to come and go through the dining room entrance. I guess we're free to leave, aren't we? It's early, but we're just standing around, and they didn't say anything about letting us back in today."

"Do they know how to get in touch with you?"

They disagreed on the answer to that, and finally Patti proposed, "What if we give you our phone numbers? You're going to be here anyway, and you can call us if we need to come back for something."

"In the next hour or two," Emily cautioned. "I don't know about you, but I've got plans tonight."

"Why don't you talk to Jamie?" I proposed. "Be sure she has your contact information where she can access it. The Assisted Living building isn't closed off, is it?"

They glanced at each other, suddenly hesitant.

"Tell her," Emily said.

Patti squirmed in her chair and looked around the apartment, stalling. "Well, here's the thing." She looked nervous. "You may not like this, but Jamie says she's leaving. Like, immediately. Today, maybe. I think you're going to be in charge here."

I laughed.

Patti and Emily looked at each other.

Emily shrugged. "Well, think about it."

Patti twisted one of her curls absently. "What we mean is, you're what they call 'professional staff.' That's what Lee was, and Jamie, and Nelson, even though he's out of the picture. Then there's the vacant position for a Resident Services person—vacant until Monday, anyway—but for somebody with degrees and certifications and all that. The rest of us are just office staff or aides or maintenance—not in charge of anything."

"I haven't even started to work officially." I felt a little less certain of my interpretation of the facts. The *ohmygod* chorus was beginning to whisper in my head again. "Is there somebody we can call? Where *is* Jamie?" I reached for my phone and searched for her number.

Jamie was curt when she answered. None of the cheeriness she had dished out in recent phone calls. I put her on speaker and told her what I'd just heard.

"I'm really sorry if it puts you in a bind, but I'm not giving this up. I've already talked to Charleston and they want me there Monday."

"Jamie, I haven't had orientation yet. I don't know procedures. And when I do start, I'll be part-time. You can't run a big facility with a part-time, just-off-the-bus administrator. I don't even have a lease for this apartment I've moved into."

That quieted her for a minute, after which she sounded resigned. "Yeah, we might need to do something about that."

Patti and Emily were quiet, too, frozen in position but listening to every word.

Jamie said, "I'll tell you what. I'll write up the lease and leave it in the office. There's another one I need to do, too."

Emily looked at Patti and I heard her mutter something.

I asked Jamie, "You know they've been put out of the building, right?"

"Who has?"

"The office staff. Patti and Emily are here with me right now, and the police have closed the main building. I suppose the other staff members have gone already."

"Oh holy . . ." After a moment of silence, she added, "Look, I've got to go." And she hung up.

"What are we supposed to do with leases?" Emily whined.

My thinking was a bit disorganized at the moment, but slowly Emily's question came into focus as the most sensible topic in play. But why wasn't the answer obvious to a bookkeeper? "You'll add me to your list of payments that come in each month. And put the paperwork into an official file. It's no different because I work here. Handle it like any other new resident."

Emily shrugged. "I just post to the accounts. We get in trouble if we think."

I walked down the sidewalk with Patti and Emily. At 3:30 on a Friday in the middle of August, forty miles from the white sand beaches of the Gulf of Mexico, it was hot in the sun but not unbearable as people might think. A breeze carried the smell of earth and vegetation, and a siren wailed somewhere in the distance. We counted seven police cars parked around the main building, plus a box-shaped white van at the side door. The van was unmarked, but there was a definite police look about it.

Yellow tape was strung across every entrance to the porch.

The relative absence of civilian vehicles and people suggested the rest of the Harbor Village staff was already gone.

"Notice you don't see any residents out? Naptime." Emily laughed. "Even if there was a drowning."

Patti joined in. "But let the cable go out and it's like an ant hill here, everybody running over to complain, wanting to know how soon FOX will be back on. That's the biggest complaint we get. That and the dining room."

"Be nice," I chided them, just as I'd do with Stephanie. "You'll be old one day, if you're lucky. Have a good weekend."

I went back to the apartment, cut open the wardrobe box and moved all my hanging clothes to the closet. And when I finished that, I hopped into the shower and prepared for a game of dominoes and the inevitable rehashing of the day's events.

At five, I was dressed and ready to go to the Bergens' apartment, but with twenty minutes to spare. I sat down at the computer and searched for veterinary offices in Fairhope. I found the one Nita had mentioned, in the shopping center next door, and dialed the number. Voice mail told me they'd be in again on Monday or, if this were an emergency, I could press *1* and be connected with the weekend on-call vet.

I hung up and my phone beeped.

I listened to a message from Travis McKenzie. "Cleo, I need to talk with you. Call me back at this number."

Oh, great. Stephanie's father was the last person I wanted to talk to, and there was no time now anyway. I got my purse, checked the doors and stroked the cat a few times before walking over to Nita's.

Chapter 5

There were four players for Mexican Trains, and Jim had already retired to his office when I arrived.

"This isn't a normal occurrence for Harbor Village." Nita seemed embarrassed and a little angry, as though a drowning were an assault on civility.

"No, it's normally as dull as dishwater here." Dolly looked at me. "Don't expect anything exciting to happen here, not ever again."

Riley chuckled and kept turning dominoes face down on the vinyl pad. "Is Ada not coming?"

"She canceled," Nita said.

"We ought to disinvite her," Dolly said.

"We can't do that." Nita frowned.

"She doesn't come half the time," Dolly complained. "And she's always so gloomy. Cleo's got all the gossip, I'll bet. What's going on?"

I did a mental check for anything I knew that would interest them. "The police closed off the main building. I guess you know that. And Jamie's leaving."

Riley looked at me, raised a finger to his lips and then pointed toward Jim's office.

Jim was speaking loudly, and I whispered back to Riley, "Is he on the phone? Can he hear us?"

Riley gave a quick headshake.

"Are we starting with sevens tonight? What did we get to last week?" Dolly swirled the tiles around on the table.

Riley consulted his notepad. "I think we should start fresh, since Cleo wasn't here last time."

"Yes, let's do that," Nita said.

"Looky here, looky here," Jim sang out from the doorway.

I looked over my shoulder and saw him leaning heavily on his cane.

"Do you know all these people, Chief?"

Chief Boozer stepped out of the hallway behind him and scanned our group around the table. "Ms. Mack, Mr. Meddors." He acknowledged us with a nod of his head.

"And this is Dolly Webb." Nita patted Dolly's arm. "She's lived at Harbor Village for years."

"Yes, we met this morning," Dolly said. "You probably don't remember."

"You're a swimmer," Chief Boozer said.

Jim didn't seem to listen. "Hard to keep all the little old ladies straight, isn't it, Chief? You have to focus your attention on people who could pose a threat, not the ninety-pound octogenarians."

"Anybody who swims laps five days a week is in better shape than I am." Chief Boozer raised his eyebrows and gave us a smile and a nod. "Good night, everybody."

"I got a call from Travis McKenzie," I said, loudly. My new philosophy called for full disclosure. I didn't want any more embarrassing confessions.

Chief Boozer turned back, tipping his head to the side. "Oh?" He waited.

"He left a message and wants me to call back. I haven't done it yet."

He nodded. "I suppose he doesn't know many people here."

"Apparently he knows I'm here."

After a brief moment of silence, the chief said, "I didn't tell him. Well, good night, folks."

Jim went to the door with him but came to the table after a few moments. "Did somebody order the sandwiches? Want me to do it?"

"It's already done," Nita said.

"Good, good. Call me when they get here." He went back to his lair.

"Was I just insulted?" Dolly asked. "I believe Jim thinks I'm insignificant."

"We all know better than that," Riley soothed.

"Yes." I changed to a gruff voice. "Where were you at midnight, Ms. Webb?"

"Drowning the CEO." Dolly laughed. "Or whatever she is."

"Was." Nita managed to squelch the levity with a single word.

But not before I learned something. If they had heard about any *inconsistencies with drowning*, they weren't mentioning it. Maybe I'd misunderstood Officer Montgomery's whispered report.

We played dominos until 6:25, when the doorbell rang.

"I'll get it." Jim charged out of the back room and headed for the door like a shot. Or like a shot with a walking cane.

Conversation during dinner focused on the day's events.

"A lot of excitement," Jim called it, and Dolly agreed.

"I prefer boredom," Riley said.

"That poor woman," Nita said.

"When do you suppose it happened?" Dolly inspected the sandwich platter before selecting turkey with Swiss and lettuce. "I thought the pool was closed until six every morning, and I was there by six."

"It's never closed," Jim said.

I looked at him. "Doesn't a pool have to be locked? I thought there was a law."

"I don't know about laws, but I know that gate's never locked," Jim said. "What I don't know is why anybody would go in there at night, wearing street clothes. I made my usual patrol of the premises at ten thirty and there was nobody in the area."

Dolly licked her fingers discretely. "Did you look in the water?"

Jim ignored her.

"We saw her in the lobby at eight thirty," Riley glanced at me for confirmation and accepted the sandwich platter from Nita. "So she was on the premises after dinner. Probably in the water by the time you went out."

That got Jim's attention. "Really? You and Cleo saw her?"

"Well, Cleo did. Ms. Ferrell was sitting in the lobby when we got back from dinner. Right, Cleo?" He took a couple of sandwich pieces and held the platter for me.

I nodded and selected a big segment with hot, sautéed vegetables.

"Very interesting," Jim looked from me to Riley. "I didn't realize you knew Ms. Ferrell, Riley. Don't think I ever saw her before." He looked back at me. "Did you give this information to Chief Boozer?" He motioned for the platter.

"Yes."

Riley said, "Maybe I should."

Jim frowned. "I guess he just forgot to mention it, but I'd better be sure he knows. I'll phone him after we eat. Sitting in the lobby, huh? By herself."

"I didn't see anyone else. But when I saw her late in the afternoon, she was looking for the handyman. I guess he might've been there somewhere, working on the lights. They were on, and Lee was looking at them."

"I haven't gotten in the habit of checking the pool every night. I suppose I should."

Wouldn't he love to discover a body? I hoped he'd never get another chance.

At eight thirty we wrapped up our game and prepared to depart. The bill for sandwiches was cheaper this week.

"I ordered one less than last time, since Ada wasn't coming," Nita said.

We got out our money and swapped bills until everyone had appropriate change, and Jim collected the payments.

"Go back to the larger order next time, honey." He arranged the bills and stuck them into an already bulging wallet. "Doesn't hurt to have a little extra food. Cleo, you want me to walk you home?"

"No. I'll be fine. It's just across the street."

"And I'm going that way," Riley said.

"We can't just assume it's safe here now." Jim led the way to the door, sounding pleased with the turn of events. "I'll do a late patrol in a couple of hours."

Dolly paused at the door. "What do you mean it's not safe? It's never safe to go falling around a swimming pool, and there's no evidence of anything else."

"Well, maybe, maybe not. Things aren't always what they seem. Have to keep an open mind."

"You know something, don't you?"

Jim shrugged and grinned, and looked past me to Riley. "Riley, I meant to ask. What do you know about the financial condition of Harbor Village?"

Dolly was out on the porch. "You think somebody drowned her because she didn't pay the bills?"

Riley said, "I haven't reviewed anything recently. Maybe I should."

"Maybe Cleo will have inside access." Jim looked at me with a hopeful expression.

"Maybe, but I don't know anything yet."

Dolly reappeared in the doorway. "Cleo, earlier tonight—did you say somebody is leaving?"

"Jamie. She's transferring to Charleston."

"What!" Jim squawked. "Where did you get that?"

"From the office staff. She may be gone already."

Jim took a step backward and bumped against the wall. "She hasn't said a word. Does Chief Boozer know? I'll call him right now."

We said our good nights to Nita, and Dolly went in the main entrance to the building. Riley and I walked across the boulevard.

"If you don't mind my asking, who is Travis McKenzie?"

I told him. "We've been divorced twenty-three years, but he married Lee Ferrell a few weeks ago."

"And you didn't know that?"

"I knew he got married. I just learned this afternoon that his new wife was the administrator here. But she knew who I was." I told him about the remark she'd made in the lobby.

We were at the front door of my building and he followed me through the sitting room, where the mailboxes were located.

"I got part of that last night. That's why you wanted Stephanie to see her."

"Right. And just think, if Stephanie had seen her, they would've recognized each other and talked. The sequence of events would've been altered. Maybe Lee wouldn't have gone to the pool." I sighed. "Have you heard anything about the cause of death?"

"Drowning?"

"I thought I heard something else, but I must've misunderstood."

At the door to my apartment, I got out my key. He produced a flat brown wallet and pulled out a business card.

"My number is on here and I'm in the next building. Call if you need me."

I thanked him and wondered what use he'd be in an emergency. Fortunately, I didn't intend to have any emergencies.

Stephanie called an hour later. I was already in bed, working a Sudoku puzzle to stay awake.

"Did you have fun playing dominoes?" There was a tease in her voice.

"Yes. Nobody's died since you left."

"Did Dad call you?"

"Yes. What does he want?"

"Mom. You didn't even talk to him?"

"He left a message for me to call back and I haven't done it yet. What's up?"

"He thought he might be arrested and wanted me to arrange to bail him out. I told him you're there."

"Great. Why would he be arrested?"

"Oh, Mom. He hasn't got a clue. They don't arrest you just because your wife drowns. I tried to tell him that. I don't know what he's thinking. That's the problem, I guess; he's not thinking, he's just bouncing around. Grieving, I suppose, or going nuts. He's so irrational, I almost wonder if he *has* done something."

"You don't mean that."

"No, of course not."

I woke early Saturday and couldn't get back to sleep. Ten minutes before six, the clock said when I gave up and rolled out of bed. The cat stood, arched her back and stretched then meowed for attention.

I put on the jeans I'd left lying across the dresser, with the last clean T-shirt in the suitcase, and slipped into sandals. This would be a good day to catch up on the laundry I'd generated before and after the move. But first I went out to the kitchen and started the coffee.

While I waited, listening to the coffeemaker's sizzles and grunts, I added food to the cat's dish. Then, with a cup of steaming coffee in hand, I decided to see what Harbor Village looked like in the early morning, when it wasn't the scene of a fatal accident. I got my keys and phone, stuck a tissue in a pocket and went out through the screened porch.

The lights were on at Ann's next door and in the apartment at the other back corner of my building. I couldn't think of the name of the woman who lived there, but I knew she had short gray hair and a slow-walking Pekingese and had told Barry he looked like her grandson. And around the corner from her was Gloria, a chubby little blonde with gold-framed glasses, who looked like Mrs. Claus and had brought me a welcome gift, a loaf of homemade bread. I made a mental note to return her plate today.

It had rained sometime during the night and the sidewalk was still wet. A few shallow pools of water stood in low spots. I stopped at the corner of the garages, where I had a view of the big house. The lights were off and everything looked calm and quiet. Yellow tape still looped in scallops from one porch post to the next, barring admission.

I walked along the south side of the big house, sipping my coffee and taking in my surroundings. The silver SUV was right where I'd first seen it two nights ago. If it belonged to the night watchman, as I suspected, he must park in the same space every night. Such predictability didn't strike me as an ideal trait for a security guard, who was supposed to observe things people didn't want seen. But would a guard own a Lexus? I wasn't so sure.

There was a sign on the side of the building, big letters saying "ballroom." Sounded grand, but I wondered what it was like inside. Elegant or utilitarian? And what was it used for? I couldn't picture many Harbor Village residents dancing a tango.

At the back of the main building, I found a pretty little koi pond, with not-so-little orange and white fish that followed me as I walked around their pool to look in the windows of an arts and crafts room. The fish were sort of creepy, but the art room looked inviting. I could see easels and finished paintings displayed along the back wall. There was more yellow tape across the back doors to the lobby, but with the reflections on the glass, I couldn't see inside the lobby.

I retraced my path to a lush vegetable garden, where radishes shouldered up out of the earth and giant leaves of squash plants held little pools of rainwater. The cherry tomatoes looked like Christmas balls. I wished Barry could see the green tunnel the plants made, growing up and across the top of a bamboo frame. He would've raced right through it, but I didn't because of the dripping water. Instead, I took a gravel pathway that ran between raised beds. My footsteps crunched and loose gravel slid into my sandals.

Fern-like dill plants were loaded with sparkling drops of water and gave off their distinctive smell as I brushed against them. I half-remembered that they served as a host plant for some butterfly species, but I didn't see any caterpillars crawling around.

The yellow Assisted Living building had three cars parked out front. The porch was crowded with love seats and rockers and a swing, but no one was out yet.

I considered going in and looking for Jamie, in case she was still in town, but her BMW wasn't among the parked cars. Anyway, the staff would be busy at this hour, serving breakfast and morning meds and helping residents get up and dressed.

I turned toward the front of the complex and walked past the recycling shed, where I was supposed to deliver my flattened moving boxes. Across the street was a row of attractive small condos, with individual garages and tiny porches. Lights were on in one unit and a bird feeder swung from a Japanese maple.

Next came the pink building with the indoor pool, and beyond it the wrought iron fence around the outdoor pool. And there was Dolly, just exiting the outdoor pool area and closing the gate behind herself.

"Good morning," I called softly then again more loudly. "Dolly!"

"What?" She looked around, startled. "Oh, it's you."

She was wearing her white bathrobe, juggling a phone and a key ring while she closed the gate. Today she had a pink towel and it was wrapped turban-style around her head. "Are you coming to swim?"

"No. Just walking. It's so quiet today."

"And no corpses in the pool. Except me, that is. I don't usually swim on Saturdays, but I had to make up for yesterday. Oh, Cleo! I want to give you something."

"What?"

She stopped walking and dug in the pocket of her robe then stretched her hand out to me. "It's a good thing you showed up. I didn't know what I was going to do with it."

I stuck out my hand and she dropped in a phone.

"I found it. Just now."

"Where?"

She pointed to her pocket. "In here."

"Is it yours?"

"Never saw it before."

"And it was in your pocket?"

"You saw me take it out." She began walking again, briskly.

She didn't seem to want to talk about it, and I didn't want the phone. Since Dolly wasn't about to take it back, maybe she could shed light on its owner.

"How did it get there, do you know? Was anyone else out here earlier?"

"No. I don't know whose it is." She raised her other hand, which held a phone. "Here's mine."

"Do you have an old one, one you might've left in the pocket?"

"It's not mine, I tell you. I wear this robe every day and I've never seen that phone. And I don't want it. You keep it." She waved her hands. "Give it to your policeman friend. Maybe somebody reported it lost."

"Okay." I shrugged and slid the phone into an empty pocket. It reminded me that I needed to call Travis McKenzie and spoiled what had begun to feel like a pleasant day.

It was too early to call Travis when I got back to the apartment, or maybe I was just stalling. I made the bed, with the cat clinging to her spot on the duvet, and sorted the laundry and started a load. Stephanie's sheets were still in the dryer, so I heated them up and remade the guest room bed and crib and opened the blinds.

At eight I got my phone, selected Travis' missed call and hit redial. The call woke him up, although he denied it. We agreed to meet in town for breakfast in an hour. I chose the restaurant and gave him directions.

I changed the laundry from washer to dryer and started it then put a second load, dark colors this time, into the washer. At the last minute, I decided to add my jeans, which were damp from the knees down as a result of my walk through the garden. I changed into black pants and took everything out of the jeans pockets. The phone Dolly had found was small and black, a flip phone with *Verizon* imprinted on the front. Cheap. Probably old and thrown away, rather than lost. Or maybe one Dolly had forgotten she had. I put it on the dresser, added my jeans to the washer and moved on to the next task, disposing of the moving boxes.

I got the boxes out to the car by making three trips, and then I drove down to the recycling shed and made another three trips carting them inside.

I was getting pretty sweaty by then, so I turned the car's AC to full blast for the drive into town.

No matter how long ago the marriage ended, no matter how nasty the divorce, there was still a feeling you shouldn't look like a complete slob when you saw your ex again. I pulled into Walgreens parking lot and stopped the car. The emergency kit in my purse held the basics—lipstick, mascara and blush. I couldn't get a good view of my hair in the rearview mirror, so I stepped out of the car and used my reflection in the car window, giving my hair a good fluffing. And then I drove into town.

Travis was sitting in the first booth, facing the door. He was wearing a gray suit—a *suit*! On *Saturday*!—and had a few white hairs showing in his dark eyebrows. "Cleo!" He sounded glad to see me and stood to give me a phony kiss on each cheek.

"You're looking good." I slid into the booth across from him.

It wasn't true; he looked like crap, like he hadn't slept in days, with puffy, pale circles around his eyes and gray stubble along his jaw. Why had he needed an hour to get ready if he wasn't going to shave? Then I remembered he'd just lost his new wife.

"I'm so sorry about Lee."

Travis shook his head, barely moving, like he was numb. "I can't believe it yet. We were together for two years and married just a few weeks."

"Tell me all about it."

He looked confused. "The wedding? Steffi came, didn't she tell you?"

"Yes. But I meant the drowning."

He leaned across the table. "Cleo, I think they suspect me."

"Of course they do." I tried not to laugh at his child-like indignation. "Even if it's an accident, the husband is always suspect number one. Especially, I should think, if the ink isn't dry on the license yet and he stands to inherit a fortune."

"That's not true." He scowled, looking a lot like Barry. "Where did you get that idea?"

I unwrapped the silverware and spread the paper napkin across my lap. "The cops have to rule out any possibility other than an accident. Isn't that her name on the sponsor list for *Masterpiece Theatre*?"

He grimaced. "Thank her first husband for that. He wanted the Ferrells to be known as philanthropists and damn near broke them."

His phone buzzed and he looked to see who was calling. "I need to take this."

"Go ahead."

I asked the server for a cup of decaf.

While Travis talked, I considered my position. I always insisted that my students learn everything possible about an organization before they interviewed there, and yet here I was beginning a new job and—because it was only part-time, and not part of a long-term career plan, and maybe because it had just fallen into my lap with no effort on my part—I knew almost nothing about the Harbor Village organization. I knew Lee was a Ferrell, and I knew I wrote my rent check to Ferrell & Associates, but I didn't know exactly how Harbor Village was connected to the Ferrells. For that matter, I didn't know if Ferrell was her family name or acquired through marriage.

I decided to learn what I could from Travis, preferably without revealing my ignorance.

I had plenty of questions. What had Lee's role been? How could Jamie be reassigned at a time like this? And who was likely to take over this facility, to be my supervisor? Had Patti and Emily possibly been right— would someone try to throw me under that particular bus?

Travis didn't go outside to avoid disturbing others with his conversation. He put a hand over one ear and sat right in the booth, saying yes and no and okay a bunch of times.

Finally he hung up. "The lawyer. Now where were we?"

"About to have breakfast."

When he returned to the main topic, after eggs and bacon and hash browns, he sounded more like a bereaved spouse. "We had a disagreement, Lee and I. An argument. And she walked out."

He talked as though he were speaking to a therapist, or perhaps a priest. "She'd done it before but she always came back. Not this time. I have this app on my phone—we both have it, so we can find the phones if they get lost. When I remembered it, it told me she was here."

He took a long sip of coffee and signaled for a refill.

"So I drove seven hours from Houston to apologize, even though it wasn't really my fault. I went to the motel and waited, but she never came."

He closed his eyes momentarily. This was beginning to feel like an act.

"I even sent flowers that she never saw."

He snapped his fingers suddenly and I jumped.

"Gone, just like that. And I'll never see her again. Can you believe it?"

"Yes, Travis, I can. I've lost a spouse, you know."

He scowled at the interruption. "Well, I didn't *die*, for God's sake."

"I was thinking of Robert."

"Oh. Yeah. Right."

He had no idea who I was talking about. The most self-centered man I'd ever met had honed his faults in the last twenty-three years. I wanted to laugh.

He changed the subject. "What do you know about the cops in this town?"

I'd been there three days and met two cops, Boozer and Montgomery. They seemed to be reasonable people, but I didn't want to argue. "I haven't had much contact with them, personally."

"Cleo, look. I thought they were going to arrest me last night. If they do, I need you to get me out, okay? I've got your phone number now and I'll give you my attorney's number. If anything happens, call him. He'll tell you what to do."

"Why would they arrest you, Travis? Drowning isn't a crime. Is there something you're not telling me?"

A big group of people came into the restaurant, talking and laughing while they waited to be seated.

Travis leaned across the table. "She didn't drown. Her skull was fractured."

I cringed at the way he said it, such cruel ferocity about a loved one. I was picturing the scene and, in my imagination, it was night and the outdoor pool was still under construction, as it had been two months ago, with garden hoses and piles of sand and cement mixers and shovels strewn around inside the fence.

The hostess swept the crowd of newcomers into a side room.

"So she tripped." I clung to my vision. "And hit her head on something. She wasn't dressed for swimming. She went into the water by accident. If she was conscious, if she tried to swim—she could swim, couldn't she? But maybe not with wet clothes weighing her down. However it happened, they don't arrest somebody for an accident."

He began nodding. "Right. Right."

Inconsistent with drowning, I recalled Officer Montgomery saying. And now Travis' words: *she didn't drown*. I ignored a germ of suspicion and plowed ahead with my scenario. "You know the kind of shoes she was wearing. Walking around a swimming pool in the dark in those things? Anybody could fall."

"Right." He still sounded doubtful. Then he looked at me sharply. "How do you know what she wears? Did she meet with you?"

"Briefly."

"She didn't tell me." He rested his elbow on the table and rubbed his eyes. "Didn't have a chance, I guess. I wasn't sure you'd work with us if you knew. With me, I mean."

"I'm not sure I would have, if I'd known. I was just taking a job because it was offered and convenient. The one thing Lee told me was she didn't like working with family, so it must've been your idea to hire me."

I realized with surprise that the sentiment she expressed might have been directed at him, too. I wished I hadn't told him. Even more, I wished I hadn't told Chief Boozer, since it might explain why he gave Travis such a grilling.

"We didn't have much opportunity to talk. Just ran into each other in the lobby. What did you mean when you said she didn't drown?" What I wanted to know was whether Lee Ferrell was murdered, but I couldn't bring myself to use the word.

"That's what they say, based on the preliminary report. But, of course, you're right. She probably fell and hit her head on something." His voice grew insistent. "But they need to figure out exactly how that happened. What did she trip on? What caused a skull fracture? Was anybody with her? If so, why didn't they do something? The cops were out there all day and didn't even keep the area sealed off. I'm going to talk to them again and this time *they'll* do the worrying."

"What were they looking for in the main building?"

He gave me a blank look. "Evidence of some sort, I suppose. I didn't know they were there. Did they go through files and stuff?"

I shrugged. "I just know they put the staff out."

He glanced around then leaned forward. "There's something weird going on at this facility, Cleo. That's what Lee would've told you if she'd had a chance. Revenue and expenses don't match up. Too many people move out, there's too much staff turnover and too many complaints. Overhead is unpredictable. Things look fine on the surface, but something's wrong. We needed some fresh eyes here, someone without a 'corporate' label pasted on her forehead. Then Stephanie said you might move here." He tapped the tabletop. "I told Lee you were it."

"Stephanie told you?" That answered one question. "And then Jamie ran into me at the restaurant?"

"According to her, you practically volunteered for a job. Maybe it wasn't the best idea, not with a new wife. But I'm glad you're here now. Have you started work yet?"

"Monday," I answered automatically, wondering just how much influence Travis exerted with Harbor Health Services, or if he only operated through Lee.

"And another thing," I said. "What do you know about Jamie Barnes? How can she leave right now? Who will replace her? There doesn't seem to be anyone on site."

Travis' mouth clenched. "Lee approved her transfer, for some reason. Thursday night. Might've been the last decision she made. I'm sure she had her reasons. Lee never did anything without a good reason. Jamie's her sister, you know. The black sheep of the family."

Chapter 6

I was stunned.

Jamie and Lee were sisters? Nobody had said anything about that. And they were nothing alike. Lee was polished and intimidating, a winner. Jamie was assertive but scrappy, a survivor, with lots of scars and more than a little disrespect for the system.

I was about to ask if Jamie had been a Ferrell too, but Travis signaled for the check and got out his wallet. There was something else I needed to settle.

"This is turning into a big job, Travis. Even before I knew I'd be snooping, too."

"Yes, I see that. You have to take over here, Cleo. For the time being, at least. You're still free of the corporate stamp, since it's obvious you're an accidental executive. And if you really want to be part-time, you can scale back later, once things calm down."

I was shaking my head all the time he talked, but he ignored me.

"You're too young to quit working. If you don't need the money, you can start a college fund for our grandson." He laughed ruefully. "Hard to believe, isn't it, you and me and a grandson."

I barely controlled a shiver. "I'm not interested in a full-time job, Travis. I'm interested in a social life, some hobbies. A little travel."

"A year, how about that?"

"I hear this facility was already short-handed, with bad food and unhappy employees. What could I do about that if I'm busy learning the ropes and snooping? You need to get a good person in here ASAP. That's how you deal with problems."

He grinned and stood up. "See? You're figuring things out already. Anyway, there's nobody else. It won't be as bad as you're imagining.

You'll have full authority and you'll find things well organized, except for losing Lee and now Jamie. Lee was a good manager, Cleo. You're about to find that out."

"Then why is this facility off track?"

He didn't take that well but turned it on me. "That's what you're going to find out. Better get going. I need to light a fire under some cops."

"One month. That's it."

He continued to talk while we waited in line at the register. "I'm leaving this afternoon, making a round of all the places Lee managed personally. Then I'll go back to Houston. I'll be back here in ten days or so, after the memorial service. Oh, yes. Here's the card with my cell number and the office number in Houston. I put my attorney's number on the back, although now that I think about it, you probably won't need it."

We were going out the door, Travis turning right, me going left, when he thought of something else and called for me to wait. He trotted back, looking a bit like a movie star.

He got near enough for me to hear him. "See if you can find a nurse for next week. We're supposed to have one on the premises during the week and Jamie's gone already. There's probably a temp service in Mobile if not here."

"Okay." That should be a simple job. Nursing services operated 24/7 and responded on short notice.

"I'll call tomorrow night. If you haven't found someone, I'll pull a nurse from another facility. But that gets expensive, you know."

He acted like I would be paying for it. And I supposed I would, in one way or another.

I walked back to my car in a funk, thinking I'd just thrown my lot in with a faltering facility, a bullying, self-centered ex-husband and added to that a full-time job I didn't want that required me to find the problems and fix them. What a mess. To top it off, I had imposed a one-month time limit on myself. How dumb was that?

When I backed out of the parking slot, I realized I was aimed toward the bay. Just the place for a pity party.

It was midmorning already and shoppers were strolling the streets, mixed in with dog walkers, teenagers, tourists and senior citizens. There were more people and cars at the pier and not a single parking space. I drove around the rose garden in a slow train of cars. An Italian ice cart was set up near the pier, doing a good business. The car ahead of me, with two kayaks strapped on top, got lucky and pulled into a space as soon as it was vacated, but most of us made it all the way around the circle without finding an empty spot.

I did see someone I recognized. The desk clerk from the motel was standing near the fountain with a young woman. Both of them were looking up the hill, waving and acting silly. They faced each other and began to dance like marionettes, arms up and jerky.

I drove back up the hill and turned right. The parking strip on the bluff was only half full. I pulled into the end space and got out. It was shady there, with a breeze. I walked across the grass, past some bronze statuary of children, a teacher in a long skirt holding a book. I sat on one of the wooden benches and stared out at the water.

So Travis and Lee had been together for two years. I assumed he lived in Houston now, since that was where Harbor Village's headquarters were. And what did he do, work for his wife? He'd been a grad student in social work when we were together, one of the few males in a program that concentrated on public policy. The faculty had assumed that male students were on a different career trajectory, that they would become college professors or agency administrators of some sort, perhaps in Washington. The women, it was presumed, would go into human service delivery, working in health care, in counseling, at schools, with the courts, or in children's agencies. It wasn't that a woman couldn't work in a major university—I was proof of that—it was that the males shouldn't go to lesser positions. And all the classmates I'd kept up with after graduation had pretty much followed those expectations, or else given up their careers for motherhood.

Had Travis stayed in the field? I hadn't kept up with him, personally or professionally, for at least a decade, and Stephanie wasn't concerned with such things. The suit he was wearing made him look like a salesman, maybe pharmaceuticals. Or a hospital administrator.

I took out my phone and dialed Stephanie.

"I saw your father."

"And? Did they arrest him?"

"Of course not. What does he do now, professionally? Is he still a social worker?"

"Oh, I don't know. You should've asked him. Hospital administration? No, that was a few years back. I think it's clinics now. Or hospice, maybe. Is that the same thing?"

She didn't seem to know he was connected with Harbor Village.

"Honey, do you ever listen to your parents? For instance, would you know where to find your mother now?"

She giggled. "My father never talks to me, and my mother tells me everything. It's about noon right now, so I imagine she's sitting in a trendy little restaurant, looking out at flowers and water. Maybe a short, handsome man is sitting across from her. How am I doing?"

"Close enough." So she thought Riley was handsome. I'd have to take another look. And she actually thought I told her everything. "Does Travis live in Houston?"

"Oh yeah, he's been there forever. Remember he couldn't come to my wedding because a hurricane was aimed at Houston?"

That wasn't exactly the way I remembered it, but I didn't go there. I asked about Barry and Boyd and, after she reported all was well, she said she needed to get back to work, unless there was news about Lee. I told her I hadn't learned anything.

A trio of pelicans flapped by, over the water, but since I was on the bluff, they were at my eye level and looked almost close enough to touch. It was easy to forget how big they were until you saw them up close. They flapped their wings a few times and then floated out of sight, looking like prehistoric mechanical devices.

Two people came up the steep flight of wooden steps from the park down below. They were panting and gasping and giggling. I recognized the desk clerk again.

"Hi there," he called out. "Are you staying with us?"

"No. I live here now."

"Oh, congratulations. Welcome to Fairhope." Then he hurried to catch up with his friend.

I sat a few minutes longer before I decided my mood was sufficiently improved and I could go home. I still wasn't crazy about the idea of working with Travis, but we'd be in different states, and he probably wasn't involved in daily operations of the company. The Harbor Village problems were actually intriguing and I found myself looking forward to solving them.

But before I could leave my bench, the motel clerk came back.

"Mind if I join you for a minute? I'm on duty in an hour, but no sense in getting there early."

"Oh, I'd love company." I slid down the bench to give him more room.

"I would ask if you come here often, but you might take it the wrong way."

"I intend to come here often—does that count? My name's Cleo, if you don't remember."

"I'm Hunter. So you got moved?"

"Yes, to Harbor Village. It's a place for old people." I grinned, wondering if he'd remember his slip of the tongue a few weeks ago.

Hunter reddened and flung his head back. "Oh, please!" He had a prominent Adam's apple and a nasty-looking pimple beside it. He sat upright again and shook his head from side to side. Even while sitting still, there was something of the marionette about him. "For retirees, retirees! I'll never make that error again!" He looked at me. "They had some excitement up there yesterday. Did you hear about it?"

"The drowning? I heard she was staying with you."

He nodded. "I've known her a long time. She comes every month or two. Drives from Texas and stays two nights. Always gets a suite and has a pizza sent in. Funny how predictable people are."

"I met her yesterday and she wasn't very friendly."

"Yeah, well, some people are like that. Still, it's too bad she drowned."

I wondered if he'd consider motel business private and decided to find out. "And the man who came with her—Travis. Is he a regular, too?"

He hesitated but followed the "in for a penny, in for a pound" rule. "He wasn't really with her this time, not at first. She came on Wednesday. I wasn't on duty, but I looked it up."

"I was there Wednesday night, too," I said. "That was the day I moved. I looked for you."

"I usually work Wednesdays, but somebody needed to trade days. That's why I'm working today." He looked at his watch. "I need to leave pretty soon."

So Lee and I had stayed in the same motel Wednesday night. If I'd been there Thursday, I could've run into Travis, too. In fact, I hadn't seen either of them there, but maybe the suites were separated from the regular rooms.

Hunter was still reflecting. "She called Thursday night, must've been about eight. Told me to let him into the room, to tell him she'd be there in an hour. But I guess she never came."

"You guess. Would you know if she did?"

He nodded. "Probably. There's only one door open after eight, so she had to come right by the desk. It's so sad to think she's dead."

This was probably his first brush with the death of someone he knew. Maybe I should distract him. "Where are the suites located?"

"There's really just one, on the second floor. And several double rooms we can join together for families or whatever. Liaisons." He laughed.

"So Travis got there Thursday—about nine, did you say? And he was there all night?"

He nodded. "The police asked that, too. I'll tell you what I told them. I think he went to sleep. He came down to the desk about five in the morning and asked if she'd been there or called. And then he went out."

"And didn't come back?"

He shrugged. "I left at seven. He's still staying with us, but the police had him move to a different room. So they could go through her stuff, I guess. He's her fiancé or something."

"Married two months ago, I understand."

He looked at his watch again. "Too bad. I'd better go now, I guess."

I got up to go, too. "You need a ride?"

"No thanks. My car's right here."

We walked together across the grass. "And just what were you and your friend doing down at the fountain earlier? You looked like puppets dancing."

He laughed and his mood lightened. "We were dancing! We've been doing it every weekend this summer. Sometimes her friends come, too. They're all staying at Harbor Village, you know. Well, no, maybe you don't. I think it's sort of a secret. They're from Ukraine, working at the hotel for the summer. Not the Holiday Express. I mean the Grand Hotel, at Point Clear. Her family gets up in the middle of the night, goes online and calls up the Fairhope pier cam so they can see us doing Ukrainian folk dances. They go home in another week."

"And the pier cam focuses on the fountain."

"No, not necessarily. Viewers can take control of it and move it around. That's just the spot we use."

"What a great idea," I said. "Skyping on a grand scale. Saves the cost of an international phone call but lets the parents see that their kids are okay. Maybe I'll get my grandson to look for me sometime."

Now I understood the jerky movements of the camera I had seen on my first visit to the park. It had probably been under the control of someone in Ukraine.

Traffic was heavy on South Mobile Street, with congestion backing up from the stop sign at the corner. Southbound cars zipped around the curve without warning, so I didn't dare back across to the other lane. Instead, I left the park going in the opposite direction from Harbor Village. At the next intersection, I turned onto an unfamiliar street that twisted through a nice residential area. Large, new homes were mixed in with small, old cottages. The contrast was a little jarring, but the neighborhood seemed like a good place to walk, with huge trees and dark shade and lots to entertain the eye, especially now, with colorful campaign signs in many of the yards.

After a few blocks, houses gave way to commercial buildings, and at the transition point, there was a children's playground with a splash pad. It appeared to be the same one I'd seen in photographs from Barry's first visit, the weekend of Travis' wedding. Several wet kids were making good use of it today.

I drove a few more blocks, gaining a sense of direction that told me I needed to turn left, but before I could do that, a sign caught my eye. All Pet Vet was a big clinic, with people and cars moving around in the parking lot. I pulled in.

There was a nice waiting room and one woman at a counter.

"I need a cat brush."

"Right behind you."

There was a good assortment of brushes and combs on a shelf and a hanging rack, everything from a window squeegee type to a hard plastic device that looked like fangs and several brushes with needle-sharp wire bristles. I chose one that looked similar to my hairbrush and promised on its label "no pain, no scratch." With tax added, it came to a few cents under twelve dollars.

I handed over my credit card. "I'm surprised you're open on Saturday."

She scanned the sticker on the brush and then recorded my name and address and phone number in her client register. "We're the emergency clinic this weekend." She didn't seem too happy about it. "We'll be here until five."

"I wonder, if you're not too busy—" I looked around and saw one couple with a poodle waiting. "I just moved into an apartment and a cat came with it. I wonder if she might be one of your patients. Can you look up her name?"

A woman came out of the examining room and called the poodle back, and the clerk helping me frowned and pointed to the credit card machine. I swiped, but it wanted to read the chip, so I stuck the card into the slot.

"It's slow today. Now, what were you asking? How in the world would I know the name of your cat if you don't?"

"Go to the client register and search for the address," the second woman said. "Want me to do it?"

"I guess you'd better." The original clerk stepped away from the computer and rolled her eyes like I was a nut job. "You need a bag for this?" She held up the brush.

"No." I pushed it into my purse with the sales slip and recited my address a second time for the woman who took over the computer.

"Let's try just the apartment eight part and see if that works."

The computer coughed up a list of clients, including my just-entered name and address. The assistant scrolled down the list. "Harbor Village, you said? Here it is. The owner's name is Flowers and the cat's name is . . . well, this was hardly worth your effort. The cat's name is Kitty."

We laughed.

"Sometimes it doesn't pay to go to a lot of trouble," the original clerk said.

I went home and found the cat rolled in a ball on the bed, sleeping. I began brushing her, and she uncoiled and stretched and purred. Then she stood and turned from side to side, getting every little spot groomed, even her chin.

I had to clean the brush several times and wound up with a ball of hair half as big as the cat. "Kitty," I called several times while I brushed. No reaction. Once she narrowed her eyes and blinked then demanded more brushing. She turned her head one way and another, exposing her neck and chest and purring like a chainsaw.

"Kitty." I left the bedroom and took the ball of hair to the kitchen trash. "Kitty!" No response. Had Ms. Flowers just never bothered to think up a name?

While I was getting lunch, I came across Gloria's, aka Mrs. Santa, empty plate and set it out. My mother had a rule that dishes that came into the house bearing food could not be returned empty. What did I have to put on a plate? There wasn't much food in the larder, but there was a container of biscotti in assorted flavors like lemon, chocolate, or almond with sea salt. I could take some of those.

Nita phoned while I was eating. "Cleo, I feel like I'm neglecting you. Are things going well?"

I invited her to come see the furnished apartment. "Would you and Dolly like to come tomorrow? Any time is fine with me."

"I'd love that, but it's the third Sunday, you know. That's the night a group of us go to the Goldenrod Grille for dinner. At my age, I try not to schedule too much in one day, so I'd better take a rain check. And I hope you'll go to the Grille, too. But I do want to talk with you when it's just the three of us. We wondered if you'd consider coming to dinner tonight. I've got lasagna in the freezer. It's from the dining room and they always do a good job."

"May I bring a bottle of wine?"

"That would be lovely, dear. Five thirty, shall we say? Or about then. We don't have to be too precise when it's just us. And don't dress up. Anything except blue jeans will be fine."

* * * *

I stuck to my long-time routine and did the usual Saturday chores. I emptied all the trash cans into the kitchen container and tied the bag then walked out to the garages and tossed the full bag into one of the big green containers. The top was big and heavy. Some residents—Nita, for instance—wouldn't be able to lift the bag and hold the container open simultaneously. Did they just let garbage accumulate until the housekeeper came, every other week? Should management offer other options?

Back in the apartment, I got the ironing board out of the laundry area. As I tugged and steamed and smoothed a couple of linen shirts, the work to be done at Harbor Village occupied my attention. I hated to cancel the rotation Jamie had proposed—using my first week to work a day in each of the five departments—but things had changed, and I didn't have a week for a leisurely start. Find a nurse, find out what was going on with income and costs and if young people from Ukraine were actually living here, and why.

In spite of my intentions to make full-time employment into a brief commitment, questions were already eating at me. Why was the food bad, and why did the night staff fail to answer resident calls? Find out and fix it.

I assumed the police would make the main building accessible again by Monday, and whatever they had been looking for probably didn't concern Harbor Village. Lee's death had cast a pall over my arrival, but the residents didn't know her and the staff—even her sister—didn't like her. I was moving past it already and hoped that was true for everyone.

I put the ironing board away, and the fretting with it, and made up a shopping list for tomorrow's trip to the grocery.

I showered and dressed for the evening and then, since I had a little time left, I put six individually wrapped biscotti on the neighbor's bread plate, wrapped it with plastic wrap and went around the outside of the building to her apartment. She didn't answer my knock, but the lady next door came out on her porch.

"Gloria's out."

"Oh, thank you. I was just returning her plate. I'll try again later."

"Her kids are in town. Just between you and me, they're looking at that place up in Spanish Fort. They may move her out."

"Oh? Do you know why?" Might as well start the snooping.

"Probably the dining room. She goes every day and never has anything good to say. I tell her, do like I do. Open a can of soup and make some toast."

"That's not what I like to hear when I'm just moving in."

"Well, that's just my opinion. You may like it fine. Do you hear your neighbor's television at night?"

"No, I haven't noticed it."

"Oh, well, I just wondered. If mine ever bothers you, let me know."

I walked back thinking about Gloria. Nothing to do all day but watch TV, so she went to the dark little dining room, where there weren't many people to talk with and only mediocre food. I'd probably be moving, too. Now what could we do about it?

I took Gloria's plate and the biscotti back to my kitchen, put my phone on the charger, closed the blinds and locked up, leaving a light on. It would be dark when I got back. As I walked across the boulevard to the Bergens' apartment, with no phone, I felt almost like a limb was missing.

Jim met me at the door. "Come in, come in. You look well rested, for someone who's just moved."

"She's been here three days." Nita came in behind him to give me a hug and a pat. "I think that's past the moving-in stage, isn't it?"

"It smells wonderful in here," I said. "And it always looks so festive. Like a holiday." The little lights on the fig tree sparkled in the glass tabletop.

"When you reach eighty-three, every day is a holiday. Right, Nita?" Jim took the wine I'd brought, removed the bottle from the bag and read the label aloud. "We don't usually drink wine with dinner, but I think we might like a little glass of this."

"I always like a glass of wine." Nita inspected the label. "Good choice. Merlot goes well with lasagna."

Jim went to the china cabinet and got out stemmed glasses.

"I'd better help him. Just have a seat on the couch. We'll eat in fifteen minutes. Jim, you'll need the corkscrew. Let me get it."

It turned out it was Jim, more than Nita, who wanted to talk with me. In fact, he had a yellow legal pad full of notes in a large, heavy script. He even had an almost-blank page ready, with my name and a couple of topics written at the top.

"Now, about this drowning." He paused to take a sip of wine before setting the glass on the table beside his recliner. "That's good stuff, Cleo. I see you know your wine."

"Not really. It's just what the grocery store had."

Nita sat at the other end of the couch, took a little sip from her glass and cooed approval.

"Well, where were we? I have just a couple of items I'm not clear about, and Nita thinks you may have the answers." He consulted his notepad. "Number one is, who called nine-one-one?"

"I'd like to back up a minute. I don't remember if I told you this, but you should know. Travis McKenzie is my daughter Stephanie's father. We were married for two years, twenty-some years ago and haven't been in touch much since. And he married Lee Ferrell earlier this summer. He and I had breakfast together today. I just wanted to get that out of the way."

Nita answered slowly. "No, I don't think you told us that, not specifically."

"It's a small world, isn't it? But Chief Boozer fills us in on some of the minor details. I think he might've said something about it."

So they had known about Travis and me. I was glad to have it out in the open.

Nita had a question. "And how did Mr. McKenzie seem? I suppose he's in shock, losing his wife so suddenly."

"He's afraid the police suspect him of something. I'm not quite sure what, but they questioned him extensively."

Jim nodded morosely. "Oh, yes, the husband's the first suspect, until he's cleared. And you know, Cleo, he's not always the guilty party."

Nita and I smiled at each other.

The kitchen timer sounded and she got up. "The lasagna's been cooling for fifteen minutes, so it's ready to serve now. Shall we leave this discussion until after we've eaten?"

Jim struggled to his feet and headed for the table, wineglass in hand. "You thought Cleo would know the score, Nita. I see we've got the mother lode here. Bring your glass, Cleo."

Nita had a green salad, already dressed with vinaigrette, and crisp garlic toast to go with the lasagna. We each had a generous serving and Jim followed up with half as much again, while Nita picked at her food.

"Tell me, Cleo," he asked, "have you managed to capture the cat?"

I laughed at the idea of a capture. "She moved right in. And doesn't object to my being in her apartment."

Nita smiled. "I'm so relieved you like each other."

"And I found the vet and got them to look up Ms. Flowers' record. It seems the cat's name is Kitty."

"Kitty," Jim repeated.

"Kitty?" Nita tipped her head and narrowed her eyes. "And does she come when you call her?"

"No reaction at all. Maybe my voice doesn't sound right to her."

"Well, there's nothing wrong with Kitty," she said, "not if you like it. But since she's not attached to it, you could certainly change it, you know." It was obvious what she would do.

"I think I may. Help me come up with a good name."

"I like Kitty," Jim said. "Direct and to the point. No doubt who you're talking about. It even says she's a female. You wouldn't call a male cat Kitty, you'd call him Tom."

We had ice cream for dessert, mint green with little shavings of chocolate. It looked pretty in the small dessert bowls, but Jim used a larger dish. "I have a little ice cream most evenings and I like this bowl. It fits the hand."

"And fits a large scoop of ice cream," Nita pointed out.

"Anybody want a little more?"

Nita offered to make coffee, but we turned it down. I helped her move the dishes to the kitchen. Then we went back to sit in the living room.

Chapter 7

"I'm going to have a little more of this wine." Jim poured half a glass then wedged the cork in.

Nita and I were back on the couch.

"You asked who called nine-one-one. I assume it was Dolly. Right?"

Jim tipped the recliner's footrest halfway up and picked up his notepad again. "Dolly says she did. Says she opened the gate and went in, saw the body in the pool and immediately dialed nine-one-one." He chuckled. "I'm not entirely sure about the immediate part because Dolly can't see much. She could swim laps with a dead woman in the water and never know it. But she says she saw the body and made the call then went to the indoor pool to swim and watch the rescue vehicles arrive. And before she finished her workout, the officers spotted her and ran her off."

"I can confirm that part." I told them about seeing Dolly walking away from the pool house early Friday morning, with Chief Boozer following her. "That's when I met him. He came up to the intersection and talked to both of us."

"The problem is, the police phone log doesn't agree. Dispatch says the call didn't come from Dolly's phone. It came from an unlisted number."

"What's known as a burner phone. The type drug dealers use." Coming from Nita, the words sounded so alien.

"Maybe they got more than one call."

Jim shook his head. "Not unless you count the people calling to ask what was going on out here. You've got a lot of nosy neighbors, if you don't know it."

Nita muttered, "Too bad no one noticed a murder."

I recoiled. "A murder? Is that what they're calling it now?"

"A suspicious death, possible homicide. That's the official terminology. I still say drowning, but technically it wasn't."

I didn't want to give up my scenario. "Why do they think it wasn't a drowning?"

He pushed back in the recliner. "Well, think about it. An accident happens in one place. She trips and bangs her head on the pool coping, dies instantly and goes in the water. That's an accident. But if she dies instantly, never takes another breath, then there's no water in the lungs. Still an accident, but not a drowning. What's the definition of drowning? Water in the lungs." He took a sip of wine.

"And the phrase 'inconsistent with drowning'...."

He nodded. "Exactly. It might look like a drowning, but it's not. Was it an accident?" He shrugged.

"Not if somebody pushed her," Nita said.

"Oh." My heart sank. The figure in the scene that popped into my imagination looked an awful lot like Travis. I dialed it out and listened to Jim.

"Well, Nita, there's no suggestion of that. The question is, why does the big house have all that crime scene tape around it? To me, it says something happened there. And when something happens in two places, it's no accident."

It made sense. "Maybe they're just looking for background evidence. She had an office in the building, probably some records, a computer."

"So there's the question for you, Cleo. What's in the big house? Have you picked up anything?"

I shook my head. "I won't be in there until Monday, and I wouldn't expect to have anything to do with Lee's death. Maybe it'll be resolved by Monday."

Jim shrugged again. He didn't seem to believe it. Maybe he didn't want it to be over so quickly.

I asked, "Was there blood in the pool area? Anything she might've hit her head on?"

He shrugged. "Not that I'm aware of. Of course, they might not tell me everything."

"Well, I might be able to tell you something about the call for EMTs. Did Dolly tell you she found a phone? I saw her this morning, just finishing her swim."

Nita frowned. "Dolly doesn't usually swim on Saturdays."

"This was a make-up day, after she was interrupted yesterday. She found a phone in the pocket of her bathrobe. It wasn't hers, and she didn't know where it came from. She insisted I take it."

"She never mentioned a phone." Jim seemed offended to be left out of the loop.

Nita sounded more interested in excusing Dolly. "You know she's forgetful, Jim. Like the rest of us."

"Now, Cleo, you may have just answered the sixty-four-thousand-dollar question." He dropped the footrest and got up with the usual effort. "I'll call the chief right now. You still have the phone, I hope."

Nita tried to stop him. "A call can wait, can't it? It's Saturday night."

"It's not late yet, Nita. Not for most people. Policing doesn't stop on the weekends. Chief Boozer might want to come get it tonight. And even if he doesn't, he might sleep better knowing it's here."

He went to his office, and I shifted into a more relaxed mode. "That was a delicious dinner, Nita. I think I'll go to bed early tonight. Maybe read some more about old Fairhope."

"Wait just a minute, dear, and see what Jim learns. Then he'll walk with you."

"No need for that." I stood up. "Thanks for having me over. I want you and Jim and Dolly to come to my apartment soon. Are Saturday nights usually good for you?"

Jim joined us as we reached the door. I gave Nita a hug.

"If you're about ready, Cleo, I'm going to walk you home. Chief Boozer is sending a car to pick up that phone. I'll stay until it gets here."

"Oh, there's really no need. Why don't I just call you when I get home?"

He wouldn't hear of it. "Anyway, I want to have a quick look at that phone. Hold on just a minute." He went to the kitchen and came back carrying a clear plastic Ziploc bag. "I don't suppose you put the phone in an evidence bag."

I admitted I had not. "I didn't know it was evidence. I think I left it on the dresser. And both Dolly and I handled it, so any prints may be ruined, if that's what you're thinking."

He shrugged and joined us by the door. "Well, that's just the facts, but it's always surprising what these technicians can conjure up today. They get fingerprints off skin, did you know that?"

We walked across the street together.

On the way, I asked, "What's the story with Jamie? Did you find out why she's leaving right now?"

That didn't seem nearly as interesting to him as the phone. "I saw her last night, after you told me she's leaving. Lee Ferrell was her sister, did you know?"

"Travis told me."

"Well, it's not a bad idea, not the way she describes it. She should've gone months ago. Should never have worked for her sister. But who's going to be in charge here—that's the question."

"I may do it temporarily. Travis asked me to."

"Lee Ferrell's husband? Now why would he think you could run a retirement community? You're a teacher."

Ouch. But I was willing to grant an octogenarian a few prejudices.

I changed the subject. "Do you know anything about the ownership of this place?"

"Harbor Health Care is a big outfit in Houston. Riley's looking into it. They've got several facilities, like this one, scattered around the country. They're sending Jamie to Charleston to take over one. Maybe you better say yes about the management job, Cleo, before they find someone we don't like. Would it be part-time?"

I stepped onto the curb and paused a beat for Jim to catch up. "Travis said the cops gave him a real grilling. They must think it was murder."

"She was struck with an unknown object, and it's not here. But nobody's going to leave a weapon lying around. I'm sure it's in the bay by now, or in a construction dumpster in Mobile or Pensacola."

I sighed and got out my door key. "I wonder if we have adequate security here."

"That's a thought. But I'm on it. And I can recruit a few more volunteers, just until they know if anybody local was involved. What does Travis look like?"

I unlocked the apartment door and Jim gave me the plastic bag.

"Let me see where that phone is. Maybe you can slide it in here without more touching."

We went to the bedroom and he looked around.

"I see you've got everything shipshape already. Where's the cat?"

Before I could answer, he broke into a banshee shout.

"Here, kitty-kitty-kitty-kitty! Here kitty!"

I nearly wet my pants.

No doubt he woke the neighbors, and probably people in the houses behind us, too. No sign of the cat, of course.

"Let's sit in the living room." My hands were shaking, and I was eager to get him out of the bedroom.

"Just scoop up that phone and we'll take it with us. I'll do it if you can't, but my tremor's bad tonight."

I had a tremor of my own now, thanks to his outburst, but I aimed the bag at the phone.

"Might be best to turn the bag inside out and pick up the phone. Then you can flip the bag back to normal." He acted out the movements. "That's a little tricky with these stiff bags."

He was right in my way, leaning over the dresser and blocking my view. I twisted the bag this way and that and finally got the phone inside then zipped it closed.

"Wait, let's have a quick look before we seal it." He leaned against the dresser and took the bag from me. "I'll just examine it."

He unzipped the closure but didn't remove the phone. Instead, he manipulated it, squeezing it to one side of the bag and jabbing at the flip top with his thumbnail. After a few tries, he got it open, but it didn't light up.

"Maybe the battery's dead."

"No way to see what calls were made from it? I don't suppose you have a battery charger we could use."

"I don't think so, Jim. If the phone is evidence, tampering with it doesn't seem like a good idea."

He didn't seem convinced and gave the dial another jab through the plastic.

I tried another approach. "We might erase its history."

He snapped the phone closed and handed the bag to me. "Oh. Well, we don't want to do that. Let's just see what the police can learn. They'll have experts, you know."

Officer Montgomery came alone to get the phone. She and Jim addressed each other by first names, like old friends.

"Mary, do you know our new neighbor?"

"Ms. Mack." She gave me a nod and got out her notepad. "Tell me about this phone."

I gave her the story, with liberal assistance from Jim.

"Tell the chief to call me when he learns something. And you might want me to go along when you talk to Dolly Webb. She can be difficult." He tapped the side of his head. "Turns eighty on Christmas Day."

Thirty minutes after Jim and the policewoman departed, the cat came out from under the bed while I was brushing my teeth.

"Sorry about that."

She meowed and went out to the kitchen. She was crunching on dry food a few minutes later, when I put down my puzzle book and began to drift off to sleep.

The next morning, I realized I had just one day left to settle into my new location, since my job, whatever it was going to be, would begin the following day.

I made up a shopping list, while I ate chocolate-almond biscotti and drank a cup of coffee. Then I looked up a phone number and placed a call to a home health care service in Daphne. The woman who answered gave her name as Ivy Stafford.

I told her who I was and that I was calling for Harbor Village. "I'm just starting work here and I need to line up an RN for our Assisted Living center, beginning tomorrow. I'd like to get one person who can come every day for a week or so, not a series of people. Is that possible?"

"Is this a fill-in for Jamie Barnes?"

"Jamie's out of town. I'm not sure how long she'll be gone, or if she'll come back."

"Really? So there's a chance this might turn into a permanent job? Full-time, with benefits?"

"It's possible. I can't make any promises at the moment."

"If it's likely to be permanent, I might come myself." She gave me a short sales spiel, saying she had worked at a local nursing home before she took over the temp service. "Sometimes I go out on jobs, but mostly I schedule CNAs. I miss patient care, and I've always wanted to work at Harbor Village. The timing just never worked out."

"Okay, good." I told her where to come. "Let's say eight thirty, and ask for Cleo Mack. What kind of fee are we talking about, for one week?"

She gave me a figure. "That's an eight-hour shift, whatever hours you want, with thirty minutes for lunch. If I stay longer, the fee goes up."

I agreed and wrote down the amount and her phone number beside her name, Ivy Stafford.

Next, I searched for the non-emergency phone number of the police department.

A woman answered and I gave my name and asked if Chief Boozer was in. I didn't expect him to be there on a Sunday morning, and there was no reply when I asked for him, but in a few seconds, he answered.

I told him who I was. "Chief, tomorrow's a workday. Is the administration building going to be accessible to staff?"

"We're finishing up in here now, and I'll have the tape down in a few minutes."

"Thanks." I was surprised when he said *in here*; apparently he was at the big house at the moment.

He was still speaking. "I need to talk with you. I understand you're beginning work tomorrow."

"I'll be there all day and we'll talk whenever you like."

When I headed out to the grocery store a few minutes later, two police SUVs were parked at the office door. All the yellow tape was still in place.

Grocery shopping is usually a pleasure for me. When I get home, I wash all the produce at once and repackage it, ready for use. On Sunday I bought locally grown lettuce, a cauliflower, colorful little peppers, cherry tomatoes, green onions and two cucumbers. I filled the sink with cold water and a generous splash of vinegar and washed each piece individually. Afterward, the kitchen counter looked like a farmers' market, with everything spread out on cotton towels to dry.

Quinoa and lentils and tea bags went into clear glass canisters lined up at the back of the countertop. Half the loaf of five-grain sour dough bread went into the freezer, zipped into what I now knew as an evidence bag. Beans, crushed tomatoes, tuna and soup went into the cabinet, along with plastic containers of mustard and fat-free Catalina dressing, jars of peanut butter and bread-and-butter pickle slices. I assigned cat food to a separate skinny cabinet under the counter. And while I was in the kitchen, I mixed up tuna salad and put it in the refrigerator, ready for quick sandwiches.

When all that was done, I filled my cup with leftover coffee and heated it in the microwave then read through the *Sunday Times* I'd just paid six dollars for. When I started on the crossword, I recognized how nice a quiet, peaceful day at Harbor Village could be. It was exactly what I had expected when I arrived a few days before.

Eventually I moved to the computer and checked e-mail. There were notes from friends in Atlanta, which I answered, and some accumulated messages about the approaching new semester, which I trashed without even a glance. Stephanie had sent new photos of Barry, and I admired each one before transferring them to my photo file.

And then while I was online, I typed in a string of related words. *Harbor Village Fairhope Houston corporate.* I hit enter and, after a few seconds, got a long list of potentially relevant sites. I scanned down and recognized what I was looking for.

Harbor Health Services was described in glowing terms. *One of the leading operators of senior living facilities in the US*, the site boasted; *26 facilities in nine states, with a capacity of 9,200 residents. Independent living, assisted living, continuing care and dementia care.* I was amazed. *Seventy-nine percent occupancy.*

Twenty-six facilities? That wasn't exactly the little family business I had envisioned.

The website also had a small box with a thumbnail summary of financial data, and it showed that half a million shares of Harbor Health Services stock had traded on the stock market Friday, with a closing price of $10.50 a share. It sounded like a lot of shares, but that part didn't mean much to me.

I wished for someone knowledgeable to explain this to me and thought immediately of Riley. A banker—that was what he'd been in his working life, and a banker would understand the stock market. And he'd agreed to review the financial side of Harbor Village for Jim. I clicked on a couple of pages and hit print, so I'd have something to show him the next time we met.

Next, I clicked on the "About Us" tab and nearly jumped out of my chair. Travis McKenzie was smiling back at me from a large photo.

The text beneath the picture gave his name and title: President & CEO. He had assumed that position three years ago, his bio revealed.

I scrolled and a little farther down found a photo of Lee Ferrell. She was one of several vice presidents and also Director of Senior Living, according to the caption.

So, I'd had it all wrong. Travis didn't work for his new wife; it was the other way around. Travis McKenzie ran a large, publicly traded, health care corporation and had done so for the last three years.

I was stunned. Perhaps he had told the truth when he said he wasn't about to gain a big inheritance.

Ohmygod, ohmygod, my mental chorus was singing, like crickets in my ears. Travis was a business mogul, and he was trying to make me one, on a minor scale. Well, good luck with that.

I spent several minutes staring out the window and then did another Google search.

This time I typed in PBS and the word donor, plus the family name Ferrell, and got three hits, all at a site that expressed gratitude to supporters. Lee was there, along with William Stevens Ferrell and Claude J. Dyer.

I started with William Stevens Ferrell, added Houston and the word "image" and did another search. The photos that appeared were of a man who was easily old enough to be Lee's father. He had a fringe of almost white hair, a long, creased, smiling face, and dark eyes. In addition to his name, the text said Harbor Health Services, Houston.

Putting in Lee's name got me the same photo I'd seen at the corporate website—Lee in a bright red dress and a gold necklace, with a big smile, bright lipstick and lots of wavy dark hair. And once again the text included a professional affiliation with Harbor Health Services, Houston.

I figured the third name was a glitch of some sort, especially when the photo revealed Claude Dyer to be young and handsome. Once again, the identifying text cited Harbor Health Services, Houston.

I copied his name and pasted it into the browser and got several links to explore, but the subject line of the first one answered my question. It was a news item/obituary for Claude Dyer, age fifty-two, dated four years ago. I clicked and read. Dyer was identified as President and CEO of Harbor Health Services. S*urvivors include his wife, Houston socialite Lee Ferrell Dyer, and daughter, Debra Lynn Dyer, a student at Julliard Conservatory of Music.*

There was more, but no other relatives. Cause of death wasn't apparent but mourners were invited to make memorial donations to another Houston institution, the MD Anderson Cancer Center.

So now I was getting the corporate and family history straight. Lee's family name was Ferrell, and her father had probably started the company. Claude Dyer had been her husband and the company's CEO and, according to Travis, started the philanthropy tradition that was something of an overreach. Then Claude died and Travis McKenzie replaced him, both as CEO of the business and, two months ago, as Lee's husband. And now Lee was gone.

I wondered if her father was still alive, but before I could research that, I looked at the clock. The afternoon had flown by, and now I would have to rush to meet my neighbors at the Goldenrod Grille for dinner.

I was walking down the sidewalk toward the Grille when my phone rang. It was Travis.

"I'm at the Crab Shack in Charleston, waiting for Jamie." Irritation was obvious in his voice. "She was supposed to be here at six fifteen, and I can't even get her on the phone."

"It's not six yet."

"We're on Eastern Time here, remember. But you're right, Jamie may not know that. You have any luck finding a nurse?"

I told him about Ivy Stafford. "She'll be here tomorrow morning." I told him the fee she had quoted.

"Okay, but don't make her any promises until we know what's what. Well, let me try Jamie again. I don't want to sit here all night waiting for her."

From the corner of the garage, I could see the sign for the Goldenrod Grille. There was nobody in sight, and all the crime scene tape was gone.

I crossed the porch and entered at a small foyer. A row of empty coat hooks was mounted on the beadboard wall, and the main body of the restaurant snaked off around a bar. I followed the sound of voices, walking between empty tables arranged against the front windows and empty stools lined up against the bar. About twenty Harbor Village residents were seated in a cozy back room at one long table, with only a couple of empty seats.

I recognized about half of the people and even knew a few names. Jim and Nita sat across from each other, near the middle. Jim tapped on his water glass with a knife and waited until he had everyone's attention. Then he introduced me.

"She begins work here tomorrow, so take all your problems and complaints and go see her."

I gave a weak little wave and some people waved back.

"Tell us about the drowning," one man called out. "Who was she?"

A buzz of comments and questions swirled and rippled around the table. Obviously the rumor mill was churning. I stood at the end of the table and delivered the little speech I had prepared.

"Lee Ferrell worked for Harbor Village's parent company in Houston. She was the sister of Jamie Barnes, director of the Assisted Living program here. The Fairhope police are still investigating and will announce their findings soon. And there will be a memorial service for Ms. Ferrell later this week."

As an afterthought, I tacked on another little announcement. "And if you haven't heard, Jamie Barnes has been promoted to a management position at Harbor Village in Charleston. She begins working there immediately. I'm sure we all wish her well and extend our sympathy for her loss."

That seemed to satisfy everyone. A number of conversations broke out, and I looked for a place to sit.

Nita asked, "Can you get around to that seat on the back, Cleo? That's your neighbor Ann back there, and you know Dolly."

"Or she can sit up at the window with me." Riley was standing at my side. He leaned closer and I got a whiff of sandalwood. "Unless you'd rather sit with the group."

"I'd be delighted to join you. And you're just the person I want to talk with."

We moved to the window and a table for two.

"I can't hear anything in that big group. I hope you don't mind." He held a chair for me.

I'd almost forgotten about such courtesies and nearly tripped over my own feet as I changed course. I thanked him and he pushed the chair forward. "I've brought a financial report I'd like you to look at." I laid my folder on a corner of the table.

The Sunday night menu was limited to three items—pasta with meat sauce, salad and garlic toast; an 8- or 12-ounce sirloin with salad and baked potato; or beer-baked kielbasa with sauerkraut and sweet potato rounds. None of them sounded especially healthy, but I didn't often see kielbasa on a menu, so I chose it and so did Riley. We ordered red wine, which the server said was complimentary for me, since it was my first visit to the Grille after moving into Harbor Village.

"Ready to begin work tomorrow?"

"Getting there." I pulled out my two-page report and laid it in front of him.

Riley put on skinny little glasses and scanned the pages. "Interesting," he muttered to himself.

I recalled Stephanie calling him handsome and tried to see it. I didn't think I would use that term, but there was something appealing about him. He looked up abruptly and caught me staring at him, but he only grinned and went back to his reading. I minded my manners after that.

"And all this is available at the push of a button. Sure simplifies research, doesn't it?"

Service was slow and our meals were the last to arrive. People ate rapidly and left, some of them with takeout boxes in hand, some stopping to speak to Riley or me. Jim finished his meal and went to work on Nita's. Riley put the financial report aside, face down, but glanced at it occasionally as he ate.

A couple of people promised they would see me in the office soon.

"We need a poker night," one man said.

Another asked, "Can you do anything about the mail coming so late?"

By the time we finished, Nita had moved to a different seat, still at the main table, and still engaged in conversation with other diners.

Jim pulled a chair up to our table. "Looks like you've got some interesting reading there. Anything to share with me?"

Riley flashed the papers but didn't give them up. "A financial report on Harbor Health Services. I think you'll find it interesting. Is this confidential material, Cleo?"

I shook my head. "I got it off the Internet."

Riley took a final glance at each page then pulled his glasses down and looked over their top at me. "Anything special you want to talk about?"

"I do well to balance my checkbook, Riley, so don't worry about being too elementary. Just tell us what it says."

"It's pretty simple, really." With glasses back on, he pointed to the box in the corner. "The stock price was ten and a half at the close of business Friday, down from twelve dollars the day before."

"That sounds bad."

"The company lost ten percent of market value in one day. That's extraordinarily bad. Losing a top executive may explain it, since the drop was abrupt and not part of an ongoing slide. I don't know of any other disaster in the market, or in this particular segment. I don't keep up with legislation any more, but anything that might cause such a loss would've gotten the attention of all of us. Now the price may bounce right back tomorrow, but remember, it's only a paper loss. The way to lose for real is to sell stock right now. And just between us, that group of stockholders includes me. Maybe you, too."

I shook my head, but he disagreed. "Lots of pension funds hold Harbor Health shares."

That gave it a different spin. "And if the stock dropped ten percent due to Lee's demise, then the investment community must have seen her as just the management expert Travis thought she was."

Riley nodded agreement. "This report gives me some of the information you've been asking about, Jim." He took out his pen and underscored a few numbers in the report. "They claim a seventy-nine percent occupancy rate and a capacity of nine thousand two hundred residents, overall. How many actual residents does that translate to?"

I pulled out my phone, called up the calculator function and handed it to him.

"Cleo, you should be getting a commission on all this technology." He calculated quickly. "So the actual number of residents is seven thousand two hundred sixty-eight, spread over twenty-six facilities." He entered a few more numbers. "That means the average facility has about two hundred eighty residents. I'd guess we have that many here, don't you, Jim? Counting all the condos and the houses and assisted living."

"More," Jim said. "I can give you an exact head count tomorrow. Or maybe you have access to that information in an official form, Cleo."

I nodded. "I'm sure I will, but not yet. Can you get an idea of the finances? Is the corporation profitable?"

"Think about it this way. We said over seven thousand people live in Harbor Health facilities nationwide. If every one of them paid a thousand dollars a month, we'd multiply seven thousand by one thousand dollars and that would give us seven million dollars in revenue. Got it?" He jotted that figure on the back of the printout.

"Yes."

"That's what I call profitable," Jim said.

"No, it's not profit at all. It's income for one month. We have to multiply seven million dollars by twelve to see what they take in during an entire year. That's eighty-four million, before expenses. Senior citizens are big business."

"We pay more than a thousand dollars," Jim said. "Twenty-two hundred for rent, plus another eight hundred for the dining room. But it's what we saved for, a little luxury at the end."

"That averages fifteen hundred each, but you've got one of the nicest apartments. I get by on the cheap side." He grinned. "You know me."

"One person, and no garage." Jim nodded.

"And no meal ticket."

"This facility has an Assisted Living unit," I reminded them. "And some of the other facilities offer nursing care. Residents of those units pay considerably more than a thousand dollars a month."

Riley agreed. "I just used a thousand to simplify computations. Our eighty-four million is a low figure. The true amount may be twice as much. Or more."

"Stick with eighty-four million and tell me how much goes out for expenses."

Riley pushed his glasses up and looked at the report again. "Hard to say from the information we have here. They give a couple of margin ranges in the fine print, but those things are difficult to interpret. You can hire a few new employees and change all your figures."

That reminded me of Patti's concerns about job security. "Are you saying that firing staff makes the figures look better?"

He looked over his glasses at me. "And there'll be taxes to consider, too. I'd guess, off-hand, that Harbor Health Services clears a few million each year—six or eight, maybe—and pays out probably half that to stockholders in the form of dividends. I can guess that because I know what kind of stocks I buy."

He put his glasses and pen back in his shirt pocket and looked around the little restaurant. "This is all very interesting, Cleo. But now, if we've answered the pressing questions, we'd better go home so these people can close up. Can I keep this report?"

I handed him the folder to put it in. "I can print out the whole thing if you want it."

He nodded. "Yes, that might be informative."

"And Cleo's got to work tomorrow." Jim got up slowly. "You'll walk her home, Riley."

"Oh, that's not necessary."

"I'm going that way," Riley said.

Nita and Ann and Dolly joined us and we walked out together.

Nita asked, "Did you hear us talking about your cat, Cleo? Ann thinks the calico wasn't named Kitty."

"Oh, really?"

Ann, my neighbor, shook her head with certainty. "Kitty Baby was the male, the white cat. I think he was deaf. She took him with her."

"And left this one to fend for herself? That seems heartless."

"Yeah, she was a snippy old woman. But I can't remember what the calico's name was. I never saw much of them. Inside pets, you know. Maybe it'll come to me. Or maybe somebody else will know."

So much for Jim's theory that a male cat wouldn't be called Kitty.

Ann joined Riley and me for the walk up the back sidewalk. "It's nice to have a little mystery to solve," she said. "I'll talk to the other neighbors tomorrow. If they don't remember her name, we can hold a lottery to come up with a new one. Can't have a pet without a name, can we?"

Ann went in at her apartment and I asked Riley, "Do you want to come in for a minute?"

He shook his head. "Let's do it next time. You'll have things to do, preparing for tomorrow."

Chapter 8

My husband for almost twenty years, Robert Mack, was tall and thin, always happy and a genius. He was a guinea pig for genetic studies and needed frequent blood tests, occasional transfusions, and now and then was hospitalized for a lifelong blood disorder. He told me when we met he wouldn't live a long life and he did not, but he lived it fully. He was passionate about mathematics, consulted with high tech industries and the military, even the space program, and critiqued the work of colleagues all around the world.

In contrast, I freely admitted I could barely balance my checkbook.

But I did acquire one quasi-mathematical skill from Robert. I had become a devotee of Sudoku puzzles. I purchased the Will Shortz collections from the bookstore and worked on them daily, usually before I fell asleep at night. I started at page one and went straight through to the end of the book.

According to Robert, Sudoku wasn't actually mathematics, but a logic puzzle. "You could work them just the same if you substituted emoticons or the first nine letters of the alphabet for the numbers one through nine," he told me more than once. Nevertheless, he solved them without difficulty.

And now I solved them, too, sometimes with considerable difficulty. I never gave up on a puzzle without solving it.

Somehow Sudoku seemed like a link to Robert, all those numbers arranged in tidy squares. Ridiculous I knew, but it was part of my daily routine now and I was convinced it exerted a calming influence, like meditation did for its practitioners.

Robert's approach had become my way of dealing with life, too. Use logic, he would say. Be systematic. Try different approaches. Find out what's true and, just as importantly, find out what's impossible. Complete every cell, every box and every puzzle. The difficult ones would yield at some point.

As I prepared to go to bed Sunday night, I resolved to spend the next month applying the Sudoku approach to Harbor Village and its problems. I planned to use logic, to be systematic and to try new approaches when necessary.

Find out what was wrong with this facility and how it could be fixed. Find out why the staff was unhappy, why Jamie left so abruptly and why no two people had exactly the same view of the place. Figure out what was wrong with the financials and how the problems could be fixed. Make residents and employees want to stay here.

I flipped off the bathroom light and added a final objective. Find out why Lee died. I didn't expect to infringe on the law enforcement role, but I was about to be in a unique position to access inside information. I certainly hoped Travis wasn't involved in any way—after all, he was Stephanie's father—but I wouldn't start with preconceptions. Travis was one cell of the puzzle. If I was going to do this job, I'd try to do it right.

I got into bed, picked up my Sudoku book and a pen and waited for Stephanie to call.

* * * *

At a few minutes before eight on Monday morning, I gave the cat with no name a good brushing, checked her food and water supply and walked down to the big house. I was wearing khaki slacks, a nubby black sweater set, my gold chain and matching earrings and black sandals. In other words, I looked like a cross between an Atlanta college professor and a tourist, and nothing like a business executive.

My plan for the first day involved three simple tasks. I wanted to meet all the staff and figure out who did what, get my new office organized and equipped to my liking and get an RN on duty in assisted living.

Patti Wagon was walking from the side door toward the reception desk as I crossed the lobby. We waved to each other and converged at her desk.

"Oh, you're here! I'm so glad. Have you seen your office? It's right this way."

She led me down a hall. Executive Director, the sign on the door said, and below that was my name and a string of letters signifying the degrees I held, of interest to pretty much no one outside academia. The top sign would be easy to remove, I saw.

"Mr. McKenzie had Stewart put it up." Patti looked a little starry eyed. "Even with all the problems he has right now."

I assumed she was referring to Travis' problems, not Stewart's, but I wasn't sure which of them was responsible for the starry eyes. My own eyes were wide open, I fancied. Travis must have hatched the idea of making me Executive Director on Friday, in order to have nameplates in place at the beginning of the workweek. Less than twenty-four hours after his new wife died, the CEO was taking care of business. Could that be normal?

The office Patti took me to was furnished simply but felt stale and unused. Pathetic was another word that came to mind. There was a desk in front of the single window, a three-tier letter tray on its corner and a large desk chair with a mesh back. In front of the desk three chairs were arranged in an arc. I walked to the desk and began opening drawers. All empty.

Looking back toward the door, I saw a plain worktable and two green file cabinets in the corner. No computer. Not a scrap of paper in sight. Where should I start?

Patti sensed the despair, I guess, and made a weak apology. "We gathered up some furniture when we thought you'd be taking over Resident Services. There wasn't a lot to choose from. Things got sort of cannibalized over the last year."

I looked around again. "Did Lee have an office here?"

"The cops were in there Friday and the tape's still up. Maybe they just forgot to take it down?"

I didn't know anything about Lee's office. "I think I'm going to need your help, Patti. Can you get someone else to handle the driving today, so you can follow me around?"

"I'll call Goldie." She rushed off to her desk.

Ivy Stafford arrived early, wearing white running shoes and a white uniform with buttons that pulled open across the bosom. "I didn't ask if you wanted me to wear a uniform or scrubs." Her handshake revealed rough skin.

"Scrubs are more comfortable, I imagine."

Ivy was about my age, with yellow hair curled under at her shoulders. Her eyes looked like they'd seen a lot. "Oh, definitely more comfortable, but some employers want the authority look. I aim to please. I've got scrubs in the car, just in case."

"Why don't you get them and change. I think it's better to avoid the hospital look, so people don't start thinking they're sick. And when you're ready, I'll walk over to assisted living with you."

I introduced Ivy to Patti, just hanging up the phone. "Goldie's going to drive. She's glad to get the hours."

"Good." I made a mental note to find out who Goldie was.

While Ivy went to her car, I stood beside Patti's desk and thought aloud. "I need a list of all the residents, with apartment numbers. And a copy of the standard lease form, plus any special conditions that might be included—pet policy, secondary occupants and registration and insurance requirements for vehicles kept on the premises. Anything of that nature. We may as well put the list on a spreadsheet, so we can add to it as things change. Then, in another spreadsheet, I'd like a list of all employees with their job title, salary, how long they've been here. Grouped by department—housekeeping, maintenance, grounds, dining room, administrative, whatever."

Patti's eyes were beginning to bulge.

"Somebody's got all this already," I assured her, "and there's no need to reinvent the wheel. I just need to get a copy on my computer. Speaking of which, I need a computer. Got an extra one somewhere?"

"I don't know, but I'll look."

"Is Emily working today?" I had a few questions for the bookkeeper.

Patti shook her head. "Tuesday, Wednesday and Friday. That's what the dragon lady wanted."

"Then leave a note for her. I need a financial report, showing what we owe and to whom. Are any tenants behind on rent? If so, by how much? They all pay by bank draft, I suppose, but I'd like to know if there are any problems. How much money is in our bank account and where is it and who can sign checks. It may not be necessary to put me on the account, since I'm temporary in this job, but we need at least a couple of people here who can sign checks."

Patti was jotting down notes.

"Now the apartments. This isn't the same as the residents. Who can give us a summary of the status and condition of all apartments?"

"Cynthia." Patti used her usual pronunciation.

"Okay, a list of units by building, showing which ones are empty and the base rental rates. And again, don't reinvent the wheel. Just get whatever she has. Reports from last month will be fine, or she can update them if there've been changes. And give me a list of anybody besides Cynthia who handles leases, and what the incentive is. I suppose an employee gets a bonus or something for bringing in a new resident? By the way, Jamie said she'd leave my lease here. If you will, get it for me. I need to see what I've agreed to." My laughter had a little edge of wariness.

Ivy returned wearing pink scrubs.

"I'm going to assisted living with Ivy right now. I'll be back in half an hour." I gave Patti my phone number and patted my pocket to be sure I had my phone with me.

I recognized Michelle, Jamie's assistant, standing in the front hallway of the Assisted Living building, talking with two female aides. She had gotten a shorter haircut since I first met her but was just as remote and sullen as I remembered. All three of them froze and watched as Ivy and I came through the automatic door. I wondered if there were any male CNAs on staff. I hadn't seen one.

"Ladies, I haven't met all of you yet, but I'm Cleo Mack, Executive Director of Harbor Village for the time being." I introduced Ivy. "She's an RN and she'll be overseeing the Assisted Living program for a few days. Everything going okay here?"

"When will Jamie be back?" one of the aides asked.

Michelle took a step backward and tried to blend into the wall, but she was attending to events. And it was obvious she wasn't happy to see me.

"I was hoping one of you would know. Jamie didn't tell you her plans?" Michelle stared.

Another aide answered. "She told us she'd see us today, right?"

The younger woman nodded. "Where's she gone?"

"Have you tried calling her?"

They had. "She doesn't answer."

"Goes right to voice mail. First a drowning, now Jamie disappears. I'm beginning to wonder."

I wondered, too. Did the staff still think Lee had drowned?

I opted for a pep talk. "Let's just be sure we're doing the best we can. Ivy's here to help, and you can call on her as needed. Now, who's got a key to the drug cart?"

Two of them looked at Michelle, who hesitated a moment before responding. "It should be in Jamie's desk. I'll see."

I followed a few steps behind and saw her remove something from her pocket as she turned in at the office. When I got to the door, she pretended to scramble the drawer contents before producing the key.

"And where's the spare?"

She shrugged. "Up at the big house, I guess. We only have the one."

"And who gives out meds when Jamie isn't here? What about the night shift?"

She pursed her lips, twisting her mouth sideways, and didn't make eye contact. "I don't really know."

On the job an hour and I was already making an enemy. I gave the key to Ivy in front of the three of them. "We'll let the nurse hang onto this key. Is that the way you'd like it?"

"Sure," Ivy said. "And why don't I come in earlier tomorrow, so I can give out morning meds and help with dressing and breakfasts?"

The two aides perked up at that idea, and I felt the dynamics of the Assisted Living program begin to shift in my favor.

But Ivy had more ideas. "Then I'll do afternoon meds before I leave and have a little med tray, with its own key, to leave for the evening shift. How does that sound?"

The aides nodded approval.

"And I'll do a drug inventory right now, if one of you will assist me." She looked at me. "And we'll go from there."

Wow! Clearly Ivy knew how to run a unit. And she was protecting herself, too. Maybe some of that competence would rub off on the others.

I went back to the main office and found Patti still busy. Even here, the atmosphere felt subtly changed, less musty and more businesslike, with a hum of activity. She handed me a two-page printout.

"Here's a list of the department heads, with phone numbers. If they supervise other people, those names are listed on the lines below. All together there's twenty-six of us. I took Lee's name off and put you in her place, but I left Jamie on the list and put Ivy right below her. In case things change again."

"Perfect." I scanned the list. There were three housekeepers, three maintenance men, including Stewart, and seven CNAs for the Assisted Living program, with Goldie's name among them.

"Maintenance takes care of the grounds, too. I know you named grounds as a separate department, but that's not the way it is here. Not the way it has been, I mean. And tomorrow I'll get Emily to fill in the salaries." She was breathless by the time she finished.

"Good work. I want to meet everybody today, but I don't want to interrupt work. Is this a good time to start with the office staff?"

Patti went with me. Nelson Fisher was listed as the office manager, but I'd never seen him. Patti led the way down the main hall, turned right and went to the last door. If my personal orientation system was working, we were at the back corner of the building.

She whispered, "He's a little funny." Then she knocked and opened the door.

There were windows on two sides of the room, one with a view of the parking lot through wide gaps in a bamboo roll-up shade. The other window framed a pleasant view of the koi pond and the garden area. The office itself looked like it had been lifted straight out of an English cottage. There was a navy blue rug, a pair of wingback chairs upholstered in a small print, side tables, a pair of lamps—even an ottoman. An electric heater sat under a table, its cord wrapped around the handle. Stacks of newspapers and magazines mostly obscured a mahogany desk, and music was playing softly. Nelson was in there, too, a shrunken, hunched man with a prominent nose and combed-back hair. He had a jigsaw puzzle spread out on the available portion of the worktable. And he wasn't happy about being interrupted at his leisure.

We chatted for a few minutes, but he stuck with short answers and didn't initiate conversation. I didn't get a clear picture of what his responsibilities were. "A little bit of everything," was all he said when I asked.

"Do you sign checks?"

He stared at me and shook his head. "No, ma'am. Not anymore."

"Do you handle procurement? Things like computers? The reason I ask is that I need one."

"I'll see what I can do." He was still staring.

I noticed a little tea station with an electric kettle, tea bags and a tin of imported shortbread. There were paintings on the walls, in nice old frames, and at least forty jigsaw puzzles, in their boxes, were stacked beneath the table.

"I love your office."

"It's mine." He swiveled back to his puzzle.

We closed the door and walked a few steps away before Patti twittered and I laughed out loud.

"Any idea what he does in there?"

"I should've told you, he's a member of the Ferrell family. I don't know exactly how he's related. He feeds the fish and works in the garden sometimes. I guess you could say he's semi-retired."

Cynthia Quarles was on the phone when we stopped at her door. She noticed us and waved but kept talking. She was my age, with a better haircut, wearing a double strand of pearls and a flowery dress, with a matching short jacket hanging on the back of her chair. She made sweeping gestures while she talked.

"She handles rentals," Patti said in a loud whisper. "Shows apartments, writes up leases, that sort of thing."

Cynthia waved again, and rings sparkled on her fingers. She had a big smile on her face, too. I imagined a little light beam shooting off one tooth, like in cartoons. "I'll be delighted to show you what we have available now," she told someone. "When can you come? Oh, perfect. How about two o'clock. Is that too late? Let's allow a couple of hours."

There was a large key box on the wall beside her desk, its door folded back against the wall. I saw hundreds of keys, with color-coded tags on their pegs.

"A good way to see at a glance what's vacant." I directed Patti's attention to the key box.

"I never thought of that. Do you want to wait?"

I shook my head and heard Cynthia say, "Just a minute." She put her hand over the phone. "Welcome aboard, Cleo! I thought social workers just handled adoptions, so I'm looking forward to getting to know you." She went back to her phone conversation and we walked out.

Patti asked me, "What exactly do social workers do? People ask and I'm not sure what to say."

"It's a varied field. In general, we solve problems, get people the help they need. Often from government agencies."

We reached the next office, which Patti said belonged to Cynthia's assistant, Matthew Conyers. The door was closed.

"He's part-time and I barely know him. Works weekends, I think, and does whatever Cynthia needs."

We moved down the hallway, away from Cynthia's voice.

Patti whispered, "I guess you've seen the Marietta Johnson statue on the bluff? Cynthia claims she was the model for the little girl with pigtails, but everyone knows that's Mary Lois. Her initials are even hidden on it."

"I'll have to look more closely." I had seen the statue a couple of days ago but hadn't paid much attention.

Ivy phoned as we turned onto the main hallway. "Looks like somebody cleaned out the pain meds. What do you want me to do?"

"I have no idea." I froze in mid-stride. "Can we get refills?"

"We don't use a drugstore, you know. We use a prescription service. I can call them and tell them what happened. They'll probably get replacements, but we'll have to pay, since the residents have already been billed. Are you going to file a police report?"

"I need to think about that."

Ivy offered little sympathy. "Damned if you do, damned if you don't."

"Go ahead and order the replacements. We'll need them." I would dump the question of a police report into Travis' lap. He couldn't expect me to handle that on my first day.

Patti had moved on down the hall, her footsteps clicking on the tile, but now she was stopped, waiting for me.

"Tiko is physical therapy." She ran a finger down the employee roster. I noticed that her nail polish was orange and white zigzags. "I shouldn't have put her on this list, since she doesn't actually work for Harbor Village, just rents space here. But you may want to meet her anyway. She fixed my stiff neck one day by resting her elbow on it." She moved to the next line of her chart. "Carla is in charge of the kitchen and has one helper, Lizzie." She looked up and I noticed her glasses had orange frames today. "They're the ones we wouldn't want to interrupt right now. They'll be busy serving lunch."

"Patti, do you match your glasses to your nail polish?"

She twittered and admired her fingertips. "When I can. Don't you love it?"

"What time is lunch?"

"Eleven thirty until one, officially, but everybody comes early. Just looking for something to do."

She went back to the list, nearing the bottom now. "Security won't be here until tonight, and Joyce is the head of housekeeping. She has two assistants and they're out working most of the day. Some days they come in early. We have some early risers here, and the housekeeper is like a social visit."

"And what do we offer in the way of activities to keep people entertained?"

She shrugged. "Not much really. I hope you'll have some ideas."

"Do the housekeepers work in teams?"

"Oh no. They'd never get finished then. Usually two of them do the offices, but they separate once they're here. And they come here every week. Most places they do every other week."

I silently hoped they did a better job on the apartments and condos than they did in the office area.

"How long does it take them to do a circuit of the entire complex?"

Patti didn't know. "I know they complain all the time about being overworked. And they quit. Joyce will tell you she needs more help. I think what she really wants is an office job, instead of running a vacuum cleaner. She wanted my job, but she has an old DUI."

"You know everybody's secrets."

"Yeah. Well, everybody has some. Aren't you glad you're from the big city?"

One of the residents I'd met at the Goldenrod Grille was coming across the lobby. I couldn't think of his name.

"Who is this, do you know?"

"Mr. Levine!" Patti sang out, making it sound like a greeting to him rather than an answer to me.

"Good morning. Mr. Levine, you're my first official visitor. Come back this way and see my new office. Would you like coffee? I guess we have coffee. Do we, Patti?"

"Coffee, tea or bottled water. Which will it be, Mr. Levine?"

"Water, I guess. Need to rehydrate after that walk across the parking lot."

He was puffing and red-faced, with a little ribbon of perspiration beads across the top of his forehead.

"Have you thought about getting golf carts for us to use around here?" He took out a handkerchief and blotted his brow and upper lip then took off his glasses and wiped his eyes.

He had come to complain and wasted no time with pleasantries. "The place I moved from had things happening. Dances, lectures, performances. Why can't we get that going here?"

His lips still quivered with the heavy breathing.

"Good idea. Let's do it."

"There's a municipal election coming up in two weeks. Why can't they come here and debate? Or at least answer questions and try to get our vote."

Patti brought water and then perched on the edge of the third chair, wavering between staying and leaving and trying to intuit what I expected. I smiled at her while Mr. Levine drank a lot of water.

"Do we have a club that could sponsor a debate? Current Events or Community Affairs, something like that?"

Patti shook her head and Mr. Levine nodded. "A club, yes, we can call it that. Get them to help with publicity and emceeing. It's nothing official, just the people in my building who sit on the porch every afternoon, but I'll organize them. Community Affairs. That'll do."

"You don't think the candidates will be booked up already?"

"I don't think they're booked at all! No place to go and hear them."

"How many people does our ballroom hold? I haven't seen it yet." I looked to Patti for an answer, but Mr. Levine beat her to it.

"We can go look right now."

We went. Stewart was coming in the side door as Mr. Levine and Patti and I were going out.

"Stewart! Just the person we need," I said. "How many people would you say the ballroom holds?"

"Standing or seated?" He fell in step with us.

"I think we'd want to sit."

"Sitting. Definitely." Mr. Levine was puffing from exertion.

Stewart tried the door to the ballroom. It was locked, but he had a passkey.

"I need to get a key, too, I guess. Who's in charge of keys?"

"That would be your friendly maintenance man. I'll bring you one when I go back to the shed. Seated capacity is a hundred and thirty, according to the fire marshal. I think we still have that many chairs. They get banged up, you know, with people standing on them, or driving over them."

"Driving over chairs?"

Patti twittered and nodded her head, curls bouncing. "It happened."

The ballroom was larger than I expected, with a chandelier that looked like a smaller cousin to the one in the lobby, and sconces spaced around the walls. Three pairs of garden doors opened out to the koi pond, but otherwise it was about as plain a space as ever existed. At one end there was a pass-through to a kitchen. Double doors stood open at the back end of the room, revealing a storage room filled with racks of tables and chairs with padded seats and backs.

"Who sets up chairs and a sound system before an event?"

"I do. Or a helper, if I've got one."

"What day would you like, Mr. Levine? You want to talk to the candidates first?"

"Thursday."

"This week? That's just three days from now." I was thinking of publicity and schedules. "Would that give us time to post notices in town?"

"Six o'clock," Mr. Levine said. "If they can't come, screw 'em."

"Set up chairs for one hundred thirty people, six o'clock Thursday." Stewart looked at me. "You want refreshments?"

"Don't tell me the maintenance man handles that, too."

Patti twittered again and Stewart preened just noticeably.

"No, not refreshments. You talk to Carla in the kitchen about refreshments. And talk real sweet. But I'll put up a table or two at the back for her to use. How many candidates do you expect?"

"Let's see, there are five council seats and four challengers, plus two running for mayor. What's that, eleven?"

Stewart gestured toward one end of the room. "Let's see, tables with seats for eleven plus a moderator at this end, and two tables but no chairs back here, for refreshments. We'll need the sound system, and all the microphones I can find. May have to borrow some. Do you need a sign-up table, anything like that?"

Mr. Levine shook his head. "Literature, maybe. They pay all that money for cards and flyers. Better give them a place to set things out."

It was noon when we got back to the office area. "I don't want to interrupt Carla while she's serving lunch, but I think I'll go down there and eat."

"Oh, you'd better go soon, then." Patti looked at her watch. "They run out of food sometimes. You want company?"

"Sure. But let me make a quick phone call first."

I went to my office and phoned Travis.

"Looks like some pain meds are missing from the lock box in assisted living." I gave him the facts. "Do you want me to file a police report?"

"We both know who's responsible, but yeah, go ahead."

"I don't know who's responsible."

"Three guesses. Is that all you needed? I'm in the middle of something here."

I told him bye and went back to Patti, waiting at her desk.

"Want me to bring along some of this material to review?"

"No, but I want you to lock it up while we're out. Let's not leave personal information lying around for just anyone to see. And while we eat, we'll just chat with whoever's in there."

"Oh, an undercover operation." She sounded delighted.

"Not at all. I believe it's called fact finding."

"Even better." She almost skipped across the lobby.

"What's our policy about the ballroom? Is there a reservation book or something? I should've checked before Mr. Levine left, but I'll chase him down if there's a conflict."

"I'll check, but I don't think there's anything scheduled."

"Thursday, I think he said."

"I don't think there's anything scheduled, period. All the way to Christmas, maybe. We always have something then."

That was months away. "Why so long without an event?"

She shrugged. "Who would do it? He's not going to pay, is he?"

"I didn't think about it. He's a resident. Do residents pay extra to use the facilities? They don't pay you for driving them, do they? Or to use the gym, or the pool?"

She sort of shrugged again, sort of rolled her eyes and moved her head in a way that wasn't clearly yes or no.

"Where can I get a copy of the ballroom policy? What are residents told about using the facilities when they move in?"

"I should've brought a notebook, if you're going to be fact finding all through lunch."

"Who's the activity director? I remember seeing one listed on the employee roster."

"That's Melba. But she's just for assisted living."

"We don't have an activity director for—what?—three hundred residents?" My voice was rising.

"Isn't that going to be your job? Resident Services."

"No. Absolutely not. Activities are something entirely different. Game nights, book groups, concerts, trips. Things like that." No wonder people were complaining about the lack of activities; the staff didn't seem to know what they were. "How often do we have a staff meeting?"

Patti glanced at me and pursed her lips. "A what?"

Chapter 9

Half a dozen residents, two men and four women, were seated at the long table in the dining room, dirty plates in front of them.

My neighbor Ann was one of them. "I hope you didn't come to eat."

"Are we too late?" I introduced myself to the other people at the table and got their names.

Ann laid down a knitting project and went to the steam table to see what was left of lunch.

"You all know Patti."

They did, to some degree.

"You're Patti Wagon, aren't you?"

"I think it's just so amazing your name matches your job," another said.

Patti did a double take, laughed and started to explain it wasn't actually her name before she must have realized the futility of that approach. Then she laughed even harder, and I joined her.

"I think you can get enough for two plates," Ann said. "Want me to do it for you?"

"Oh, no." I went to the serving cart and got a clean plate off the stack. "We'll do it ourselves. You just stay and talk with us while we eat."

Carla came out of the kitchen and went through the same apologizing routine after I introduced myself. "If I'd known you were coming, I'd have made extra." She was young, maybe Patti's age, with square-cut, chin-length brown hair, a white apron over a polo shirt and jeans, and a tiny gold filigree butterfly in the side of her nose. "Let me get Lizzie out of the kitchen."

Lizzie was her helper, a skinny, pale-skinned girl with freckles across her cheeks, who looked like she should still be in school. She seemed stressed about being introduced and quickly went off to clear dirty dishes from the long table as Patti and I pulled up additional chairs.

"Oh, oh, oh!" Ann grabbed her tea glass from Lizzie. "You got any more tea back there?"

Lizzie, obliging, headed for the kitchen.

I asked Carla, "How do you ever figure out how many people you'll be serving?"

That opened the floodgates.

"It's impossible! Some days we come out even, some days there's enough left to feed an army. And some days, like today, we scrape the bottom of the trays. I always tell people, if they get here and there's nothing left, I'll make them a hamburger or a grilled cheese and salad. I'll take that, Lizzie. Get some ice." She took the tea pitcher and circled the table, refilling glasses.

"And what do you do with leftovers, when you have them?" I asked when she got back to me. I scooped up a bite of squash casserole on my fork.

Carla dropped her voice. "Save them for another day."

Well, that was nice to know, I supposed. "I wonder, Carla, are you and Lizzie able to provide refreshments for a political forum in the ballroom? Mr. Levine is planning it for Thursday evening. This Thursday."

"Oh, I love doing events." She seemed completely unfazed by the imminent deadline. "How many people? What kind of refreshments?"

Of course I didn't know but the people at the table immediately began voicing their ideas.

"Thirty people," Patti guessed. "Maybe more. What do you think?"

That sounded right to me, but Ann shook her head and Gloria Gibbons agreed. "Right here in Harbor Village? We wouldn't have to drive? All the night owls will come."

"And serving refreshments? Everybody will come."

"Fifty, at least," they assured me.

"Plus the candidates," Patti remembered.

I added, "Mr. Levine is organizing a committee to help."

Every person at the table wanted to join the committee. While Patti and I ate, they discussed plans.

"Get bottled drinks," Ann told Carla. "Open them as you need them and that way nothing goes to waste."

"Right. And plastic cups and ice. Lizzie, go turn the icemaker up a notch, while we're thinking of it. We'll bag some up and store it in the freezer."

"Cookies," one of the men said.

"Good idea," Ann said. "Assorted flavors. Chocolate chip and oatmeal with raisins. I always like lemon, maybe with some frosting. I'll help you with the baking, Carla, and I've got nice tablecloths we can use."

"I'll help, too," Laurel Gibbons said.

"Maybe some cheese," one of the men proposed. "You can put it on lasagna later in the week if there's some left over."

"Won't be any leftover cookies. Ha! Not in this place," Ann said.

"Now, don't forget to come," they told each other and laughed like it was a running joke. Two of the women made notes of the date, time and location.

"Can we put it on the bulletin board?"

"Where is the bulletin board?"

"I mean that little sign, the A-frame. That thing they put out front."

"I haven't seen that sign in months."

"Didn't Ms. Vetter run over it?"

"I'm going to sign up for that committee. What's he calling it? Community Action?"

Well, well. I raised my eyebrows at Patti. She smiled back. It seemed that we had found some facts already. People wanted activities. Maybe Mr. Levine had hit on something. We'd know for certain Thursday night.

"What about this woman who drowned," a man asked as Patti and I were about to leave. "I heard it might be a purse snatching."

"I haven't heard that but the police are still investigating. In fact, they're coming to interview me this afternoon." I checked the time and waved to get Carla's attention. "Do I pay you?"

She pointed to a clipboard on a stand beside the door. "Just sign. You'll get a bill."

As Patti and I walked down the hallway, I checked my phone. Travis had called back and left a message. But Patti had a serious question, one I'd been dreading.

"Do you think Ms. Ferrell's death was an accident?"

"I hope so. What do you think?"

She did a little shrug. "Nobody liked her. Stewart says that alone makes it suspicious."

Would a guilty person say that? I didn't think so. "Did you know Lee was Jamie's sister?"

Patti stopped in her tracks and stared at me, eyes wide. "No! You're kidding me. Even her own sister couldn't stand her? You should've heard the things Jamie said...do you think Jamie might've..." She pantomimed a quick little shove.

"Hard to believe. But I'm no expert about such things."

"No, you've been in a university. You had to move to a retirement center to experience real life." She grinned and bounced her curls. "How did you like the dining room?"

"To tell the truth, I barely noticed the food. Meatloaf, squash casserole and a tomato-cucumber salad, right? Good, but I think it needed cornbread rather than toast."

We reached the lobby and I cast a quick glance toward the seating area as we walked by. How long before I quit thinking of Lee there?

"You saw Carla send Lizzie to make the toast, didn't you? I'll bet she had cornbread and the early birds cleaned it out. People pay for one meal, eat the soup and salad at noon and take the meatloaf and vegetable back to their apartment for supper. That way, they get two meals for the price of one. And they probably take double cornbread, one for each meal."

"So, for one modest monthly charge—is it four hundred a month?—they get thirty lunches and thirty light dinners. What does that come to per meal? The cost, I mean."

Unfortunately neither of us could do the math in our heads. And we had no idea how many residents took advantage of the dining room meal plan.

"Carla might not keep a record, but Emily will know how many people pay," Patti said.

"The question is, does the number paying match the number who eat? The dining room is depressing, I think. Maybe that's why it's not more popular. The food wasn't bad."

"The lights were off. I didn't even think about it while we were in there, but I'm sure they were off. Maybe Jamie has Carla on a budget."

"I wonder if she'd like to have a committee to advise her about meals. She certainly seemed open to Ann's suggestions just now. Maybe they could plan some food events, a cook-off or something."

"Oh, I love that idea! See? I knew you were going to fix things around here. And a murder is kind of exciting, too, isn't it? Just the possibility that that's what it was. I can't wait to tell people about a cook-off."

I got to my office and listened to Travis' message. Lee's body had been released by the coroner and would be cremated. The memorial service was scheduled for Thursday, in Houston.

I called Stephanie and gave her the news.

"I guess I should go." She sounded miserable.

"Yes, I think so, for your father. You can fly and make it a quick trip."

"What about you?"

"No. I didn't know her. And I've got things to do here." I told her about Mr. Levine's political forum, even though it seemed somewhat trivial under the circumstances.

When we hung up I phoned Chief Boozer and told him about the missing drugs. "I suppose I should file a police report."

"Yes, definitely." He reminded me he'd be stopping by soon. "We'll write up a theft report while I'm there."

Stewart came in as Patti and I were just settling down to work in my office.

"Geez, Patti, couldn't you have told me to paint this dump? What color do you want?"

I looked around. The walls had been white a few years ago. Now there were black marks, scrapes, a few gouges and a generally dingy appearance. The floor was carpeted in medium gray and the baseboards looked fuzzy with dirt and dust. Clearly housekeeping had marked this room off their regular cleaning schedule.

"What do you think, Patti? Nothing garish but maybe a little warmth?"

"How about a pale, pale coral, almost white?" Stewart held his hands up and turned, framing various views of the walls. "Then get some plants to go near the window, with lots of lacy leaves to let the wall color shine through. Happiness in a gallon bucket."

"I love it!" Patti's voice soared into the stratosphere. "Can you do mine, too? Please?"

"And clean these nasty carpets. We'll do it all tonight and you can get back to moving in tomorrow."

"You work at night?"

"Only on special occasions, but this office is on life support. I'll get one of the guys to help. It won't take two hours and the carpet can dry overnight. Three hours tops. Everything will be done in the morning and we'll bank some comp time for hunting season. We'll put yours off, Patti, since it's hard to see where your office ends and the hallway begins."

She looked disappointed.

"But you're on the list. Be thinking about a color. I brought you a key." With a swoop and a bow, he laid it on the desk in front of me. "If you'll just sign this card…"

I signed and got out my key ring. "You keep these cards?"

"Yes, ma'am. Locked up with the key machine."

"Do you have a record of who has keys to the drug cart in assisted living?"

Chief Boozer knocked on the open door. "Am I interrupting?"

"Come in." I got up and walked around the desk. "Do you know my assistant, Patti Snyder, and the head of maintenance, Stewart...?" I fumbled, and he mumbled his last name as he stuck out his hand.

"Stewart Grainger."

The men shook hands, presenting quite a contrast, Boozer big and dark and bald and perfectly tailored, Stewart small, wiry, wrinkled and covered by tattoos.

Patti was staring at me, wearing a silly grin. "Your assistant? Did I just get a promotion?"

I laughed. I'd have to tell her about my one-month agreement with Travis. Any promotions I made, even if official, might be short-lived.

Chief Boozer addressed Stewart. "That was a good question, about keys to the drug cart. Do you have a set? Or know who does?"

Stewart threw his hands out, fingers splayed, palms facing the cop. "I don't know anything about drugs. I do door keys, that's all. Not desk keys, not cart keys." He looked at me. "I assume we're talking about that gray box they roll around?"

"Right."

Stewart shook his head emphatically.

Officer Montgomery looked in at the door but disappeared again.

"Chief Boozer, would you like coffee or water or something?"

"Coffee would be good."

Patti headed for the door. "I'll make fresh. It'll take a few minutes."

"And I'm on my way to the paint store." Stewart hustled out.

Officer Montgomery came in a moment later, unsmiling as usual and directing who should sit where. She spread her materials out on the desk and signaled to Boozer she was ready.

"Officer Montgomery will take notes. First, what drugs are missing?"

"Pain meds, according to the temporary RN we brought in this morning."

"You check her recommendations?"

"Actually, no. She runs the temp agency. But she asked one of the CNAs to help her do a pill count and she called a few minutes later with their findings."

"The medications are kept in a locked box?"

I nodded. "Should be, anyway. I asked for a key this morning and I think it might have been in Michelle's pocket. But she didn't admit it. She's a CNA and was Jamie Barnes' assistant. That's Certified Nursing Assistant, you know."

Chief Boozer nodded and watched Officer Montgomery change to a new page in her notebook. "I know you're new here, Ms. Mack, so you may not know if this has happened before."

"No, I don't know."

Patti tapped on the door and brought in a tray holding three filled cups, plus napkins, spoons, sweetener, and packets of powdered cream. The smell of fresh coffee crept through the room.

I thanked Patti and asked her to head off any interruptions until we finished, and she closed the door as she left.

Boozer poured in a packet of sweetener, stirred and took a sip of coffee before returning to the topic. "Do you know how many pills we're talking about?"

"It wouldn't be many. The prescription service delivers frequently and we only have about twenty-five residents in assisted living. I doubt all of them take pain meds."

I had unwittingly pushed some of Chief Boozer's buttons. "This state has a big problem with prescription drugs, the biggest in the country. If half your twenty-five residents take Percocet three times a day, that's thirty-five pills. Say street value is ten bucks each, so three hundred fifty dollars a day. More if the dosage is higher. Don't think this is pocket change."

I confessed I hadn't thought about the way numbers and values mounted up. One of the problems of being innumerate.

"Think how many hospitals, nursing homes, private houses we have in town, every one a target for medication theft."

"You think they're being sold? I guess that's preferable to having a staff member using them." I sipped my coffee.

"That's even worse, somebody working in a place like this, depriving people of meds they need. Do you suspect any staff members of a drug problem?"

"I haven't even met all the staff. But Travis McKenzie said he knows who's responsible."

"Is Mr. McKenzie here?"

"No. Well, it's hard to tell with cell phones. Last night he said he was in Charleston. I didn't ask where he was today. I got a message that the memorial service will be in Houston Thursday, so he'll be there soon."

Chief Boozer watched Officer Montgomery and waited until she quit writing.

"We'll need to talk with your nurse. And find out when the last drug delivery was. We can ask if residents are getting their meds, but I'm not sure they would know. Officer Montgomery can take care of all that when we finish here. She'll bring a complaint back for you to sign." She nodded and he asked me, "Any questions?"

I said no.

"Why don't we take a short break, give Officer Montgomery time to set up. Then we'll move to another matter."

I didn't even know where the ladies' room was but Patti directed me around a corner. Patti was coming out of my office when I returned. I told her there was no soap and that paper towels were running low and she made a note for the housekeepers.

"Jim Bergen was here looking for you. They want to take you to dinner."

"That's nice." I knew he really wanted a report on the day's events. And chances were he'd have some news for me, too.

I had two phone messages, one from Ivy and another from Mr. Levine.

I listened to Ivy reporting that the pharmacy service had made a delivery and all was well in assisted living. "I'll be leaving soon, but I'll be back at seven in the morning." So that situation was under control.

Before I could listen to Mr. Levine's message, Officer Montgomery came looking for me. I stuck the phone in my pocket.

"Ask them to bring our lamp back," Patti said.

"What lamp?"

"The parrot lamp from the lobby. We always leave it on at night and the police took it."

"Oh yes. The pretty one." I went back to the office.

The recording device, looking like a cross between a cell phone and an electric razor, was positioned on the edge of my desk. Chief Boozer had moved his chair up closer, facing mine. Officer Montgomery once again took the desk chair. There was a bottle of water beside my coffee cup.

Boozer began by stating the date and time. "Present are Ms. Cleo Mack, acting Executive Director of Harbor Village Retirement Center, Officer Mary Montgomery taking notes and operating the recorder, and myself, Ray Boozer, Chief of Fairhope Police Department. Ms. Mack, let's begin with background. What did you know about Lee Ferrell prior to last Thursday?"

I'd known these questions were coming, but I had intentionally avoided thinking about the process until now. I cleared my throat.

"My daughter told me a couple of months ago that her father was getting married again. I don't remember her mentioning the bride's name, but it wouldn't have meant anything to me." I told the recorder about Stephanie sending a photo of the wedding party. "Jamie Barnes told me that Lee from corporate would be here when I began work. She may have mentioned the name Ferrell. But I met Ms. Ferrell for the first and only time Thursday afternoon in the lobby here at Harbor Village. And I first learned she was Travis' new wife from you, Chief Boozer."

"Can you elaborate on that?"

"Friday afternoon you and Officer Montgomery came to my apartment and asked why I hadn't told you she was Travis' wife."

Officer Montgomery smiled quickly. That was a first.

I continued. "I didn't tell you that because I didn't know. I didn't put the two weddings together. Travis' wedding was in New Orleans, but I didn't know where he lived. And Lee Ferrell was always referred to as Lee from corporate, which is in Houston."

The chief was listening, nodding occasionally. He looked through his notes. "I believe you talked with Ms. Ferrell on Thursday. Take your time and tell me all about that. What did she say, what did you think of her. Tell us whatever you remember."

I checked my coffee cup and found it empty and reached for the water bottle instead. "Late on Thursday afternoon I walked from my apartment to this building, the administration building, with my grandson. He's two. We came into the lobby and Lee was standing there, looking glamorous in a green dress and the highest platform wedges I'd ever seen. I remember noticing her perfume. She knew who I was and welcomed me to Harbor Village. It's possible she recognized my grandson since he'd been at her wedding, but I'm not sure she even looked at him."

Boozer scratched his chin and doodled on his notepad but didn't interrupt.

I got back on topic. "Lee said something I found odd at the time. She said she didn't like working with family, that it never works out, and that I shouldn't expect any favors. I knew we weren't family, and the warning about not expecting favors seemed...well, it seemed like a rude welcome to a new employee. I realize now that her remark may not have been aimed me. She worked with her husband and her sister and either of those relationships might have been problematic. I don't remember her saying anything else, except wondering where Stewart was. He's the handyman here, and it's possible she had an appointment with him."

"He's the guy who was in here earlier?" Chief Boozer jabbed a thumb toward the door and I nodded.

"Right."

He made another note. "What time did you see Ms. Ferrell in the lobby Thursday?"

"The first time? The office staff was still here and they leave at five, so let's say it was four thirty."

"And she was looking for Stewart Grainger? Did she find him?"

"He came into the office while I was there. I said Lee was looking for him and he went off in the same direction she'd taken."

He asked what direction that had been, and I told him. "And what do you know about Ms. Ferrell's sister?"

"Jamie Barnes? I met her on my first visit to Fairhope in June. I didn't learn Lee was Jamie's sister until a day or two ago."

"How did you come to get a job here? Did you apply through normal channels?"

"No. The day Jamie and I had lunch, I was still debating whether I should retire. Then when I came here to see about renting an apartment, Jamie said she'd been trying to track me down to talk about a job." I told him about her contacting all the motels. "She gave me a tour and, over the next week or so, we worked out the job details by phone. She arranged for me to get an apartment—which I do pay for, by the way. And then Saturday, with Lee dead and Jamie leaving, Travis McKenzie dropped the director's job into my lap. I've agreed to take it for a month. He's got some problems here he wants me to investigate."

"Tell me about those."

I shrugged. "I don't know much yet. Financial oddities, too many residents moving out, staff issues, a general instability."

Officer Montgomery made a little sniffing sound. Maybe Jim Bergen had shared his thoughts about my lack of qualifications?

"Let's go back to Thursday, after you left the lobby. Trace your actions for the rest of the evening."

I closed my eyes and gave details about our dinner on the pier with Riley. I told about seeing Lee in the lobby when we returned then finding the lights turned off when we walked around the corner for a better look. I even told about the cat moving in that night.

"Did you see Ms. Ferrell at the restaurant?"

"No. But I sat with my back to the room, looking at the marina, so it's possible she was there."

He paged through his notes. "Did any of the people with you see Ms. Ferrell in the lobby?"

"I wanted them to. That's why we walked back for a look. Just think, if Stephanie had seen her, they would've recognized each other. They would've talked and...things might've turned out differently."

"Let's stick to what did happen," Boozer said.

I sighed. "Riley Meddors may have seen her, but I don't think so."

"And Mr. Meddors lives here?"

"He'll be in the resident directory. Or I'll get his address for you."

"Okay, now back to Jamie Barnes. Why did she leave town so soon after her sister died?"

I shook my head. "She got a promotion, but I wonder about the timing. I understand Lee Ferrell made the official reassignment Thursday night and Jamie jumped at it. It looks bad, I think, leaving right after her sister died. It looks bad that Travis took off, too, but I assume they had reasons. They've got a business to run. Jamie is ambitious. She told me the promotion was an opportunity she'd wanted for years."

"What about the message Ms. Ferrell sent? What did it say exactly?"

I shook my head. "I haven't seen it, but it named Jamie to head up the Charleston facility."

Chief Boozer asked if I knew anything else that might be helpful, if we'd seen anyone out walking Thursday night, someone who might've seen something.

I thought back to Thursday night. It seemed such a long time ago.

"I did go out again. We were about to go to bed when my daughter asked me to check her car, to see if it was locked. While I was out, I checked the back door of my garage, and then I went home and went to bed, probably by ten. And here's something, probably insignificant. When we returned from dinner there were two cars, SUVs actually, parked side by side in the center of the lot, one aimed east, the other facing west. When I went to check Stephanie's car, I walked to the garages and clicked her remote. And just as I clicked, maybe a second or two later, lights on both those SUVs came on. One was just a flash but one started up and drove away."

"Did you see the driver?"

"No. I checked the back door of my garage and went back to the apartment. The other SUV stayed there for a day or two, a silver Lexus. It may belong to a security guard, but a Lexus...I don't know. I haven't met the security people yet."

"What color was the vehicle that left?"

"Dark. Black or red, maybe."

"And you're sure lights flashed on both of them before the one drove away?"

I nodded. "I'm sure. I saw headlights flash on one, and taillights on the other as one started up and drove in a big arc. I don't know which way it went on the cross street, since I didn't stay to watch. It might've gone over to the next street or out the boulevard."

"It might've gone to the swimming pool?"

I shrugged. "I suppose."

Chief Boozer didn't seem happy. "Would you recognize the cars if you saw them again?"

I hated to disappoint him, but I didn't think so. "A silver Lexus, and I only know that because I walked past it later, and the dark-colored SUV, about the same size. I don't think I know any more than that."

"Do you know what kind of car Jamie Barnes drives?"

"I do, actually. A BMW two-seater convertible."

Boozer looked at Officer Montgomery, raised his eyebrows inquiringly then sighed and launched into another little pre-packaged speech, announcing the end of the interview and giving the time.

Officer Montgomery picked up the recording device and turned it off. "What kind of husband was McKenzie?" she asked, casually.

Ohmygod, the tinnitus chorus erupted immediately. Not Travis; please, Travis, don't be involved in her death. "That was twenty-three years ago." My voice sounded tense. "I've tried to forget everything about it but I don't believe he'd harm anybody."

"Why did the two of you divorce? Was he abusive?"

I hesitated and Chief Boozer said, offhandedly, "Divorces are public records."

"No, he wasn't abusive, not physically. It was no-fault, I guess. It was a long time ago."

Boozer continued. "And he's been married twice since then, in addition to Lee Ferrell. Any idea why those marriages ended?"

I shook my head. "I never met the women. I don't know much about his life since we parted company. He was happy to be rid of me. No alimony and not much child support since he was a student at the time."

Montgomery spoke casually, like she was chatting with a friend. "Why do you suppose he left here so suddenly yesterday? Is business more important than finding out who killed his wife?"

I decided to defend him. "I can think of a few possible reasons. He likes to be in charge, he's not good at waiting and he needs to stay busy. I know he was afraid you were going to charge him with something. Personally, my guess is, since they're both in Charleston, he wanted to talk with Jamie."

"Isn't that a little odd? Both of them in Charleston? There's not something between them, is there?"

It reminded me of a good cop/bad cop routine, but Montgomery wasn't very good and Boozer was just listening.

"I have no idea. She went for a new job, he went to talk to her...that works for me. It's not like we don't know where they are, and they do have a business to run. If you want low probability, consider that they might both be hiding from somebody, someone with a vendetta against Harbor Health Service. Maybe Lee was just the first target."

Officer Montgomery snorted.

I gave her another smile. "I said it was far-fetched."

Boozer inhaled noisily and slapped his leg. "Well, I guess we're done here."

Chapter 10

I had begun hearing noises in the hallway outside the office, bumps and squeaks and the distinctive clank of a metal ladder, as well as a variety of muttering voices. The painting crew must be waiting.

Officer Montgomery gathered up her gear. "That nurse is probably gone already."

"Is it after five." I looked at my watch and saw that it was, barely. "She'll be back by seven in the morning, but she'll be busy for the first hour, helping with the morning routine." I stood and looked at Chief Boozer. "Can I ask a question?"

"You want to know how she died." He pulled off his glasses and dropped them into his uniform pocket. "A single blow to the back of the head, delivered with a rounded object. It happened right where you saw her last, out there in the lobby."

I held my breath for a moment then blinked a few times. "So not an accident. Homicide?"

"Undoubtedly. But don't worry about finding any traces. The bleeding was mostly internal. We had a disaster crew come in to clean up, just in case. You'll get a bill." He paused for a second or two. "Probably dead when you saw her."

"Are you kidding? In the window, with all the lights on?"

He nodded. "Got any ideas?"

I shook my head. "Hard to process it all at once."

Officer Montgomery had her equipment packed up and ready to go. "You know, for somebody who just moved here, you're awfully involved in this case, if you don't mind me saying so. You met the victim just before

she died, you were married to her husband, you got hired by her sister
and you found that mystery phone. And now you've taken over her job."

I was offended. "And we stayed at the same motel last Wednesday.
But don't get ideas. I didn't know she was there until the desk clerk told
me Saturday. And I wouldn't have known who she was if I'd ridden in the
elevator with her. In fact, everybody who works here knew Lee better than
I did. I hadn't heard from Travis in years, and I didn't find the phone. I
just turned it in. And I've told you everything I know. It's up to you now."

Chief Boozer spoke up. "That phone you turned in was used to call
nine-one-one Friday morning. What do you make of that?"

"Used by Dolly Webb?"

"She denies it. Says she used her own phone and didn't find the other
one until the next day."

"Dolly could be confused about that. She might've picked it up reflexively.
But that means somebody else left it at the pool. How did Lee get there if
she was killed in the lobby?"

He shrugged again.

Didn't know or wasn't telling me. I drew my own conclusions. "Whoever
moved the body left their phone, probably by accident. The question
is, whose phone is it? Aren't they easy to trace? And what about the
weapon, Chief?"

Another shrug. "Probably in the bay."

"That's what Jim Bergen said." I paused to think. "About the phone...
where is Lee's phone?"

He shook his head. "Not with her. We haven't found it."

"She had a computer?"

"A laptop in her office down the hall here. Supposed to have an iPad
and a phone but they're missing, along with her purse."

"So it could have been a robbery."

"Anything is possible, but why add additional complexity?"

"Travis said..." I was thinking a split second ahead as I spoke and
caught myself in time to edit out the part about them having an argument.
No need to make things worse for him if he didn't deserve it. "He said he
used an app to learn she was here, before he drove over from Houston.
Have you tried the app, to see where her phone is now?"

"An app on his phone that tells him where her phone is? Yeah, I've got
that, too. The detectives probably looked into it, but I'll ask. We don't get
a lot of murders to practice on. She had dinner at the pier Thursday night.
You said you didn't see her there."

I shook my head and got in another quick question. "How did her body get from the lobby to the pool?"

He grinned, but all at once the wall between cop and witness was firmly in place again. He pushed up from the chair. "We're working on that. Thanks for your help. Call if you think of anything else. And let me remind you not to play detective. That could be dangerous. I assume you won't be leaving Fairhope. We may need to come back at some point."

"I'll be here."

The hallway outside my office looked like a construction zone. There were paint cans, trays and rollers, a cart with an air compressor and what looked like scuba diving masks, another cart with a steam cleaner, hoses and drop cloths, a ladder and a vacuum cleaner. Boozer and Montgomery and I threaded our way single-file through the clutter.

The painting crew was lounging in the lobby.

And so was Jim Bergen. "Hello, hello." The couch was low and soft and he needed a couple of tries to swing up onto his feet, where he balanced by stabbing his cane against the floor.

Stewart and his helper bounded into action and headed for the hallway.

"It's all yours," I said, "if you're sure you want to start on it tonight."

"We'll be through before dark, what'd'ya bet. Start the clock."

"Chief, Mary," Jim acknowledged them. "Are you making progress?"

Boozer's voice was quiet compared to Jim's. "Got a couple of angles to pin down still. But it's coming together."

"And what do you do first, Chief? Arrest or get a warrant?"

"We're meeting with the DA."

"Good work." He nodded, looking a bit like a shaggy buffalo.

Officer Montgomery looked at me. "We'll be here first thing in the morning to talk with your nurse."

The four of us headed for the door together.

"Cleo," Jim said, "we were hoping you'd be available for a steak dinner tonight. We thought we'd go up to the steakhouse in Daphne."

"Sounds good. Shall I drive?"

"No, Riley will. Just the four of us, so we'll fit in a booth. Why don't we pick you up in about twenty minutes? That may sound early, but it'll take us thirty minutes to get to the restaurant and longer to get food on the table."

"Let me stop by my apartment for a minute and then I'll walk to your place."

He agreed, which meant I had to get moving. I was eating out too frequently, but these were unusual times.

I thought about Stewart as I walked to the apartment and freshened up. He had appeared uncomfortable around Boozer and Montgomery and been quick to avoid them. I wondered why. He seemed like a nice guy, but the question was, how had he gotten along with Lee Ferrell? Could he have been on her hit list for dismissal? Or maybe he had a history with cops. I wondered if his personnel file would hold any clues. With a chief executive who was only occasionally present, Harbor Village might've dropped the ball on screening employees. It was an important consideration, given the vulnerability of older residents and the recent increase in opioid abuse.

The cat met me at the door and watched while I changed shoes and selected a sweater from the dresser drawer. Restaurants were always so cold around here. I went to the kitchen and added dry food to the empty cat dish.

Was this weekend's theft from the assisted living drug cart related to Lee's death? And why had Lee Ferrell been looking for Stewart Thursday afternoon? Had she really been looking at the lights in the lobby?

I locked up and walked through the building and across the boulevard. I could see Jim and Riley standing on the porch and Nita sitting in one of the big white rocking chairs. I'd ask Patti if there'd been any problem with the lobby lights. I was playing detective, exactly what Boozer had warned against, but I had to have confidence in my staff.

Riley's car was a black BMW station wagon. Jim claimed the front passenger seat because of his long legs, but he opened the back door and helped Nita in.

"Nice car." I slid into the seat behind the driver.

"No more driving than I do, I'll probably keep it forever."

We went north on the four-lane in light traffic, although the southbound lanes were still clogged with commuters returning home to the Eastern Shore. The sun was on my side of the car, dropping low in the sky, and dark clouds loomed to the north.

"Looks like it'll be a pretty sunset."

Nita smiled. "It'll be hard to beat your first Fairhope sunset. I'll always believe that's what persuaded you to move here."

I gave her hand a squeeze. "I think some nice people played a big role, too."

"Oh, how is your cat?"

Jim spoke up from the front seat. "Now remember, we're not going to talk about anything important until we get to the restaurant, where everybody can hear."

Nita rolled her eyes and looked at me. "I didn't realize he considered cats important."

The Bergens knew the hostess, who took us to their favorite booth, where Jim and Nita sat with their backs against the kitchen wall.

I ordered tilapia with mango chutney on a bed of rice. Riley and Nita got petite filets with potatoes and salads, and Jim ordered the large version, a 10-ounce portion with a sweet potato and a Caesar salad "with a few extra croutons. And bring us extra napkins, a big stack."

Then the inquisition began.

"Well, Cleo, how was your first day on the job? I see the police are still on the premises."

I told them about the missing pain meds and summarized the questions Boozer had asked in our interview. "I couldn't tell him much about Lee Ferrell, but he asked about my history with Travis, twenty-three years ago."

"Well, it's quite a coincidence, you know, although some people say there's no such thing. You're aware it's officially a homicide."

"I think they'd like to pin it on me. Officer Montgomery thinks it's suspicious I have so many connections to this case."

"Mary's a good officer. That's just the way they're trained, to look for anything out of the ordinary."

"It's hard to think a local did such a thing," Nita said.

Riley took a wry view. "Hard to accept when you claim to have a perfect little community."

"I do it, too," Jim admitted. "Catch myself thinking a stranger came in, grabbed her purse and something went wrong. And who's to say it didn't happen that way. Where is her purse?"

Nobody knew.

"Well, there you go." He shrugged.

Our salads were delivered and right behind them came the rest of our meals, so food absorbed our attention for several minutes. Then I told them about the two SUVs. Jim produced an index card and made a sketch to be sure he understood precisely where the vehicles had been located and what they had done.

I asked Riley, "Did you notice them, parked in the center of the lot beyond Stephanie's car?"

He couldn't be sure. "I don't think I could be specific about how many vehicles or what type."

"That's what I would've said, too, but when I went out later to check Stephanie's car, the lights of both SUVs flashed and then one of them drove away. That brought them to my attention."

"Must've been those keyless cars. With the fob you keep in your pocket. Or purse."

All three of us looked at him.

"You know what I mean. You walk up and the doors unlock automatically. Then you touch a button on the dash and the engine starts up. No key needed."

"All automatic." Jim was awestruck. "I'll have to go to the dealership tomorrow and educate myself. Something I've missed out on. Now, Cleo, the question is, who did these cars belong to?"

"I can't answer that. One was a silver Lexus. It sat in the same spot, or close by, for a day or two. I haven't seen it since. The dark one left that night, and I wouldn't recognize it if I saw it again."

"A silver Lexus." Jim paused thoughtfully. "That wouldn't be Lee Ferrell's car, would it?"

Lee's car! "You know, I never thought of that. I don't know what kind of car she drove, although the cops do, I'm sure. I'm clearly not cut out for this sleuthing business."

"The question is," Nita asked, "was she in the car when the lights flashed? Could she have been signaling to you?"

"Ohmygod." I shivered. Had I ignored a signal for help? "Chief Boozer thinks she might've been dead when I saw her in the lobby."

All three of them stared at me.

Jim shook his head. "I think he's got that wrong. What murderer would choose a victim seated under spotlights, right in front of a wall of windows?"

"He said there was 'forensic evidence' there." I did little air quotation marks. "But I don't know how they determined the time of death."

"Stomach contents." Jim nodded.

I was afraid he was going to elaborate, but Nita gave him a stern look. Just the thought was enough to make me opt out on dessert. Riley and Nita shared a slice of banana cream pie—a specialty of the steakhouse, they said—and, of course, Jim had a whole piece all to himself.

I got a cup of decaf and took a sip. "I have a question for you. Who answers emergency calls at night? The security guard?"

Riley and Nita looked to Jim, who blotted meringue off his lips. "There is a security guard, the same man for years. I think he catches a few winks during the night. Any calls from the alarm system go to the Assisted Living office. But there weren't any calls Thursday night. That's the first thing I asked."

I smiled at Nita. "He's amazing, do you know? Thinks of everything."

Riley changed the subject. "What's the story with Jamie? It looks bad, her leaving with her sister just murdered. That's the main thing people are talking about."

"Let's not use the m-word," Nita said. "Can't we just say deceased, or that she died."

Jim pulled his eyebrows together in a scowl. "We can say she went for a moonlight swim, Nita, if you like that better, but it was still murder." He took a deep breath and covered Nita's hand with his. "Sorry, honey." He looked at Riley. "Jamie had a rough life, and she got the short end of the stick in the brains department. But I know her pretty well and I can't see her bashing anybody over the head. We don't even need to consider it."

"Jim!" Nita's eyelids fluttered like she might faint.

I took another sip of coffee. "I learned something else since we talked. Lee didn't run the business. Travis does."

Jim seemed stunned. He put down his fork. "Did he marry the boss and then bump her off? It's an old formula, but he had to work fast. Only been married a couple of months."

"He's been CEO of Harbor Health Services for three years."

There was half a minute of silence as everyone digested the news.

Then Riley interrupted it. "Tell us about that girl who worked with Jamie. The little one with all the funny business going on."

Did he mean Michelle? She was close to Jamie's age, not what I'd call a girl.

Jim was agreeing with him. "Sneaking around, wanting to empty people's trash. Got people cruising the parking lot in the middle of the night."

I didn't know what they were talking about, but I didn't like the sound of it.

"Don't forget Dolly's ring," Nita reminded him.

"Twelve thousand dollars, according to her, but that was her fault, leaving it in a drawer."

"And she might've dropped it anywhere," Nita added.

"Whoa, whoa," I said finally. "You're losing me. Is this Michelle you're talking about?"

"See what you can find out about her, Cleo." Nita was frowning. "She's worth a closer look."

"And it's all rumors. But let's correct another thing." Riley looked at Jim. "It's not a family business, it's a corporation, like GE or Regions Bank. Marrying the founder's daughter, or being engaged to her, didn't give Travis control. That came from stockholders and the board of directors."

"And about Jamie," I said, "she didn't just leave. Lee sent out a message Thursday night, promoting her to director of the Harbor Village in Charleston. It was a job she'd wanted for a long time."

"She wanted away from Lee," Jim said, and Nita nodded agreement.

"And why shouldn't she go immediately? It's not as if the funeral will be here." Nita seemed to be growing more sympathetic. "The body's not even here. Maybe Fairhope is just too negative a place for her under the circumstances. Maybe she needed to get away."

"Now about Travis McKenzie." Jim looked at me. "I'd have more questions about him if you weren't vouching for him."

"But I'm *not* vouching for him. I don't really know him now. I just can't imagine that he…" I wasn't sure what to call murder, if the word was off limits. "The truth is, I hope he's not involved because of the impact on Stephanie and Barry. Totally selfish, I admit it."

"And perfectly natural," Nita said. "I hope so, too. Will you go to Houston for the memorial service?"

I shook my head. "I didn't know her. And I've got a job to do here. Did you hear that Mr. Levine is arranging a political forum for Thursday night?"

They had heard and were interested.

"We need things like that, Cleo," Nita said. "To keep our minds working."

"Murder does that, too." He ignored a dirty look from Nita. "Well, I wouldn't want it to become a regular event."

Jim had brought a handicap placard for Riley's car, so we didn't have a long walk, which was good since a drizzle had started while we were in the steakhouse. The parking lot was black and shiny.

The rainfall increased as we drove back to Harbor Village.

Nita watched it out the side window. "We need rain so badly. Some summers it rains every day, but the farmers are hurting this year."

Jim swiveled partway around. "It wasn't supposed to be heavy until morning. I just brought the little umbrella."

We got back to Harbor Village and Riley stopped at the curb in front of their building. "Take your umbrella and go, Jim. I've got a big umbrella and I'll walk with Nita. You wait right where you are, Cleo."

"I can walk from here." But I made no move to get out of the car.

He left the flashers going while he helped Nita out of the car and walked her to her door. Then he jogged back to the car, made a U-turn through the intersection and parked in front of his building. "Just wait. I'm going to walk you to your door."

We took the sidewalk that ran between buildings. I entered the screened porch and held the door open.

"Have you used this porch at all?"

"About five minutes the first night I was here. But it'll be nice in a few weeks, with cooler weather." I turned the lamp on and stepped back. Its glow was a welcoming sight on a wet night.

"Very nice. I'll come join you some evening if you invite me."

"I will." I unlocked the door to the living room. "Do you think we need more security here? Is that why Jim is always patrolling the premises? I admit I haven't met a security guard yet."

"Better safe than sorry, Jim would say. And he'd still do his patrols even if you had a dozen watchmen."

I flicked the lights on inside.

"Very nice." Riley looked in, apparently not eager to depart. "You're already settled."

"Would you like something? A glass of wine, a cup of tea?"

"Rain check."

We laughed, since it really was raining.

"See you tomorrow. Well, hello, kitty."

The cat was rubbing against the coffee table. She gave a soft little *brrrp* and trotted to him, and he bent over to rub one finger against her black and orange cheek.

"She likes you."

"Did you find out what her name is?"

"Not yet, but I haven't given up."

Riley said good night to the cat and to me, and I locked up behind him.

I loved rain, but the drone of the bathroom exhaust fan obscured any sound from outside while I had a long, steamy shower. I put on a cozy, terry cloth robe and went into the bedroom. Rain splatted on the shrubs and the sidewalk outside. I attended to my clothes, putting dirty things into the bathroom hamper and selecting an outfit for the next day. And I set out the closed-toe shoes I wore on rainy days. It would rain most of the week, according to Jim.

Stephanie called but didn't talk long. "Dad was here. He took us out to dinner."

"Oh, he's in Birmingham?"

"Just passing through. He was going to Tuscaloosa for the night. He asked me to ride to Houston with him, but I can't be gone all week. We went to Highlands Grill for dinner. Have you had rabbit roulade with rice grits?"

"Ugh. What kind of car does your father drive?" The question occurred to me out of the blue, or out of the drizzle, to be more accurate.

"A Lexus. Wish I had one exactly like it. A black SUV with tan leather."

Uh-oh. A black SUV? My heart sank. "Was it a rental, do you think?" Fingers crossed.

"I didn't ask. Do rentals have regular tags?"

"I think so. What state was the tag from?"

"Alabama."

Maybe it was a rental. Someone who lived in Houston wouldn't have an Alabama tag. But I pushed the whole topic into mental storage for the moment.

I wished her a good night and sent a hug to Barry. Then I made a circuit of the apartment, turning off lights and checking door locks. When I returned to the bedroom, I propped up pillows to make myself a comfortable nest and picked up my book about Fairhope. I'd been captivated from the first page and could've read all night, if not for my thoughts about morning. At least I didn't have to dread a commute.

I turned the bedside lamp off and eased out of bed without disturbing the cat. A rainy night always guaranteed good sleeping, but I wanted to open the window just a bit so I could hear the rain better. I pulled the curtain back, reached for the window lock and froze.

A man was outside, standing on the sidewalk.

I dropped the curtain into place, leaving a slit to watch through. He had a flashlight in one hand and a small umbrella in the other, and it took only a moment for me to recognize Jim Bergen. I watched him swing the flashlight in a wide arc, side to side, then fix the beam on my screened porch. After a few seconds, he turned and went slowly, carefully, toward his building. I supposed my apartment had been added to his nightly security round. And I decided to leave the window closed, after all.

It was still raining Tuesday morning, a light, misty rain that put a slight chill in the air and gave the impression it could go on for days. In Atlanta I would've said it was a sign fall was approaching.

I put on a short raincoat, opened my folding umbrella and dodged puddles on the way to the Assisted Living building. If the police were coming early to interview our temporary nurse about missing drugs, I wanted to be there. It was the police department's responsibility to find out who had taken the missing pills, but it was my job to ensure it didn't happen again.

The aroma coming from the dining room just inside the door worked like a magnet, and the staff treated me like a royal visitor. All except Michelle, who wasn't there yet.

"What time does she come in?" I asked one of the CNAs.

The aide—Rutie, her name tag said—shrugged. "Whenever she feels like it. You know that girl. She works for Jamie, not like us." I loved Rutie's New Orleans accent. "Jamie keeps her own hours, too. Makes it hard for us. This a good one we got now." She took a step toward Ivy and gave her a hip bump, like a high five when your hands were occupied.

Ivy gave her a grin but kept working. She was quite efficient, bringing residents to the dining room, giving every arrival a cheery greeting, consulting a seating chart and getting people into their assigned places. "Makes it easier to be sure everybody gets the right meds. She gave me a wink and directed a resident to an empty seat. "Just change the chart up every month for social stimulation."

When a critical mass of residents was reached, she began passing out the little pill containers and watching the pills go down.

Other staff members were rounding up late risers. "Miss Amy don' wanna get up," Rutie reported to Ivy.

Ivy wasn't bothered. "It's so nice to sleep in when it's raining. I'll take her meds in later. Tell Goldie to put aside a muffin for her, too."

Concierge service, and why not? The residents were paying customers, not inmates conforming to the warden's schedule.

When everyone was in place and the food had been served, I got a cup of coffee and a cranberry muffin and sat near the floor-to-ceiling windows, at a table with three residents and a vacant chair. The topic of conversation was pets, and I told them about my three-colored cat.

"What's her name," one of my tablemates asked.

"I'd like a cat," another said.

"Does anybody here have one?" I was certain I'd read or heard pets were allowed, even in assisted living.

The women at my table shook their heads. "I haven't seen a cat in years." She sounded so sad. I felt a little stab of sympathy before I considered she might have a memory problem.

"Maybe we can find one for you to pet."

"We have a bird feeder, but it's empty. Haven't seen a bird in years, either."

"Maybe the cats ate the birds," the other woman said.

"What cats? There aren't any."

I'd read about pets in nursing homes and assisted living. Research said they had strong therapeutic benefits. I got out a note card and wrote myself a reminder to check on a pet for the residents. When I looked up again, Officer Montgomery was running through the rain, heading for the front door.

I got her a muffin while she prepped her coffee, then we headed for the office Jamie had used. Ivy followed us with the drug cart. And whom should we find in the office but Michelle, sitting idle with the lights off.

"Oh, Michelle! I didn't know you were here. Would you mind letting us use this office for a few minutes?"

She left, giving a passing glance at the drug cart and trailing a sullen air in her wake. I flipped the lights on and closed the door.

Ivy had wedged her cart into the tight space, so I sat in the doorway to the back office. "I'll just listen, if you don't mind."

Ivy told about doing the pill count the previous day, gave the name of the CNA who'd served as observer and showed us the bubble wraps in which pills were delivered.

Montgomery asked, "And they were all opened?"

"No, pain pills are in their own little bubbles." She showed us one of the damaged pill packs, as well as the replacement pain meds sent in yesterday by the pharmacy service.

"Any idea how long residents went without pain meds?"

"There were fourteen residents whose meds were taken. I didn't ask all of them. Some wouldn't be able to give an accurate report. But three said they didn't get all their pills on Sunday and one said she didn't get the usual meds Saturday, either. I asked if this had happened before and she said it had."

"So your best guess would be the theft occurred . . . when?"

"Friday night or Saturday."

Montgomery looked at me. "Who would have records of the staff members on duty then?"

"I'm not really sure, since Jamie's gone. Michelle, maybe. She's the woman who just left. I haven't figured out what she does here, but recordkeeping for this program is a possibility. Ivy, what are the symptoms of drug abuse?"

"For Percocet? Depends on how much they take, and for how long. Let's look it up." She whipped out her phone and pressed a few buttons then read aloud. "Sleepiness, sweating, headaches, confusion, tiny pupils—that's interesting—vomiting, lowered respiration."

"And have you noticed anything of that nature?" I wished I had noticed Michelle's pupils and wondered if drug use made someone want to sit in the dark.

"We're all sweating," Ivy said. "Or were, before the rain started. Let's see what they say about Norco." She read the results of a new search. "Malaise, dizziness, mental clouding."

I had a question for the two of them. "Do you think we have adequate drug security here?"

Montgomery answered, "When did you last drug test this building?"

Of course I didn't know.

"Just tell all the employees they have to take a drug test within twenty-four hours."

Ivy agreed. "Some may quit rather than take it, so be prepared."

"There are two or three labs within a few blocks of here that can do it. Pick one and give them a list of everybody who's supposed to come in."

It sounded like a good idea.

Ivy put the meds back into the cart, locked it and removed the key. "There's a drug test policy posted in the front office, so staff members are on notice they can be tested."

Officer Montgomery asked for Ivy's contact information, and we seemed to be finished.

"I thought you were doing a fine job, working with the residents this morning," I told Ivy.

"It's second nature by now." She smiled and pushed the cart out into the hallway.

When I got out to the porch a few minutes later, Officer Montgomery was still there, talking on her phone. I stopped nearby and watched the rain until she disconnected.

"Did you learn anything about that phone I turned in?"

"Learned all we're going to." She dropped her phone back into a case attached to her belt. "Which is basically nothing. We may never know who owned it."

"What about Lee's phone. Did you find it?"

She shook her head. She was a large woman, 5'10" maybe. The uniform and cop gear made her look like a big round pumpkin on stilts.

"She sent a message Thursday evening to Travis McKenzie and the HR office in Houston, reassigning Jamie Barnes to head the Charleston facility. Probably one of the last times she used her phone."

"What time?"

"I can find out. Will you be able to tell from the message where she was when she sent it?"

She shrugged. "That's not my specialty."

Both of us were staring across the garden, watching the gusting rain. A green plastic bucket came tumbling out of the garden, bounced across the street and crashed into a UPS truck stopped in front of the condos.

"Come have lunch with me one day," I said. "I might know something without realizing it's important. We can do a little brainstorming."

She nodded absently. "Lots of dead spots for cell service in this town. Only works about half the time down at the pier. So she might've waited to make her calls from here."

"Chief Boozer said she had dinner at the pier."

"Autopsy said so, or some other place with crawfish and fried green tomatoes, which is their house specialty. And died within two hours."

"Hmm." I imagined the analysis of stomach contents and got a little queasy. "Well, I'll ask Houston for a copy of that final message. I'm not sure why I brought it up. I'd better get to work." I opened my umbrella and set off for the big house.

Chapter 11

My office looked like a different place.

Even on a gray, rainy day, it glowed with the new paint. It was actually a shock and a pleasure to enter the room. The carpet was clean, there was a six-foot tall tree with a braided trunk sitting at the window and the file cabinets were now a matched pair, painted a subtle lime green color.

"I cannot believe it," I said over and over, as I circled around looking at everything.

Stewart and Patti were lurking to see my reaction, beaming from the doorway.

"The tree's on approval," Stewart said. "It's a hundred nine dollars plus tax if you decide to keep it."

"It even smells good in here."

"That's the tree, cranking out oxygen and improving your thinking ability. You're getting healthier already."

"It does do a lot for the room," Patti said. "Gives it some life. How about flowers, too? Couldn't we find funds for a little bouquet to go on this table?" She glided across the room and swept her hand over the worktable. "And maybe another little arrangement for the lobby? Wouldn't that be pretty? I could pick up something at the grocery store and it would last all week."

"You know, I need to have a look at our budget. I have no idea what funds we have for anything. Is Emily here today?"

"Yes, and she's already looking for you. Want me to call her?"

"Not just yet. I've got a little chore to do first. If you'll fend off visitors for a few minutes, I'll draft something for you to format and print."

"Oh, I love doing that," Patti said. "I'll keep everybody out until you get ready."

I made a couple of phone calls and then asked Patti for a copy of the employee handbook and a sheet of paper. I wished I'd brought my laptop, but once I'd read the relevant section of the handbook, it took only a few minutes with pen and paper to draft a memorandum.

MEMORANDUM
TO: All Assisted Living Unit Employees, Harbor Village
FROM: Cleo Mack, Acting Executive Director
SUBJECT: Drug Testing
In accordance with the Harbor Village drug free workplace program, outlined in the Harbor Village employee handbook, and as a consequence of a recent incident involving the theft of pain medications, this memorandum will serve as official notice that all employees of the Assisted Living unit will participate in a drug test within 24 hours. The cost of this test will be paid by Harbor Village, and the testing lab selected for this procedure is located at ...

I drew a blank line where Patti could fill in the street address.

"Put today's date on it and leave room for my signature. Call the lab back. Here's the phone number. Get their street address. Sorry I didn't think to do that when I was talking with them. Then deliver a copy of this memo to each employee in the Assisted Living building, ASAP. Ask Ivy to phone any staff members who won't be coming in today and tell them what the memo says and that a copy is there waiting for them. Why don't we copy the relevant page from the employee handbook, too, and attach it. Here, I'll put a paperclip on the page."

"I'll start on it right now. And there's someone waiting to see you."

Dolly was my first visitor of the day. "I love your office. It looks new. How did you do it so fast?"

"I didn't do a thing. Stewart, the maintenance man, did it, after I left last night. Isn't it amazing?"

"Stewart? I know him. I want my apartment painted this exact color! And you owe me a paint job. I didn't get one when I moved in. Now you and Nita have got me all fired up about redecorating. Can I see your apartment, too? You've had a week to work on it, so I expect something special."

"You and Nita come tonight. We'll have a glass of wine and you can look at the apartment and visit the cat."

"Does she have a name yet? And is she friendly? I'm not sure I would be if I'd been thrown to the wilds for a month."

"She's friendly. And I'm going to try again today to learn her name."
I was thinking of the clinic in the shopping center next door, the one that

had been closed Friday afternoon when I called. Maybe Mrs. Flowers' two cats had separate vets.

Mr. Levine came in, puffing. "Why haven't you signed up for the Community Affairs committee?" he asked Dolly. He shook rain off his pants then pulled a chair around and sat down heavily.

Dolly blinked like an owl. "Affairs? Here? Is that legal?"

"More political than legal, I'd say."

"No, I mean—oh, never mind," Dolly said. "I'm not much into politics. Affairs either, for that matter. Exactly what are you planning?"

"We're sponsoring a forum Thursday night for the city council candidates."

"Oh, well, I don't drive at night. Sorry."

"You don't have to drive, Dolly." He was catching his breath but growing irritated. "It's right here, in the ballroom."

"In our ballroom? Well, yes, in that case I'll come. What time?" She got out a little notebook and pencil. "I have to write everything down."

"Six o'clock."

She wrote. "Will it be over by eight? I keep early hours, you know."

"Over by seven thirty. You don't have to stay for refreshments if you're in a hurry. We've got a schedule and we'll hold them to it."

"Oh, this is exciting! New paint and a political forum. Well, Cleo, I just wanted to welcome you aboard. Sorry I didn't get in yesterday. And I'll see you tonight. Did we say what time? I need to write that down, too."

She made her note about visiting my apartment and left.

Mr. Levine wanted to see the ballroom, to see if preparations for his forum had begun yet.

And Emily the bookkeeper was waiting in the hallway.

"I'm walking around to the ballroom with Mr. Levine. Go in and admire the lovely new paint job and I'll be right back." To Mr. Levine I said as we walked, "I don't know if Stewart has gotten anything done yet. He worked on my office last night."

We went out the door at the end of the hallway and turned toward the ballroom, staying under the roof all the way. "I talked with Carla in the kitchen about refreshments. Ann is going to help her."

"Maybe Ann can help her with some lunch menus, too. That dining room should be your number one priority. Don't let this murder business distract you. That's a police problem. Doesn't concern Harbor Village."

"I hope you're right. And hope everyone looks at it that way"

The ballroom looked just as it had the last time we saw it.

"I'll check back tomorrow and there better be progress. But right now, I'll speak to Carla. Maybe I'll stay for lunch since I'm here. I've got some good books to donate to the library. Is Patti Wagon still in charge of it?"

"I think so." Actually, I hadn't known there was a library. I wondered where it was but didn't want to ask Mr. Levine.

When I returned to the office, I saw a group of young people waiting in the lobby. They sat on the couches or stood near the windows, looking out at the rain.

Patti had a sheaf of memos. "You're certainly popular this morning. I've got copies made and I'm putting names on the envelopes right now. I'll be out for a few minutes to walk them over to assisted living."

Emily was sitting beside Patti's desk. She popped up and waved some papers at me when I looked at her. Leases, I learned, reading the bold print. I saw my name on one of them.

"These were on my desk this morning." Her voice was indignant and her face was even redder than her hair. "I don't know anything about them, and now these people . . ." She waved the leases toward the lobby. "These people are here wanting their deposits back. How am I supposed to know if they ever paid a deposit? The leases don't give any names. They say *per Marjorie Zadnichek*, and Marjorie Zadnichek has nothing at all to do with Harbor Village! She's a manager at the Grand Hotel at Point Clear."

I scanned the leases while Emily vented. They applied to two units in one of the U-shaped buildings at the front of the complex. The rent quoted was cheaper than mine, but the tenants were directed to make deposit and rent checks payable to Ferrell & Associates, just as I had.

From the corner of my eye I could see the people in the lobby coalescing and moving in our direction. There weren't nearly enough chairs for them in my office.

"Let's go out there, where we can all sit down." I moved in that direction, with Emily right behind me, and the group turned around.

"Hi there," someone said.

I turned to see a familiar face. It was the desk clerk from the motel.

"Hunter! Good to see you. And this group must be the students from Ukraine, right?"

"Yes, yes," they answered, happily.

I wasn't really superstitious, or not very, but I hadn't adjusted yet to the idea of sitting on the couch where Lee Ferrell had died. Instead, I pulled a chair from one of the card tables and sat facing the group. Emily did the same, staying a couple of feet behind me.

"I'm here to help with communication." Hunter introduced the members of his group.

I identified the pretty blonde as his girlfriend; her name, she said, was Angelika.

"I am going home." Her pronunciation was crisp. "And I need my money."

"Her deposit on the apartment," Hunter clarified.

I nodded and looked at the leases, scanning for names but not finding them. And not finding the amount of the deposits initially, but finally there it was, in small print—$1,400. "What documentation do you have? A copy of the lease showing your name? A receipt?"

"Receipt, yes." She whipped out a small piece of paper.

It was a plain receipt torn from a pad you could buy at any office supply store, with no indication it came from Harbor Village. The dollar amount said three hundred fifty, and the date was three months ago. The signature was a heavy scrawl but I had no trouble making out the first letter *J*, followed by what might be a capital *B*.

"Jamie Barnes," Emily whispered, looking over my shoulder. "It's her signature, but she never gave me anything, I swear. No cash, no check, no deposit slip. Nothing!"

I might as well bite the bullet. I smiled at the students. "We would normally return the deposit after the unit has been vacated and inspected. But I understand this is a special situation, since you'll be leaving the country. Are you all leaving at the same time?"

Hunter got involved, repeating some of my words with slight variations.

Angelika smiled at me. "We go Saturday. All eight. To Washington, DC."

Today was Tuesday, so that gave us a couple of days. Maybe the hotel would be willing to guarantee the condition of the apartments? I wondered why the hotel hadn't paid the original deposit anyway and realized that since there were no names on the lease, and no name on the receipt, I couldn't be certain who had paid what. I'd better talk with Marjorie Zadnichek before I made any promises to these young people.

"Do all of you have receipts?"

They did.

"Hunter, if you'll collect these, Emily will go with you to make a copy for us. Then I'll talk with the hotel manager and we'll have the refunds ready Friday. How's that?" I hoped I'd be able to deliver.

"Friday. Okay." Angelika spoke in a mixture of English and something else—Russian or Ukrainian, I supposed—to the others. They all gave me big smiles.

One international crisis averted.

Hunter and Emily were back in two minutes and redistributed the original receipts.

Another student spoke in a low voice to Angelika and pointed to the window. "May we look at your garden?"

"You'll get wet. But yes, of course. Hunter, thank you for coming."

Emily waited until they were out of earshot. "What do I do now?"

I took a moment to consider. I didn't know about Emily, but I was beginning to have an unpleasant inkling about the situation. What were the odds that someone had rented these two apartments outside of official channels? The students had been here for three months, paying rent that could be pocketed without much fear of discovery. And when the summer was over, and the apartments vacated, they could right go back on the list of available units and no one would ever suspect anything.

I couldn't be certain about who was involved. Jamie's name, or something similar to it, was on the receipt, but anyone could've signed it.

"You saw what the receipt looked like," I said to Emily. "Go out to the Assisted Living building and find Nurse Ivy. Take her with you to the office Jamie used. Ivy can show you. See if that receipt book is there. If you find it, bring it back here, and don't let Michelle interfere with you. Don't even tell her what you're looking for, just search the desk. Act like it's something you do routinely, and don't mention my name."

She stared for a second then straightened her back and gave me a cocky smile. "I'm on it."

While I waited for Emily, I went back to my office and tried to relax. That was only partially successful, so I got out my phone and searched for veterinary offices in Fairhope, found the one in the shopping center and dialed the number.

"I inherited a cat that belonged to Ms. Flowers in Harbor Village," I said to the woman who answered. "She lived in apartment eight. I'm calling to see if she might've been a client of yours and if you can tell me the cat's name."

"Can you hold?"

"Yes."

I was still holding when Emily appeared at the door. I motioned her to the worktable, where we could spread out the materials she was carrying.

"Now, tell me again what the owner's name was," the woman on the phone said.

"Flowers."

"We have a Bob on Fish River, and a Kimberly...this must be it. Kimberly Flowers, apartment eight, Harbor Boulevard?"

"That's it."

"She has two cats. Kitty Baby and Tinkerbelle."

"That's it!" I was so pleased to solve the puzzle. "Tinkerbelle."

She spelled it for me. "Belle like a southern belle. That's unusual. Three years old on the fourteenth of April, and she's due an annual check-up next month. She's a longhaired calico. I've got a picture of her here if you need to see what she looks like."

"I'm so glad to know her name. Can't wait to get home and see if she answers to it."

The woman on the phone laughed. "Well, you said she's a cat. Don't expect miracles."

"Tinkerbelle," I repeated to Emily after I hung up. "I've been trying for days to find out the name of the cat that adopted me."

"I've got five cats. A momma and four kittens. Do you want another one?"

"No, one's enough for me. But I'll know who to call if I need a cat sitter."

We pulled two chairs to the table and she laid out a stack of folders. "Here's the receipt book."

"It was in Jamie's desk?"

"The top drawer of the desk in the first office, just like you said. Michelle was sitting there, but I asked her to move. And I've looked; there are eight receipts for three hundred fifty dollars each in the middle of May. None of them show a name. That amounts to twenty-eight hundred dollars that was never turned in, never deposited, and I don't want anybody blaming me."

There were a lot more than eight receipts missing from the book. I looked forward to seeing what the others were for, but now I turned my attention to Emily and the bookkeeping reports.

Harbor Village was bigger than I had imagined. Emily listed two hundred twenty-four apartment units, not counting assisted living or the privately owned condos and houses. Owners of those still paid a monthly fee for yard maintenance, cable, water and sewer, gym membership and emergency call service. Emily's charts showed resident names alongside one hundred seventy-two rental units, which translated to fifty-two vacancies, I calculated, writing all the figures in the margin.

"What percentage is that, approximately?" I recalled the financial reports Riley had reviewed with me. They claimed the entire corporation had a seventy-nine percent occupancy rate.

Emily produced a calculator and punched a few numbers. "Twenty-three percent vacant."

That meant seventy-seven percent occupancy. Only a little below average, but it sounded bad. I hated being below average in anything.

"That's fifty-two units we maintain and insure, heat or cool and pay taxes on, while they produce no income, not for us or the dining room or the rental businesses. That's a lot of waste."

"But remember, those Russians are in two units I show as vacant."

"Oh, right. Where's my apartment? Does it show up as vacant?"

It did.

"Are you paying rent?"

"Eighteen hundred a month."

"Wonder how much the Russians are paying."

I hadn't thought beyond the deposits. So there was three months of rental income missing, too? "What's the usual rental rate for those units?"

"Two bedrooms, upstairs, in that building, with no incentives…" She was looking down the list. "The normal rate is sixteen hundred dollars a month."

"So that's how much? For the summer."

She didn't need to use the calculator app. "Sixteen hundred a month for three months is forty-eight hundred dollars, plus the fourteen-hundred-dollar deposit that will be refunded if the units are in good shape. In all, sixty-two hundred dollars I didn't get."

"A nice little sum."

"Times two," she reminded me. "For the two units."

"Twelve thousand dollars?"

"Twelve thousand four hundred dollars."

"Ohmygod."

Emily flexed her financial acumen. "But we don't actually know how much they were paying. Sometimes new residents get incentives, like free meals for a month. Since the deposits totaled fourteen hundred a unit, I'll bet that's what the monthly rental was, too. But it still totals…" She punched at the touch screen. "Eight thousand four hundred dollars for the two units, after you return their deposits."

"So much to think about." I wished for greater accounting expertise for myself. "I may learn more when I go through the rest of the receipt book. Wonder if any other units are rented off the record."

This was beginning to look like it could be a significant under-the-table income for someone. But instead of the usual *ohmygod* chorus, my personal reaction was more of a sinking feeling in the stomach. I remembered my first visit to the Bergen apartment. When I told them I'd like to live at Harbor Village, hadn't Nita said the complex was nearly full? Hadn't Riley commented about all the new people upstairs in his building? And yet, Emily's roster showed fifty-two vacancies.

"Keep this information to yourself for a few days, Emily. We don't know who's involved in this. I haven't even met Cynthia Quarles, except to wave at her. I'll talk with her right away and see what the rental operation looks like from her end. I don't want anybody to know what we've discovered, in case they try to cover it up."

Emily pantomimed zipping her lips. "Do you want to go over the other financial data now?"

"I don't look forward to this part, so let's get it over with. You may have to explain things."

She giggled and plucked a thick blue folder from her stack of materials.

We spent the next thirty minutes going over printouts. I asked about bank accounts and she produced different folders, with in-house reports and official statements from the bank, and showed me certain points of agreement between them.

"So there are no discrepancies in the bank account?"

"Absolutely not. I'll stake my life on that."

"That's good. And I see the bank name here. Is this the only account we have?"

"The only one *I* know about."

"And who can sign checks? Do you do that?"

She laughed and her face turned red again. Apparently I had made a blunder she was too polite to point out.

"You never have the bookkeeper signing checks. Technically, I shouldn't be handling both revenue and expenses—that's inflow and outgo—but we're a one-person office."

"So, who signs the checks?"

"Jamie, so far as I know, and it's always been a pain to run her down. She didn't keep regular hours. We can ask the bank if anybody else is on the account. They usually want a couple of people, for a big operation like this. Otherwise, what happens if someone is out sick?"

I nodded. "I'll check on that. In fact, let's do it right now." I got the phone number off the statement.

A woman answered and I gave her my name and title and a bare-bones statement of what I wanted to know.

She put me on hold and, after a long pause, a man answered and asked me to repeat my question then put me on hold again. Bad music with a poor speaker.

Finally he picked up again. "Ms. Barnes, are you calling about the Ferrell account, or Harbor Village?"

"No, Ms. Barnes is gone. I'm Cleo Mack and I replaced her. I want to know who can sign checks for Harbor Village in her absence, until I can get added to the account."

"Oh, Ms. Mack, yes, I see now. In that case, the names currently on the Harbor Village account are Lee Ferrell—and the bank and I extend our condolences about Ms. Ferrell, so very sad—and Jamie Barnes and Nelson Fisher. And you say Ms. Barnes is leaving?"

"That's right. Transferring to another facility within the organization. What will I need to bring in to be added to the account?"

"Are you a local resident, Ms. Mack?"

"I just moved in to Harbor Village."

"In that case, I hope you'll do your banking with us. You're going to be here permanently? Why don't we go with your letter of appointment, on corporate letterhead, and the usual personal identification? That should be sufficient."

An official letter of appointment. Yes, that would be nice, wouldn't it? If only I had one. I needed to talk with Travis.

My phone beeped when I hung up, but I didn't look to see how many messages had accumulated during the morning. Emily was showing me the balance in the bank account and its trends over the last year.

"Is there ever any problem making payroll or paying the bills?"

"Corporate handles payroll and does everything by direct deposit. We do everything else locally and have plenty of funds for insurance and maintenance and such. I suppose corporate might like to transfer some funds out of here occasionally. I mean, that's the whole idea, isn't it? But they haven't done that, not since I've been here."

"Now what about the annual budget? Are we meeting projections?"

She pursed her lips and then pressed them together, tightening her cheeks until she looked like a red-haired chipmunk.

"The annual budget." She blinked a couple of times.

"Well, that's what I would call it. Maybe you know it by a different name. How much money is allocated for different expenses, how much we're supposed to have left over at the end of the year."

"Oh, I know what you mean. I just don't think I've ever seen one here. Houston must prepare it." She was listlessly paging through documents. "I do a monthly summary for Ms. Ferrell."

"Can you make copies for me?"

"Sure. Give me a few minutes."

"Don't skip lunch. It's about that time now. I think I'll eat here since it's raining. And I've got another project to attend to after lunch, so let's get together about two or three."

Emily was stacking folders.

"Let me make a note about that vacancy figure." I got a card out of my pocket and found a pen. "Twenty-three percent vacant out of two hundred twenty-four units. Right?"

"Right," Emily said.

There was already one note on the card. I turned it around to read, in my handwriting, "pets for AL." I tapped the card on the table as I thought.

"How old are your kittens, Emily?"

"Eight weeks. Ready for new homes."

"And what colors do you have?"

"Any color you want. One solid black, one tuxedo, one gray striped with white feet, one orange tabby."

"Maybe you could bring them to the Assisted Living unit one day. I think the residents there would enjoy seeing them."

"They're the cutest things in the world. Just beginning to play. And those little tails sticking straight up—oooh!"

She nearly swooned.

Chapter 12

I checked phone messages when Emily left and saw half a dozen, including three from Travis. I hit call back and he answered on the first ring.

"Any problems?"

"Yes, several, but I'm working on them. I filed a police report and called for a drug test of all employees in the Assisted Living building."

"There are state laws about employee testing. And some people may quit."

"We want them to, don't we? I checked to be sure the policy was in the handbook and a notice was posted in the unit office. We'll have the results tomorrow. I haven't found a budget yet. Would someone in Houston have a copy? And I need an official letter of appointment from you so I can get added to the bank account. We need to issue some deposit refunds in a couple of days, and there doesn't seem to be anybody to sign checks except Nelson Fisher. Are you in the office, and can you send an appointment letter today? And just so you know, I'm in the process of checking out a little discrepancy in rentals."

"Great, great." He didn't seem to be hearing me.

I tried again. "What can you tell me about Nelson Fisher? He doesn't seem to do anything, but he's listed as office manager."

"No, that can't be right. You're looking at an old roster. Are you coming for the memorial service?"

"No. But Stephanie will be there." I made a note to ask Patti if the employee roster she'd given me was up to date.

"Good, good," Travis was saying. "And I'll take care of...now what was it? Listen, you'd better talk to my assistant. Tell her what you need and she'll take care of it. You're doing a great job, Cleo, and I'll be back there soon so we can talk. Let me give you Yolanda's number."

He gave me the phone number and said he'd tell Yolanda to get me whatever I needed. Hmmm. Nothing like a blank check.

I waited fifteen minutes and called Yolanda at the Houston number Travis had given me. We made the usual polite comments and then I repeated the items I'd mentioned to Travis, starting with a formal letter of appointment on corporate letterhead.

"I'll take care of it," she said.

"And a copy of this year's budget for the Fairhope facility."

"You don't have that? Well, it's probably in Ms. Ferrell's files, but I'll send you a copy, certainly."

"And if there's any company policy concerning employee bonuses, for things like initiating leases, I'd like a copy of that."

"I don't know about that but I'll check."

"And finally, a copy of the message Lee sent, naming Jamie Barnes director of the Charleston facility. I understand it was sent last Thursday night, but I don't know if it was a text message or e-mail, or maybe voice mail."

"Yes, Ms. Mack. Anything else?"

"No, not right now. I don't have a computer in the office yet, so you'll have to use my home e-mail." I gave her my address. "And I suppose I may need to call you back if I have any other problems while Travis is involved with the memorial service."

"Of course. Use this number and there's voice mail if I'm not available. And welcome to Harbor Health Services, Ms. Mack."

Patti was waiting to give me a report on the drug test memo, which she had delivered to all the Assisted Living staff.

"I assume we have some way to screen out job applicants with a history of drug use." I was angling for an opening to explore Stewart's wariness around the cops.

"Oh, absolutely. That's sort of my job." She wiggled her brows at me. "The small-town grapevine, you know. Plus we have Stewart. He's a sponsor."

"A what?"

"You know, clean and sober and obsessive about it. Are we having lunch in the dining room? If we are, we'd better go."

We were walking out when my glance fell on the receipt book. I moved a file folder to cover it and closed the office door behind us.

I assumed the day's continuous rain would cut back on business for the dining room, but the opposite was true. There was a full house when we arrived, and Lizzie was clearing dirty tables.

"Nobody wants to go out in the rain," Ann told us. "We may just sit here all afternoon. You got any coffee, Carla?"

The food tray still had a good selection, and I took a little sample of each of the vegetables, plus a bowl of hot, cheesy potato soup and a wedge of cornbread, with actual corn kernels visible.

"This is perfect for a rainy day," I told Carla. And then I ate every bit. It was perfect for any day.

Patti told me about her visit to assisted living and the reaction of staff members to being drug tested. "I think Michelle was upset but, oddly, everybody else seemed happy about it. Now why would they be happy about having their pee tested?"

"Maybe they're happy because Michelle's *not* happy."

"That's mean." She giggled.

I asked about progress on finding me a computer. "I could give you mine, but there doesn't seem to be one that's working and not being used."

"Well, then, how about office supplies? I don't even have a notepad, or a telephone, except my own."

"I'll take care of supplies as soon as we get back. There's a supply closet. I should've done that already. I guess we can make a purchase order for a computer. Do you know what kind you want?"

I told her what I had at home. "But it might be more expensive."

"What about Jamie's?"

"We can't leave assisted living without one. I'm sure they submit reports online and look up medications."

"Check their e-mail, read movie reviews."

People in the dining room were talking about Mr. Levine's political forum, just two days away. He had assigned several of them the job of making up questions, and they wanted ideas from everybody. But in the midst of that, the topic suddenly shifted to Lee Ferrell's death.

"I heard she didn't drown," someone said.

Ann looked at me. "Is that right?"

"That's what I heard."

Everyone began to talk at once.

"Was it an accident, or wasn't it?"

"Maybe she was on drugs."

"Homicide?"

"Is she married? Check out the husband."

"What does Jim Bergen say about it," a man asked. "He's out there patrolling every night. He ought to know."

"Better check him out, too," was followed by laughter.

"Carla, this soup is excellent. Have you got a little container so I can take some home with me?"

Curiosity had its limits. Everything revolved around food and, when the subject came up, everyone got involved. They were busy getting containers for soup and plastic bags to carry the containers in. They divided up all the cornbread in the tray.

I gave Patti a signal and we signed for our lunches and returned to the office, leaving the same group of residents still holding court.

* * * *

Cynthia Quarles was on the phone when I got to her office after lunch. I took a chair and eavesdropped. She didn't seem to be talking with a prospective resident, but she seemed in no hurry to hang up. She was a pretty woman, a blond version of Lee Ferrell. Same age, same gold jewelry, same Pilates' trainer, no doubt. I imagined the two of them pledging the same sorority at some expensive little women's college on the Atlantic seaboard. And now who was prejudiced? I gave myself a demerit and walked over to take a look at the key box, which was standing open.

It was a large, shallow, metal box attached to the wall, with black felt covering its interior. A vinyl grid marked the surface into sections representing the apartment buildings, each section containing rows of numbered pegs from which keys dangled. There was a colored tag on each peg: yellow, green or red. At the bottom center was a section representing the big house, with keys for the rooms and apartments on floors two and three. Three other sections ran along each side of a central space that represented Harbor Boulevard, I supposed. I identified the section corresponding to my building and saw that apartment eight, my unit, had a red tag, one of a dozen or more on the entire grid. Assuming the codes were up to date, red must mean a special category of rental, since there were relatively few red tags.

Cynthia's conversation sounded much like my side of a call from Stephanie. Since I showed no signs of leaving, or perhaps because I was examining the key box, she was trying to get off the phone.

Finally she said, "I must run, sweetie. Call you later." She hung up, came around the desk and attempted to push me out of the way so she could close the cabinet.

I stood my ground. "I've been admiring your system here. Makes it so easy to keep everything up to date."

She swung the door toward me. "Yes. It's something I brought with me from real estate. This is the way we organized keys for listed properties.

G.P. Gardner

But now electronic lock boxes have replaced the key system." She pushed at the door again.

I could be as stubborn as anyone. "Tell me what the colors mean and let me see if I've guessed correctly."

"It's just an indication of the status of each unit." She was annoyed but also a little nervous.

I moved to stand in front of the rectangle I had identified as Nita's building and put a finger on what appeared to be their apartment. It had a green tag. "Green means what? Rented?"

"Right."

"I thought so, since that's the most common color. And yellow indicates a unit is available, I guess." There were a lot of yellow tags. I ran my finger up to the next row of keys and stopped on one of them.

"I think you've got it." She grasped the door again.

This time she swung it partly closed, but I stayed put, right in the way, so the door bumped my arm. Cynthia might think she was going to dislodge me, but I wanted to establish a proper relationship with her from the outset.

"Oh, sorry." I looked at my arm and then at her. I didn't budge from my spot in front of the key box. "I want to take a good look at this. Do you mind? Part of my orientation." As I eased the door back to the open position, I saw a flash of anger in Cynthia's eyes.

Confrontations weren't unknown in the academic world, and I'd had my share, but this one felt different somehow. I actually felt a physical threat. Cynthia had an ugly expression and took a half step toward me. I didn't back down.

"And red—what does a red tag mean, Cynthia?" I locked gazes with her.

She looked away after a couple of seconds. Thank goodness. I saw a slight tremor as she swallowed.

"Just...whatever." She exhaled and seemed to deflate emotionally. "Different things, depending on the circumstance."

I felt emboldened. Cynthia was clearly evasive, and her natural arrogance was now at war with nervousness. I turned and walked back to my chair. As I did, I heard the key box click.

"You may need that open, Cynthia. I want a count of available units." I sat down and unfolded my copy of Emily's rental register. "I need to compare your figures to the list I have."

She started forward with a look of panic and stuck her hand out for the list. I ignored her and clicked my pen, preparing to write in the margin.

"But I keep the official list."

I pressed harder. "Oh, then that's the answer. A copy of your list will be fine." I folded the paper. "How often do you update it, once a month? The one from July will work for my purposes."

She was frowning, unable to decide on a cover story. "I'm not sure…I've been so busy lately. I just use the key box mostly."

"Surely you turn in a report to Houston. Or to Lee Ferrell? That's probably how they evaluate your annual performance, isn't it? How long have you worked here, Cynthia?"

"There's about twenty," she said, abruptly.

I looked at her. She clasped her hands together and twisted them.

"Twenty what? Vacancies? Open the key box, Cynthia, and look at all the yellow and red tags. There are a lot more than twenty."

She did it, distracted by the effort to get her story straight. I felt a little sympathy for her, but only a little.

She scanned the board and said, after a minute, "Thirty-six yellow tags. That's a rough count." Her voice cracked.

"Okay, now the red tags."

"They're in transition," she said suddenly. "Not rented but not ready to rent. Maybe the painters haven't finished."

"Okay. And how many are there?"

"I see nine. If the box is up-to-date."

I jotted her numbers on the edge of my paper and paused to add. Forty-five vacancies, compared to fifty-two on Emily's list. Not a big discrepancy, but why should there be any difference? And I knew that at least three of the red-tagged units were actually rented—one to me and two to the students.

I raised my phone and snapped a few photos of the key box before she could close it again.

Cynthia had turned a pasty white. I wondered if I might not look a little different, too. I was surprised and sort of horrified I was enjoying this confrontation when it was obviously torture for her. Maybe I was executive material after all. I stood up.

"Here's what I need, Cynthia." I raised a finger as I said each item. "The number of rental apartments, the number currently rented, the number vacant and ready to rent and how many need to be prepared for rent. For any unit that's empty but not ready to rent, give me the specifics. Building and unit number and what needs to be done to get it rentable. Be sure to include the units occupied by the students working at the hotel and any other units that fall into that category. Got it?"

I thought she might pass out. Or attack me.

I pressed on. "An hour, shall we say? If I'm out, you can leave your report with Patti." I turned and walked out of her office on rubbery legs.

Patti was down the hall, standing at an open door and probing inside. It was the supply closet, and her left arm held a disorderly stack of legal pads, index cards, a box of tissues and a tape dispenser. In her right hand she gripped a stapler and a few pens.

"I have to make another trip." She hadn't looked at me.

"Let me help." I still felt a little shaky, but it didn't seem to be visible.

Patti gave me the stapler and pens. I looked into the closet and saw a jumble of office supplies, the same products Patti was holding, plus boxes of plain and hanging file folders in various colors, labels, name tags, letter trays, markers and old plug-in telephones. Everything you'd need to start an office supply store, but no spare computers. One item that caught my eye was sitting on the floor, beneath the bottom shelf. It was a square red lampshade with gold satin lining. I'd seen one like it in the lobby on my first visit to Harbor Village.

I touched the lampshade with the toe of my shoe.

"Pretty shade."

"Hmm." Patti peered over the armload of supplies. "Oh, is that from our parrot lamp? Did you ever ask the cops to bring it back? I hope somebody didn't just walk off with it."

She closed the door with her hip and hitched her load higher in her arms.

We walked around the corner and down the hallway toward my office.

"I'm afraid I just gave Cynthia a heart attack."

"Good. How'd you do it?"

"I asked for a report on the rental status of all units." I sighed. "Doesn't sound like much work for the rental agent, does it? But Cynthia doesn't seem to take orders well."

"Probably the first time anybody ever gave her one. With Jamie in the Assisted Living building and Nelson in the witness protection program, Cynthia has been a real diva ever since she got here. Except for two days every month when the dragon lady showed up. Do I sound awful, calling her that when she's dead?"

We went into my office. Patti dumped the supplies on the table and went out.

I added my items to the flow then sat at the desk, looked up a phone number and placed a call to the hotel at Point Clear. "Marjorie Zadnichek, please," I said when someone answered.

After a brief delay, she answered in a breathy, musical voice.

"I'm Cleo Mack, calling from Harbor Village, about the students who've been staying with us."

"I hope they haven't caused any difficulties." She sounded concerned.

"Not at all. They seem like very nice people. But I've just taken over the director's job here and I'm hoping to save myself a search through old receipts. The students want their security deposits returned, and I need to be sure they paid the deposits personally, that it wasn't something the hotel did on their behalf."

"Oh, they told me they'd been to see you. It's so nice of you, getting their checks ready before they leave. They've been the nicest employees we've ever had, and I hope they'll all come back next summer. And yes, they paid the deposits themselves. Do you suppose we'll be able to work out the same rental arrangement next year?"

"I'm too new on the job to answer that definitely. Who was your contact person here?"

"I think her name was…oh, she used to be a realtor. Cynthia something. From one of the old-time families."

"Yes, I know her. Cynthia Quarles. But you'll want to speak to me next spring, if you decide to call back. That's assuming I don't retire before then."

"Oh, don't do it," Marjorie Zadnichek spoke with urgency. "Worst mistake of my entire life. That's why I'm here, you see. I'll tell you what. Come down and have lunch with me one day and I'll talk you out of retirement. We'll go to the Birdcage Lounge. I'm sure you've heard of it, even if you're new in town. And you must join the League of Women Voters, too. Let's get together soon. Do you have a free day next week?"

I promised to call her back in a few days. And it wasn't just a stall; I actually looked forward to it. We hung up and I got one of the legal pads Patti had brought in and stapled my note with Marjorie's name and phone number to a page. *Call about lunch at the Birdcage*, I wrote.

Patti came back with more supplies and laid out everything in an orderly fashion then began stowing things away in the desk drawers.

I got out of her way, stepping around the braided tree to look out the window. I wanted a look at the materials Travis' assistant Yolanda was sending, but the rain was too heavy to walk to the apartment right now. I checked e-mail on my phone and saw that one message from Yolanda had just come in.

"Can I print something from my phone?"

Patti shook her head. "You don't have a printer yet."

"I mean, can I use your printer?"

"You could if I had one. I'm sharing with Deidra."

I gave up without looking at Yolanda's message.

"Here are some purchase forms." She laid them in front of me. "Have you decided what computer you want?"

I hadn't. In fact, I wondered if it were really a good idea to order a new computer, since it might not arrive before my one-month commitment ended. Maybe Harbor Village could buy a printer and I'd bring my own laptop every day? The weather outside at the moment made that seem like a bad idea. I didn't think computers and water mixed well.

Cynthia looked in through the doorway. "I'll come back later."

"No, no, that's fine." I motioned her in.

"I'm just leaving. I think." Patti looked at me for direction before scurrying around the desk and out, leaving the door open.

Cynthia sat in one of the armchairs. She had nothing in her hands, no paper, no notes, no report. She stalled, crossing her legs and placing her fingertips together carefully then looked at me and flashed a toothpaste smile. "I'm so glad you're aware of the little rental problem we've having. I've been wondering what I should do about it."

"Yes?" I waited, as noncommittal as possible. No doubt she would claim she'd been on the verge of reporting it.

She arched her eyebrows and smiled again, waiting.

I didn't step in.

"Since there's no clear line of authority…" She paused. "I decided to let the problem work itself out, you know? And it looks as though that's happening, so maybe it won't be necessary to do anything. Jamie's gone and the students are leaving. What do you think we should do?"

"How did you hear that the students are leaving?"

"Oh, I forget. Just in the course of business."

"And when did you first report this problem?"

"Well, as I said, there wasn't anybody in charge. So…" She shrugged.

Both Jamie and Lee had been in charge and everybody knew it.

"Do you have the unit report ready for me?"

"Oh, I don't have anything yet. I wanted to be sure I understood exactly what you want. This may be a simple job or it may take a while, and I didn't want to go off on a…a misunderstanding, you know?"

"Let's keep it simple." I pulled the legal pad around and jotted down the essence of my categories, leaving room for her to insert the answers. "Here's a template. Just write the numbers in. How long do you think that will take? Can I get the list before we leave for the day?"

"I'll try."

She got up quickly, took the sheet of paper I'd written on and left the office.

She had to be involved. If not, how would she know which units got a red tag? How would she know not to rent my unit to the next person to walk in?

I was willing to bet she'd just tried to reach Jamie by phone, to get their stories coordinated. Jamie was certainly involved. After all, who arranged my rental and warned me not to mention it to HR? Who wrote up two leases over the weekend? Whose signature was on the students' receipts?

But another thought occurred to me. If Jamie left Saturday and the building was sealed off all weekend, how did those leases get onto Emily's desk? Was there anything else Jamie might've done while she was in here alone?

I needed to talk with Travis, but he wouldn't be available for a few more days. And I couldn't wait that long.

I walked out to Patti's desk and asked if she'd seen Chief Boozer.

"He was outside earlier."

"If he comes back, I need to talk with him."

Patti looked curious but didn't ask questions.

I closed my office door and sat at the table, finally going through the receipt book Emily had retrieved from Jamie's desk. The first receipt, numbered 001, was dated January eighth. So there might be another book, or books, from last year.

The final two receipts were dated a few days ago and made out to me, one for my deposit and the last one, numbered 061, my first month's rent.

I turned through the receipt copies rapidly. About half were made out for three hundred fifty dollars, covering deposits and rent payments for the students. The highest amount I saw was two thousand dollars. I didn't take time to add up the dollar amounts but estimated it at sixty thousand dollars. The rent scam business wasn't just pocket change.

I was still looking at the receipts when someone knocked at the office door. I closed the book and covered it with a folder before I went to the door.

It was Chief Boozer. "Hello there. You're looking for me? Got time for a cup of coffee? I thought we might find one in that dining room down the hall."

"Good idea. I don't know if anyone's still there, but let's find out."

I put the receipt book in my desk drawer, hesitated, and took it out again. No sense in taking chances with it at this point. I dropped it into my handbag, which I hung over my shoulder.

Out in the hall, Jim Bergen was leaning on his cane and flirting with Patti.

She wiggled her fingers beside purple eyeglasses and giggled. "I have six different colors to match my nails."

Jim and I traded smiles that said we both found her adorable, and I told Patti, "If Cynthia brings a report for me, she can leave it with you. I'll be back before you leave."

"Okay." Patti's eyes sparkled, probably at the opportunity to needle Cynthia. "Remember to ask about the lamp."

"Oh, right. I will."

Jim, Chief Boozer and I walked through the lobby to the dining room. It was late but Carla and Lizzie were still there, along with Ann, Ada and Gloria. Ann kept knitting without looking at her hands but they stopped talking and stared at us.

"Chief," Ann greeted him. "Have you found the murderer yet? People want to know."

"You wouldn't want to rush the investigation and ruin it, would you?"

She laughed. "Well, I'm locking my door until you give us a signal."

"I still have your cookie plate," I told Gloria.

"I know where it is if I need it." She gave me a sweet smile. If we had a Christmas program, she had to be Mrs. Claus.

Ann asked Jim, "Did you smell the cookies baking? Did they grab you by the nose and pull you right across the street?"

He laughed good-naturedly, eyeing the cookies spread out on wire cooling racks on the back counter. I saw oatmeal with raisins or nuts or both and chocolate with a drizzle of white icing.

The women were baking for the political forum, but they were delighted to have us sample the merchandise. Lizzie went to start a fresh pot of coffee while Ann made up three small plates, each one with a sample of flavors.

"We're not going to get in your way," Chief Boozer promised them, hinting for a little privacy.

"No. We've got business to discuss," Jim said.

The problem was he wanted cookies, too, and the cookies were with the people. "How about we take this booth back in the corner?" He gestured toward the booth nearest the cookie racks.

"I like this one." Chief Boozer was already at the opposite end of the dining room, turning one of the little tables in front of the window.

I settled the question by joining him and Jim wasn't far behind me.

We talked about the rain first. Boozer mentioned minor accidents around town.

Jim seemed impatient with small talk. He looked at me. "What have you learned?"

"More problems." I didn't elaborate.

He grinned.

Chief Boozer took a sip of coffee. "We sent two detectives to Charleston and nobody's there. McKenzie is driving to Houston. Jamie Barnes could've gone with him but didn't. She waited and flew out this morning. By the time we can get to Houston, they'll be holding a memorial service, and I don't like to interrupt that. And when it's over, they'll hit the road again. Meanwhile, here we sit with multiple suspects, no clear motive and no murder weapon." He looked at each of us in turn. "That pretty well sums it up."

Jim asked, "What about motive?"

Boozer shrugged. "The answers are going to be right here." He tapped on the tabletop. "Harbor Village. So I thought I'd come have a cup of coffee and see if anything jumps out at me."

"Well, I haven't seen anything jumping out, but there's something I'm trying to drag out. I haven't talked with Travis yet, but you're going to inherit this at some point, I'm sure."

Chief Boozer gave a little wave, giving me the floor.

"First, before I forget, I'm supposed to ask when we can get our lamp back."

"What lamp is that?"

"The one from the lobby. Shaped like a parrot."

He shook his head. "I'll check on it."

"The bad news is, we've got an embezzlement problem. A few apartments are being rented off the books, including mine. The rent money isn't coming into the Harbor Village account."

"Uh-oh," Jim said. "That could be serious. Connected to the murder?"

"I don't think so." I hadn't really thought about it. What would the connection be?

Boozer was waiting for details, looking at me and bouncing his fingers silently on the table. I told them about the Russian students wanting their deposits back and Emily saying she hadn't received any funds from them all summer.

"And you have confidence in her," Jim asked. "That's the most likely scenario, the bookkeeper juggling funds. Is she the redhead?"

"Yes. She's young but seems to be honest."

"Maybe there are multiple accounts," the chief proposed. "One she doesn't know about. Have you looked?"

"She says there's only one checking account and the bank agrees. But I did learn something, by accident. I called the bank to see about getting added to the account. I guess the message was garbled somehow and the manager picked up thinking I was Jamie Barnes. He asked if I was calling about the Harbor Village account or the Ferrell account."

The chief's brows went up. "And the students are paying into the Ferrell account?"

"Exactly. And so am I, for my apartment rental. But since it's not a Harbor Village account, I don't have the authority to check on it. The banker wouldn't have told me anything, except for the mix-up about who was calling." I pulled out the receipt book and dropped it on the table.

"I sent the bookkeeper to assisted living to get this out of Jamie's desk. It has receipts for this year, beginning in January. I haven't added it up, but it looks like sixty or seventy thousand dollars. There are receipts at the right time periods, and in the right amounts, to match the Russian students. And my two checks are the last ones listed." I opened it to the right spot. "I left my checks in the office Thursday, for Jamie to pick up."

Chief Boozer picked up the receipt pad and fanned through it. "Anybody involved besides Jamie? Pretend I said allegedly."

"Michelle is Jamie's shadow, so she might be involved. And I think our rental agent, Cynthia Quarles, has to be in on it, too. She's the contact person for rentals and has to know not to rent apartments that are already occupied off the books. Marjorie Zadnichek, at the Grand, said Cynthia was the person she talked with about putting their student workers here. If she didn't know how their rent was paid, she was negligent."

The chief grimaced. "You said Quarles? She's a big fish in town."

"She's a difficult person. And you can pretend I said allegedly, too."

"Have you talked with her about this?"

I nodded. "She's supposed to be preparing a report on rentals for me right now. Which units are rented, which ones are available to rent and which ones are out of the rental loop. She knows I'm onto the scheme."

"But you didn't say anything specifically about—"

"Yes, I did. I told her to be sure she includes the units the Ukraine students are in, and it looked for a minute like she might jump me. She came down to the office later, an hour ago, saying she didn't report anything because there was no chain of command, or something like that. But her routine doesn't work when she's talking to a woman. Her charms were wasted."

The chief had been looking through the receipts. "Looks like seventy-five thousand, give-or-take, and that's for eight months. At that rate, in a year it could exceed a hundred thousand. Not peanuts. And we don't know how long it's gone on?"

I shook my head.

"But divided two ways," Jim said. "Not much when you think about ruining your career."

"Divided three ways, if Jamie and Cynthia and Michelle are all involved. Or four, if Lee Ferrell was in it."

Boozer stared. "Lee Ferrell? Why would you suspect her?"

I reflected. "I don't, not really. But the name on the account is Ferrell and she's the only one who uses that name. And while you're adding up the take, don't forget the missing pills. Might all be one big operation."

Boozer slid sideways in his chair and looked out the window. After a minute, he said, "I don't think the drugs are related. Probably somebody uses, maybe a boyfriend or a husband. Might even be somebody with a legal prescription they can't afford. But embezzlement...that could be just what we're looking for."

Jim was fidgeting. "Talking about a motive, a hundred thousand a year gets anybody's attention."

They ignored me and talked back and forth, posing questions to each other.

"Do any federal funds come in here?"

"What difference?"

"If Ms. Ferrell found out and threatened somebody with federal charges...."

Jim nodded. "You don't know if it's a disagreement among thieves or if she found out and they killed her. But tell me this, is this the sort of thing a woman would do?"

Boozer looked at me and smiled. "It's an equal opportunity world today, Jim."

I asked, "Who do you think killed her? I can't see Jamie doing it, not to her own sister. Not putting the body in the water, just to throw off investigators. Regardless of how they got along. And Cynthia Quarles is upper crust. Although, she clearly wanted to assault me this afternoon. Michelle...I don't know about Michelle. She may not be involved at all. So who does that leave?"

Boozer looked at me, not speaking.

"Travis?"

He shrugged. "He was here."

Jim disagreed. "I'm a good judge of character, you know. The only point against him is he's the husband. That, and opportunity."

The *ohmygod* chorus began warming up.

Boozer interrupted it. "The Ferrell name on the bank account. Is that the only reason to think Lee Ferrell might be involved?"

I nodded. "I guess. It's a habit of mine, considering every possibility. The money wouldn't have meant much to Lee. She had a big salary and a husband who makes even more. Surely she wouldn't risk everything for a small amount of money."

Jim raised one eyebrow. "She's got more than one facility. Was there monkey business at the other places?"

I didn't know.

Boozer didn't rule out the possibility. "Some people need a thrill more than money. Jamie's her sister. Was she well-fixed, too?"

I shook my head. "Jamie's a nurse. She makes good money but she's not a top executive. Not yet."

Jim nodded. "She's a little rough, I recognize that."

Boozer said, "But her sister promoted her just before she died. I have a little problem with that, I don't mind saying. Why at this time? Was she being blackmailed, maybe because someone had found out about the scam? If that's the case, we have to consider other people, even the ones who rent those apartments."

"Okay," I said, "that was my line of thinking, too. I wondered if Jamie's promotion might've been a payoff of some sort. If the scam was Lee's project and Jamie suddenly found out how it worked, or if she was about to, then Lee might want to get her out of here. In that case the move to Charleston makes sense. It throws Jamie off the trail, or sends her out to start her own bogus rental project. Otherwise, I don't get it."

"Jamie's name is on the receipts." Chief Boozer twisted the pad around so Jim could see the signature. "I guess that's her signature."

"Anybody could write that." Jim waived it away. "Lee Ferrell is here once a month. She could write the receipts and sign Jamie's name. And Lee was here when you turned your checks in last week."

I reflected. "Yes, she was. And a few hours later, she was dead."

Boozer turned on Jim. "Why are you so supportive of Jamie? Is she a friend of yours?"

There might have been a little accent on the word *friend.*

Jim seemed troubled when he answered. "I saw her at night sometimes, out at the pool. She smoked a little marijuana and drank a beer on the job sometimes, but she's basically a sensible girl."

I cringed at the word *girl,* but what could I say, he was eighty-something. "There's another thing that troubles me. How did Lee's body get from the lobby to the swimming pool? Could one person acting alone manage that?"

"That's nothing," Jim said.

The chief and I looked at him.

"This place is full of walkers and wheelchairs. I'd have no trouble putting a body in a wheelchair and rolling it out there. Any reasonably fit person could do it. Even you." He nodded at me.

I had a sudden image of Jamie, the day we first met and lunched, down by the bay. "Jamie has a strong handshake, and her arms look like she works out."

"Oh, she did." Jim nodded his head. "Went to the gym right here, three times a week. But she's not a bad person."

He certainly knew a lot about her. But then Jim knew a lot about everybody.

Chapter 13

"Let's see how hard it is to find a wheelchair," Chief Boozer shoved his chair back and stood. "Thank you, ladies! The cookies were exceptional." He threw some bills on the table and said to me, "I'll keep this receipt book, if you don't mind." He wedged it into one of the pouches on his belt.

We made a sweep of the big house, starting with the Physical Therapy department. Tiko, the PT, was out at the pool house with a client, but her office manager, a woman named Cassidy Gee, showed us around and answered questions.

"We have a lot of clients with mobility problems, and we always have a few wheelchairs in the department. These two get daily use, I'd say." She pointed to two wheelchairs in a little corral off the main hallway. "They're a little narrower than some, with a tight turn radius, which makes it easier to get around between stations in here. And there are one or two more in an equipment closet back here." She showed us to a large storage room in back of a treatment room. It was full of treatment equipment or medieval torture devices. Two wheelchairs were almost covered up by bolsters, exercise balls and pulleys; I would've needed ten minutes to get one out of the closet.

"You've shown us just what we wanted to see," Chief Boozer told her.

Cassidy Gee knew Jim and chatted with him about his knee replacement. He'd had therapy at her clinic.

"We'll let ourselves out where we came in," I told Cassidy, "but I want to try my key as we go, to see if it works in that door. I'll leave it unlocked."

She followed us back to watch what we did.

My new passkey operated the lock without difficulty. "Now I know."

When we were out in the hallway, I said to Chief Boozer and Jim, "Anyone with a passkey could get in there. I'll find out how many people have them."

Just to be compulsive about it, we looked in at the Hair Salon, but the stylist, who stopped in the middle of a haircut, assured us there were no wheelchairs there.

The big haul was in an unlocked storage room behind the kitchen. There were three wheelchairs lined up, one of them electric. Two had "HV" in large black letters on the back, and one had "TH," which Jim said meant it came from Thomas Hospital.

"So there are at least five wheelchairs between the lobby and the pool." Chief Boozer called off the search and we walked together toward the lobby.

"What about access?" I stopped to look down the hallway, ten feet wide, running past the elevator, between the dining room and the hair salon, to double glass doors that opened to the wrap-around porch at the end of the building. "There's a ramp at that end of the building?"

"Right," Jim said. "Two actually, if you count the one for the PT office."

"And the gate in the fence is wide enough to get a wheelchair through?"

"Oh, yes. Everything here is handicapped accessible. It's the law now. ADA, you know."

"They had to cross a wide-open space, where anybody could see them." I was thinking aloud and looking at the parking lot.

"Do you know how many people I see when I make my patrol at night? Sometimes Ms. Perkins is out walking her dog. That's about it. You could march a naked brass band through here at ten and nobody would know."

Chief Boozer said, "There's a lot of strength and skill required to move a body. They're heavy and limp and there's nothing to hold to."

"Dead weight." Jim ignored the literal wording. "But prison is a big motivator."

I stopped behind the rattan couch and looked around the lobby. "And what was the weapon, Chief? Is that why you took the lamp?"

He was annoyed. "What is this about a lamp? I don't remember any lamps in here."

"It was striking. No, bad choice of words. I mean, you wouldn't forget it. Two-and-a-half feet tall, at least, with a square red shade."

Boozer shook his head.

I turned to Jim. "You remember the lamp, don't you? Shaped like a parrot? Patti says it was always left on at night."

"Well, yes, that's right. There was always a light on in the lobby. I might recognize a lamp if I saw it."

I looked down. An electrical outlet was recessed into the floor beneath the end table. "This is where it would have been plugged in." I rubbed my shoe across the bronze plate.

"Thursday night, when we got back after dinner, the chandelier and all the ceiling spots were on." I gestured toward the ceiling. "Lee was sitting right here, leaning back and looking up." I looked toward the chandelier and then made a sweeping gesture to the parking lot at the end of the building. "Then we parked, got a two-year-old out of his car seat and walked around this corner of the building. Not more than three or four minutes later, I'd think. When we could see the windows, the lobby was totally dark."

"Was the lamp on the floor? I can't imagine somebody hanging around to pick up the pieces, not even if it was dark in here. And we didn't find any."

"It wasn't pottery. It was metal. Look, I've got a photo I took a few weeks ago. I thought the lamp was attractive. Actually, it was the shade I liked." I scrolled through my phone's photo file. "Here it is. And the shade is still here, in the supply closet, but the lamp's been gone for days."

I showed them the photo I'd taken back in June, when I wanted to show Stephanie what Harbor Village looked like. This shot was a close-up, showing the upholstery fabric and part of the couches. The parrot lamp was on the table between them. I could see its metal surface, overlaid in spots by colorful stains rubbed into feather-shaped crevasses.

Jim bent forward and took a good look. "Um-hmm, Um-hmm, that's bronze, isn't it? Must weigh five or six pounds. You think that could be your weapon, Chief?"

Boozer stared at the photo for several seconds then handed the phone back. "You say the shade's still here? Let's take a look."

He lagged behind Jim and me, talking to his office while we walked across the lobby. I heard him giving directions for testing the wheelchairs.

Patti was ready to leave for the day, purse and umbrella already in hand, but she was waiting to give me a message. "Cynthia had to leave early." She rolled her eyes and wobbled her head merrily. "Her daughter got sick, poor thing. Cynthia had to rush home, or to school, or someplace." She grinned.

"So no rental report today. Well, I've got Emily's roster. I can begin working from it."

Jim, Chief Boozer and I continued down the hallway and turned right at the cross hall. At the last minute, it occurred to me the shade might not be there, but I opened the closet door and it was still sitting on the floor.

"Don't touch it." Chief Boozer stretched out one arm to keep Jim and me away from the closet. He produced a flashlight from his belt and got down on one knee for a close look. He leaned against the doorframe while he ran the beam of light up and down the shade, inside and out.

Jim bent in for a closer look over the chief's shoulder. "See any blood stains?"

"Might be prints on these metal rods," Boozer said.

I couldn't see anything from my position. "Does this mean your people are going to be in the building again tonight?"

"You won't have to stay."

"Then I think I'll go now. I'm expecting guests tonight." I looked at Jim. "Nita and Dolly are supposed to come. Do you think they will, in the rain?"

"Am I invited, too?"

What snacks did I have on hand? "Of course. Oh, Chief Boozer. Do you want to see the key box in Cynthia Quarles' office? I'd hate for her to disassemble it before you have a look at it."

"You've informed me of an apparent crime—embezzlement, I mean— and you're the local representative of the owner. Do you give us permission to search her office?"

"I do. Is that all you need? No warrant?"

He got up. "We have to investigate, to keep any evidence from disappearing. Which office is hers?"

All three of us walked down the hall.

"I have a passkey that should work on the door, but I can't open the key box. And I imagine it's locked up tight tonight."

Boozer took my key and used it. The door swung open, showing a dark office with a window view of the garden behind the building. The night lighting had come on, illuminating big leaves of a banana plant from underneath. I had a close-up view of bananas developing there.

"Nice," Jim commented, "I think I'll put a couple of bananas in my courtyard."

"Just leave the door unlocked," Boozer said. "I've got some help on the way, and we'll take a good look. And I'll give you a receipt for the lampshade and receipt book, plus anything else we take. That way there's no miscommunication about who has what."

I was duly chastised for assuming the police had taken the missing lamp.

I walked across the street and up the sidewalk and clicked the corner lamp on as I passed through the screened porch. The glow created a snug little sanctuary, protected from the rain. I shook raindrops off my umbrella and left it open in a corner.

I called to Tinkerbelle as soon as I entered the apartment, and she came blinking out of the bedroom. "Tinkerbelle," I said a few times, testing it out. "Did you sleep all day, Tinkerbelle? Do you sleep better in the rain, too? Tinkerbelle. What a pretty name you have."

She twined around my legs and made her little *brrrp* sound, but I couldn't say she appreciated all the trouble I'd gone to in finding her name. Maybe she had enjoyed living incognito. Wouldn't that be just like a cat?

I stopped at the computer and checked e-mail, looking especially for messages from Yolanda, Travis' PA. There were four. I cued them up to print while I went to the kitchen and toasted two slices of bread and made myself a tuna salad sandwich. Yolanda's messages were ready to read while I ate. Tinkerbelle was in the kitchen, crunching away on the dry food in her dish.

The budget for Fairhope's Harbor Village was a two-page numerical quagmire and would take some analysis, so I put it aside for later. There was a note saying Yolanda couldn't find any incentive programs for employees, for any purpose whatever. The letter of appointment was straightforward, scanned and attached, but Travis' signature looked like a rubber stamp, which it probably was, unless he'd gotten to Houston already. Was a banker going to accept something so phony looking? The fourth item was Lee's text message, a one-sentence note directed to Travis and Jamie and the head of the HR Department at Harbor Health Services: *I hereby appoint Jamie Barnes administrator of Harbor Village in Charleston, effective immediately, with profit sharing and all other benefits.*

The message was transmitted Thursday night at 10:34 P.M. I read it three times while I ate and nothing jumped out at me, except the time. Chief Boozer would have to revise his estimate of the time of death.

I put my plate into the dishwasher, wiped off the counter and toaster oven and set out all the necessary items to make a pot of tea when my guests arrived. I found cheese and a few grapes in the refrigerator and crisp sesame crackers in the cabinet. I angled a fringed, red-checked dishtowel across the wooden serving tray, added a stack of paper napkins and got out dishes.

There were some other chores to do. I attended to the cat box, used a sticky roller to remove cat hair from the duvet, tidied the guest bath and put out fresh hand towels then did a bit to improve my appearance. By six fifteen I was ready for visitors.

The first one to arrive was Travis McKenzie.

"I wasn't expecting you," I greeted him.

He shook his umbrella and left it, opened, on the porch beside mine. "I planned to be in Houston tonight, but I got stuck in Tuscaloosa longer than I expected. So I decided to come through here on the way. There's nothing for me to do in Houston, anyway."

"I'm expecting guests tonight. Some friends who live here. They're going to talk about events."

"Good. I want to know. Do we have time to get some dinner first?"

"You mean go out? No, but I can make you a sandwich."

"And some coffee?"

"Come back to the kitchen with me."

There was enough tuna salad left for another sandwich. I put coffee on first and then toasted the bread. Travis was restless, wandering around the apartment, picking up photographs and commenting on the people he recognized.

I heard him greet the cat and then he called out, "The bathroom's back this way?"

"To your right." I was glad I'd just checked towels and soap and tissue. I wasn't comfortable with him in the apartment. I especially didn't like the idea of my guests finding him here, but there was no alternative now.

The toaster oven pinged and cut off, and I spread the tuna mixture on the bread. I added crisp pickles and cut the sandwich on the diagonal. As I took the plate to the dining table, Nita and Dolly and Jim arrived with much clatter and chatter.

"Come in." I went to the door to meet them.

"Where is she?" Nita stepped inside and smiled as she looked around for the cat. "Oh!"

Travis appeared in the doorway from my bedroom.

"I don't believe you've met Travis McKenzie." I frowned at him. Why couldn't he have used the guest bath, and how did he pick that moment to walk out of my bedroom?

Nita and Dolly stared, but Jim stuck out his hand. "Jim Bergen. I've seen you around here a few times. Don't think we ever met. Are you a native of Alabama, Travis?"

"Georgia," Travis answered automatically.

I introduced him to the two women.

Nita hesitated momentarily then reached out with both hands and went to Travis. "Oh, you poor thing. Just married and losing your wife in such a tragic way. I am so sorry."

Travis wrapped her in his arms, put his cheek against the top of her head and sobbed.

Jim gave me a helpless, embarrassed look.

I went to the guest bathroom and got a box of tissues. I pulled out two and handed them to Travis, who released Nita to wipe his eyes and blow his nose.

"I'm so sorry. It just hit me all at once." He was red-faced but recovering quickly.

"Don't apologize. Grief is part of life." Nita stayed right beside him, patting his arm, smiling sweetly, saying all the appropriate things that never occurred to me at such times. "You've had a terrible experience. You'll need time to recover."

Dolly sat on one end of the couch and watched casually. Jim left the drama to Nita and paced around the room, investigating the sandwich on the table, looking in the kitchen. Finally he returned to where Travis and Nita and I still stood.

"We all feel for you, Travis," I said. "Do you want to sit down now?"

"Cleo's got a sandwich here for you. Cleo, I smell coffee."

I directed Travis to the table. "Coffee for Travis and tea for everybody else?"

"I'll take coffee, too, since you've got it. I'm not much of a tea drinker. It's more of a female thing. Dainty cups and those little spoons." Jim joined Travis at the table.

"Go look at the bedrooms while I pour coffee and get the tea started," I said to Nita and Dolly.

"Oh, yes, the cat," Nita said. "I don't suppose you've had time to look for her vet."

I brought Nita and Dolly up to date on the cat's name while I poured two cups of coffee and delivered them to the table.

"Tinkerbelle," Nita repeated. "That's just perfect. Two nice hard consonants." She gave two little chops with her delicate hands, so thin they looked blue with blood veins. "That's what pets need. And it's not a silly word."

"Well, I don't know," Dolly said. "Wasn't Tinkerbelle a fairy? That's pretty silly, in my book. Where is she?"

I pointed toward my bedroom and the two of them went that way. I added boiling water to the tea bags already in the pot and heard Travis talking to Jim.

"I thought if I stayed busy, you know? But it's not working. I've got to go back to Houston and deal with it."

"We can come back another night," Nita whispered, when I found them in the bedroom a minute later, stroking Tinkerbelle. "You may have personal things to discuss."

"There's nothing personal between us, believe me. Travis wants to know what's going on and you can help tell him. And maybe there are some things he can tell us, too. Jim is talking with him now. I've got cheese and crackers and tea ready, but it's not fancy."

"Travis looks just like that man who does those commercials," Dolly said. "The handsome one. Maybe you ought to give him another chance, Cleo."

"Oh, Dolly, no no no, don't even think it. It's a different world today. We're different people."

She wasn't totally dissuaded. "Well, the world's changing, they say. But you're right, Robert Mack was a better pick."

"I can't believe you've been here just a week," Nita said as I got the tray and carried it to the coffee table. "Your apartment is so organized and comfortable."

"It's easier now, after the estate sale. I have just the essentials. Everything I need and nothing extra." It wasn't quite true, but it was something I could work on.

I moved a chair with arms from the dining table to the circle around the coffee table.

Travis finished the sandwich and took his plate to the kitchen. "Want more coffee, Jim?" He appeared in the doorway with the carafe in hand. "There's just enough for refills."

Everyone found a seat in the living room and I set the conversational ball in motion. "Travis wants to know what's happened here, so let's tell him."

"I've filled him in on a few things already." Jim helped himself to cheese and crackers. "Cleo, tell him about the rental problem."

I did, and Dolly heard it for the first time. Nita, who knew all about it from Jim, I was sure, listened attentively. "I don't have exact figures yet, but it appears to have gone on at least since January, and to involve about seventy thousand dollars since then."

"And who is this Cynthia woman?" Travis asked. "I've never heard of her."

Nita answered. "I've met her. She's an old-fashioned beauty, late thirties and quite elegant. Remember, Jim, I told you about her jewelry."

"Well, she's got a temper." I told them about her reaction when I confronted her about the key tags. "She's the rental agent here, and Chief Boozer says she's a big fish in town. Lee probably hired her. Now, Travis, don't take this the wrong way, but you're going to be asked. Is there any chance Lee participated in such a scam?"

He answered emphatically. "No. Absolutely not."

I plunged ahead, risking his wrath. "She didn't have any debts hidden from you? No bad habits?"

"I'm not saying she was perfect, and Lord knows I'm not, but this sounds like a stupid operation with clear criminal liability. My first thought is Jamie. And she told me you weren't paying rent."

"Well, I guess that's right, from your perspective," I said. "She was explaining ahead of time. If you happened to look for a payment from me in the Harbor Village accounts, you wouldn't find it."

He rubbed a hand through thick, dark hair that sprang back into place immediately. "Maybe Lee just found out about it. That could be what they argued about at dinner."

Jim pounced. "They argued at dinner? Jamie told you that?"

Travis nodded.

"Do you think Jamie would harm her sister?"

"Jim!" Nita whispered.

"No, I don't," Travis answered firmly, looking at Jim. "That's really why I went to Charleston, you know, to explore that point. And I believe her. She's totally wiped out over Lee's death. She said they had dinner together down at the pier, on the outdoor deck. They argued about Nelson Fisher's office and some other crap Jamie didn't want to tell me about. It was a scene, I guess, but she swore Lee was fine, standing in the parking lot beside the office, talking on the phone the last time she saw her."

I was sure Dolly had been paying attention, but she spoke up suddenly. "And who is Nelson Fisher?"

While Travis answered, Jim leaned toward me and spoke softly. "Does the chief know he's here?"

I shook my head.

Jim flicked a glance toward the bedroom and mouthed the words. "Call him."

I wasn't sure why Chief Boozer needed to know Travis was in town, but Jim knew a lot of things I didn't. I let a couple of minutes elapse, then muttered, "Excuse me," and went to my bathroom. I closed the door, turned on the exhaust fan, and called Chief Boozer.

"My detectives are on the way back from Charleston right now," he said, when I'd given him my message. "Is he staying with you tonight?"

"Oh no. At the motel, I guess."

"Okay. Thanks."

When I returned to the living room, Travis was telling them about Jamie's promotion. "She's wanted it for a long time. Not Charleston, necessarily, but a step up. Maybe Lee wanted her to prove herself here."

At the first lull in conversation, I asked, "Travis, where is Lee's phone now?" I wanted to know what calls she'd made and received Thursday night. Had she perhaps texted someone about her actions?

"I don't know. Is it missing?"

"Have you used that app that finds it? Does it show anything?"

Travis reached to his pocket and pulled out his phone. "I knew where Lee was, so I haven't thought about looking for her phone." He touched in a code, scrolled and touched an icon. "It's been a few days. The battery may be gone by now."

"Well, I have another question. What time did you get here Thursday night?"

"Mmm, after dark. About nine?" He was distracted by whatever he was seeing on the phone. "Why? I can ask the motel if it's important."

"I don't mean when did you get to motel. I mean, what time did you get here, to Harbor Village?"

He raised his head and seemed to travel back in time. "Last Thursday? I wasn't here, not until Friday morning. Before sun-up." His attention returned to the phone. "This is odd. It's saying Lee's iPad is right here somewhere. They told me her car was impounded. Have they released it?"

Jim asked, "She was driving the silver Lexus?"

Travis nodded, fiddling with the phone still.

"And you drive a black Lexus?" I already knew the answer because of Stephanie's report, but I wanted to hear it first-hand. My stomach tied itself in a knot.

Travis glanced up. "Well, that's what I'm driving at the moment."

Jim and I glanced at each other.

"But it's Jamie's car. I'm taking it to Houston for her. Why are you interested in cars?"

The dark SUV was Jamie's car? I felt a little tide of relief wash over me. But another thought occurred right away. "I thought Jamie had a BMW."

Travis nodded, distractedly. "Yeah, she did. Her buddy Michelle wrecked it, you know."

"Right." Jim nodded. "Five or six weeks ago, wasn't it?"

"Why all the questions? And why is this thing saying Lee's iPad is right here?" Travis got up. "I'm going to check it out. You want to get wet, Jim?"

Jim definitely wanted to go, but the body was weak. "I'd just slow you down." He followed Travis to the porch. "I'll watch from here. Whatever you find, bring it back here."

"I'll go." I eased around Jim.

"Oh no, Cleo," Nita protested. "You'll get soaked."

My umbrella was still on the porch, along with Jim's. I got mine and went through the door, popping it open with the button. "Where are we going?"

Travis headed off down the sidewalk, past the garages and across the street, which was streaked with washes of gravel and sand, compliments of all the rain. I stayed right behind him, wondering if the city would send a street sweeper to clean up the mess or if Harbor Village had to make its owns arrangements about such things. The rain was moderately heavy again, slanting at a steep angle across glowing streetlights.

"Her iPad is supposed to be right here. In one of these cars, I guess, or on the ground. We should've brought a flashlight. There's no way this app would be picking up somebody else's iPad, is there?"

Jim's Buick was there, and the black Lexus Travis was driving, and the boxy white van that belonged to the police department's crime scene crew, backed up to the door at the end of the building. A couple of other police SUVs were parked against the curb beside the ballroom.

"This is Jim's car." I pointed. "I can't imagine why anything belonging to Lee would be in it."

"How well do you know him?"

"You can't think an eighty-year-old man goes around stealing iPads and murdering women."

We went to the black Lexus and the headlights flashed as the doors unlocked automatically, just the way Riley had described. I was torn and looked toward the big house. If Chief Boozer was still there, I wanted to get him. But I also wanted to see anything Travis might find. I went to the passenger side of the car and opened the door.

Travis was holding his umbrella with one hand and feeling around the driver's seat, the floor, the console. I attempted the same thing and dumped water off my umbrella onto the leather seat. I dried it with my sleeve and held the umbrella at a different angle, managing to direct a rivulet of cold water onto the small of my back. I repositioned the umbrella again and began the same searching maneuvers around the front passenger seat. Crumbs in the seat, sand on the floor mat. Rain splatted my face. A fast-food paper wrapper was balled up on the floor.

Travis moved to the backseat and repeated his actions there.

I reached into the dark beneath the seat and my fingers brushed against soft leather. "Look at this." I inserted one finger through a leather loop and pulled a dark shoulder bag out onto the carpet then held it up.

Travis was in back, peering between the front seats.

"What is it? A purse?"

"Is it Lee's?"

"Look inside. Or hand it to me."

"I don't think so." I dropped the bag onto the floor and backed away. "The cops are right here. Let's get them."

"Where, in the administration building? Go get them."

"No, we both go. Come on." I closed the door and he did the same, after only a slight hesitation. I heard a soft beep as the doors locked when we walked away.

We left our umbrellas on the porch and entered the building. Bright lights were on all the way to the lobby.

"Hello! Hello," I called. "Chief Boozer?"

"Yo!"

Officer Montgomery stepped into sight from the cross hall, looking huge against the light. She pointed at us. "Hold it right there."

Only a fool would have disobeyed that voice.

"Can you get Chief Boozer? Or can you come outside?"

Boozer stepped into view and started our way, saying something over his shoulder.

"Mr. McKenzie, Ms. Mack. What's up?" He sounded almost cheerful, but it didn't last long.

We told him what we had and he called back to Montgomery, "Get Frankel and come out here."

Travis and I waited under the porch roof, where it was dry, and Travis clicked the remote to unlock the car.

Montgomery and another officer had questions. Why was Travis driving this car? Where was the owner? Where had the car been for five days? Why had Travis not discovered the handbag before now?

"I just got the car from Jamie yesterday," he told them. "I've been driving or working ever since." He looked at me. "I assume it's not Stephanie's purse? She sat in that seat last night."

I stood an arm's length away, watching people come out of the building and don rain gear and disposable gloves before going to the car. Flashlights and umbrellas bobbed all around us, and water drained off the roof, through the downspout attached to the pillar beside us. Boozer was back and forth, listening to Travis, looking over the technicians' shoulders, watching as one of them prepared to slip the purse into a brown paper bag he had already marked with an identifying code.

"Can you tell us whose purse it is? Does it belong to Lee Ferrell or Jamie Barnes? Or perhaps to my daughter?"

"The wallet has Ms. Ferrell's ID."

The tech stapled the paper bag closed.

"It'll be inventoried at the station, with multiple observers and a video record," Boozer told Travis. "I'd like to look through the car while we're here, if you don't mind. There might be something else in it."

"Go to it." Travis waved a hand as if to hurry things along. "I want to know what happened and if this tells us something..." His attention was focused closely on what was happening at the car.

To me, Lee's purse was personal, an eerie link to the living Lee. If her phone was in there, the cops would soon know exactly what calls she made and received in her final hours.

"Look," I said to Travis. "I need to get back to my guests. I'll see you tomorrow if you're going to be around."

Chapter 14

Jim was waiting on the porch. He took my umbrella and shook it off before we went inside, where Nita and Dolly waited. I reported what we had discovered.

Jim was looking at something behind me. I turned to see Travis' car backing slowly, quietly, up the wide sidewalk, the exhaust making little puffing sounds.

We went out to the porch and Travis came around the car. The engine was still running, with the lights on and wipers going.

"That didn't take long. And they didn't find anything else. I thought I'd drive your guests down to their car, if they're ready to go."

Jim seemed reluctant to end the evening, but Travis was offering convenience. I happened to be looking at him the moment he must have realized he could invite Travis into his office and continue their conversation without interruptions. I smiled to myself, got my umbrella and walked Dolly around to the seat behind the driver.

"We could just walk to Jim's car," she complained. "Oh, never mind. What kind of car is this? It smells new."

Jim was holding a supersized umbrella for Nita, but the SUV was too tall for her. She tried and failed to hoist herself onto the rear seat.

"Cleo, give me a hand." He thrust the umbrella at me, and I held it above them while Jim grasped Nita under the arms and lifted her, easily, onto the backseat. "There. See how easy it is to move a body?" He grinned as he retrieved his cane from the crack between the door and car. Then he backed cautiously away from the car.

Nita seemed more peeved than appreciative of Jim's assistance. She wriggled into position on the seat and tugged at the seatbelt. "Thank you for having us over, dear. I'll talk with you tomorrow."

"Good night," I told everyone.

Travis walked around the car. "Meet me at that breakfast place in the morning, okay? Seven o'clock." It sounded like an order.

I agreed without hesitation. I still had a few questions to ask him, and I was sure I could generate more by morning.

He put the car into gear and eased forward, down the sidewalk. I brushed rain off my hair and shoulders, turned off the heron lamp and went inside, locking the door behind me.

It took a few minutes to wipe down the dining table, put the chairs back into place and clean up the kitchen. Then I checked the cat's food and water dishes, turned on the dishwasher, turned off the lights and headed for the shower.

I hadn't tried running the dishwasher and taking a shower at the same time, and I decided not to risk running out of hot water and getting chilled on such a cool, dank night. So I undressed, put on my robe and went back to the dark living room to sit at the computer table, waiting for the dishwasher to finish its cycle. There was something hypnotic about staring out at the rain, which formed yellow halos around the sidewalk lights.

So the black SUV wasn't Travis's. That was a huge relief and, coupled with his emotional reaction tonight, left me almost willing to remove him from my list of suspects.

Jamie was another matter. She and Lee had an unpleasant dinner together Thursday night, Travis had said. One thought led to another and, within a couple of minutes, I was online, looking at the Fairhope pier cam Hunter had told me about.

I could see the fountain, or a glare of white where it should be. There was a scattering of cars parked around the circular drive. There were four bright spots beneath streetlights, but drivers must prefer the shadowed areas. That was where all the vehicles were. An occasional car moved slowly around the circle, headlights glowing yellow, taillights red. One pair of headlights stood out with the icy blue of halogen.

At the bottom of the screen were several controls, and I began to experiment. The camera swung right or left, up or down, on command, revealing the entire rose garden and parking lot. There was even an indicator of how many seconds it would remain in my control. And there was a zoom feature, which I used to focus in on the one person visible, a man pulling a wagon toward a pickup truck. I couldn't make out his features, but if I'd been looking for someone, and if it weren't raining, I could've identified him.

I wished it was possible to see Lee and Jamie together last Thursday. Did they arrive before or after my group, and how long did they stay? How had they interacted? Were they angry or friendly with each other? Just as importantly, had anybody been with them? Maybe Michelle? Or Cynthia? Maybe Stewart?

Too bad there was no way to run the camera backward, from tonight to Thursday.

On a whim, I looked up the phone number and called the motel.

Hunter answered and I told him who I was. "You told me about the pier cam and I'm looking at it right now. I don't suppose there's any way to see who appeared on it at an earlier time, say a few days ago."

"The short answer is yes," he said, "but only if it's within the last thirty days. After that, it drops off the archive. But it's a complicated procedure. You sort of trick the equipment and access it on the cloud. Are you here in the motel? If you are, I can show you."

"No, I'm at Harbor Village. Any chance we can get together sometime tomorrow?"

He told me he would be off until six, and I told him where my office was. "I've got a breakfast appointment, but I'll be at the office by nine, for the rest of the day. And I'll have my laptop with me."

"You have to take your own computer to work? I've never heard of that."

"Maybe you can advise me about what type of computer the company should buy me."

"Oh yeah, sure. I like spending other people's money."

He promised to come by before noon. I offered to treat him to lunch in the dining room, and we hung up.

The dishwasher was doing Its final pumping and when it clicked into the drying cycle, I went to take my shower.

Afterward, I worked on a particularly difficult Sudoku puzzle until Stephanie called, a little later than usual. I told her about seeing her father, and the continuous rain, and she told me she had decided to drive to Houston. "You wouldn't expect driving to be faster, but with the crazy schedule, and layovers in Atlanta, both directions, it was going to be a three-day trip."

I told her to drive safely in the rain and to let me know when she got there. Then I turned the light off and fell asleep immediately.

Just after midnight, a rumble of thunder woke me. I got up and unplugged the laptop, printer and TV then lay in bed and thought about Lee Ferrell.

If Travis was right and she hadn't played a role in the rent scam, perhaps she had discovered the scheme and talked about it to the wrong person.

But who was that person? I had marked Travis off the list, but I supposed Stewart was still on it, along with Jamie, Cynthia and Michelle. And Jim was a strong guy, out patrolling the grounds every night; could I skip him? What about the aides, housekeepers, residents and office workers I barely knew? Even Riley. No, I couldn't go that far.

What I needed to do was to solve some problems at Harbor Village. Jamie's promotion left me with one vacant position to fill and the rent fraud was likely to result in another one. There were other things to do, too. The drug tests and deposit refunds had to be acted on right away.

Finally, I dozed off and dreamed crazy dreams.

At seven the next morning, I was sitting in the front booth at Julwin's, having a cup of coffee. Travis arrived twenty minutes late, and I gathered up my paperwork spread across the table and slid it back into my leather case.

"I stayed up too late, talking with Jim." He slid into the booth and signaled for coffee. "What's all that?"

"I've got a few questions for you."

But we didn't take them up immediately. Instead, we ordered, ate and talked about the rain and his travels.

He told me what he'd planned for the memorial service. "She was Episcopal. And I'm nothing, I guess."

"Why are you driving Jamie's car? And where's yours? Did you leave it in Charleston? Do you have to go back for it?"

"Jamie didn't want to drive to Houston alone, and we're not compatible enough to go in one car. I turned in my rental and I'm delivering her car. Michelle's going back to Charleston with her, did she tell you?"

"No. I suppose she didn't take the drug test. I should get the results today."

"Yeah, she'll leave. Jamie can't function without her. They're the poster couple of co-dependence."

"Are they a couple?"

"Oh yeah."

"Do you think Michelle would do something really, really stupid out of devotion?"

He frowned.

"Travis, it isn't just a matter of Lee being gone. Somebody killed her, and that somebody was connected with Harbor Village. Maybe it wasn't Jamie, but she was certainly defrauding the company, and you can't ignore it. She'll be prosecuted. She won't be around to run things in Charleston."

He knew it, of course, but he seemed to be imagining some system of parallel futures in which Jamie could simultaneously be fired or jailed and continue to manage a Harbor Village facility.

"Maybe it was Michelle."

I shook my head. "Maybe Jamie, maybe Cynthia, maybe both of them. I'm not a hundred percent sure Michelle was even involved."

Time was ticking by, and I still wanted Travis to answer some questions. I took out the paperwork I'd brought and we started with the Harbor Village budget.

He took my pencil and coded sections from two documents, the annual budget Yolanda had sent and Emily's monthly expenditures. He matched specific charges to broad categories, muttering under his breath as he did it. "This could be cleaned up some. The percentages look good, but the expenditures are curiously low." Travis was good with budgets, and I actually began to get the idea.

"If I want to buy a computer, does the budget allow it?"

"Of course." He showed me the correct account.

"And if we want to spruce up the office, get some flowers, say?"

He tapped his pen beside a different account and then picked up a new document. "What's this?"

"My letter of appointment as Executive Director. Yolanda sent it yesterday. The bank wants it to put me on the checking account. I may not have this job long enough to bother, but there doesn't seem to be anybody else to sign checks right now, except Nelson Fisher."

"Nelson? Are you kidding? Maybe I should sign this letter again. My signature looks phony."

"I agree. Here's a pen, if you want to add a real signature."

He added a note of explanation, signed and dated it then held it at arm's length. "Maybe I'll just stop by the bank before I leave town. And what's this?"

"Let me see."

It was the message Lee had sent Thursday night, announcing Jamie's promotion. I read it again and something didn't look right.

"Let me see the letter you just signed."

I laid the two pages, Jamie's appointment and my appointment, side by side and compared them.

"What's my job title?" I quizzed Travis.

He frowned. "Executive Director. That's what Lee was, here and three other places. Spread too thin, I know, but I couldn't convince her. That's what we've been arguing about for weeks."

"And what is Jamie's new position in Charleston?"

"Same thing. Executive Director."

"So who's the administrator?"

He looked annoyed. "There aren't two separate positions, if that's what you're thinking. Administrator is just a generic term."

"So why does this letter say Jamie's to be the Administrator?"

He scowled. "That's not…Show me."

I handed him both documents.

He read first one then the other, going back and forth a couple of times. Jamie was appointed *Administrator* of the Charleston, SC, facility, Lee's note said, yet my title at Fairhope was *Executive Director*. And we were filling identical positions.

"Maybe she was just imprecise."

He snorted. "Never."

He put the pages down and stared out the window behind me.

"Her message was sent at ten thirty-four," I said. "But Chief Boozer thinks she was dead by nine at the latest."

He didn't respond.

"Was the message delayed somehow?"

He shook his head and brought his focus back to me. "No. I think I understand it now. Lee didn't write this message."

Travis answered a phone call, and I took the opportunity to call Patti, telling her where I was and that I'd be at the office in thirty minutes. "Is Cynthia there?"

"Oh, yes. In her office with the door closed. Do you want to talk to her?"

"No. We'll wait for her to talk to me now. Did we get the results of the drug tests yet?"

When Travis hung up, I clicked off and looked across the table at him. "Cynthia Quarles is there but hiding out in her office. Michelle didn't take a drug test but arranged to be off today and tomorrow. Everybody else tested clean."

Travis nodded. "She's probably gone to Houston to meet Jamie. If she resigns right now, there won't be anything on her record. She can go to Charleston and get another job. Better make arrangements to replace her."

"Tell me about Nelson Fisher. What's his role here?"

He looked surprised. "I guess he's my responsibility now. Jamie wouldn't take him, even if she could. He's their uncle. And a significant stockholder. He's had dementia as long as I've known him, although it doesn't seem to get any worse, knock on wood. He was the office manager years ago, and Lee let him keep his office to maintain his daily routine."

"No children?"

"No. Lee's daughter is his heir, and maybe some people he worked with. He likes to putter in the garden and ride a lawn mower. Is he hurting anything where he is?"

"No. I just needed to know. No tendencies toward violence, I suppose?"

He shook his head. "Not that I ever heard of."

"So we don't have to consider him a suspect. He's still on the payroll, you know."

He laughed. "Impossible. No way!"

I nodded.

"I don't believe it. Where does his paycheck go?"

I shrugged, palms up. "I just learned he's not actually working. I'll find out."

"Well, let's get that stopped immediately. I suppose I could guess who arranged it."

"You said the same thing about the missing medications. Who do you think took the pills?"

"Jamie, of course. But I don't *know* anything, in either case. Michelle's the same song, second verse. Let's hope it was one of them. I'd hate to have a third crook on staff."

I gathered up my papers, preparing to leave. "Travis, when did you last talk with Lee? Sometime Thursday?"

"I was in Mississippi when I finally got her, so seven or a little after."

"And where was she then?"

He shook his head. "I don't think she said. She was mad."

"At you?"

He laughed without humor. "You know the story. We had a great relationship until we got married. But it wasn't just me. She had problems here, too."

"The rent scam, do you think?"

He shrugged. "If she found out about it, she didn't tell me. Maybe because it supported my position that she was trying to do too much. Maybe she thought she should've discovered it earlier. Look, I'll be in Houston tonight. I'll talk with Jamie and get her an attorney. It's screwy, I know, but what else am I going to do."

"I have a feeling the Fairhope police will be in Houston, too. Maybe before you are. You might want to review your plans in case Jamie doesn't make it to the service."

"They'd make her miss her sister's memorial service over seventy thousand dollars?"

I stared at him.

Travis seemed to deflate. "She wouldn't hurt Lee. That's just not possible."

"If I had a list, and I do, she'd be on it. The cops are getting the details nailed down, and there'll be an arrest soon. Just be prepared. I need to get to the office. Take care of yourself, Travis."

"You've got my number." He got up. "I gave it to Jim, too. Call me the minute you learn anything."

I said I would. "Jim has better contacts than I do. He'll know what happens immediately."

We paid our checks and walked out to the sidewalk and, before I knew what he was doing, Travis gave me a quick peck on the forehead and walked away.

Once again, my car was aimed for the pier instead of Harbor Village. I decided to drive a few extra blocks and make a loop around the rose garden, to confirm my impressions from the pier cam. I also wondered how Mobile Bay looked in the rain. So far, every time I'd seen it, it had looked totally different.

Today was no exception. There was a bank of low, gray clouds over the water, with dark rain beneath them. The western shore was totally obscured and the bay was the color of dark chocolate. A snappy wind created little white crests on the choppy waves and blew gulls around in the sky.

A city garbage truck, equipped with a robotic arm, blocked the circular drive. An operator in the cab emptied garbage containers as his helper rolled them out from their wooden corral near the end of the pier. When the truck finished, it retracted its mechanical arm, clanked into gear and drove slowly around to the trash can beside the walking path. I followed the other cars past the truck and up the hill, then on through town.

While I waited for the traffic light at Section Street, I reviewed the critical events from last Thursday. At 4:30, Lee had been at Harbor Village, in the lobby, looking for Stewart. At approximately twenty minutes past eight, we returned from dinner and saw her sitting in the lobby, perhaps already dead. What happened in that four-hour interval? Anxiety gnawed at me.

I parked in my garage and loaded up with all the items in the backseat—my shoulder bag, with the garage remote clipped in the pocket, the laptop, an umbrella, and a leather briefcase containing printouts, budgets and resident lists.

I juggled things around so I could press the remote and started for the side door. But on an impulse, I detoured to the ballroom, where the door stood open.

No one was there, but chairs and tables had been arranged for Thursday night. I used my elbow to flip the light switch. The little chandelier, suspended from a low ceiling, was like an inferno in the semi-dark room. I could imagine tablecloths, trays of food and lots of people. The room was going to look quite presentable for the political forum. I turned the light off.

My next stop was Patti's desk. "Has Mr. Levine said anything about a program to hand out?"

She shook her head, eyes wide.

"Why don't you draft something and talk with him about it. A list of candidates, plus his name and the committee members. Harbor Village in bold at the top. Add something saying refreshments are complimentary from the dining room. You might give Carla's name, too, if there's room. Make it look good and we'll have it as a model for future events."

She perked up. "Does that mean there are going to be lots of events?"

"I hope so. Start thinking up ideas. We want frequent, tasty, engaging events that aren't too much work. Maybe we have some musicians living here who would do concerts. Everybody likes games and food, so come up with a competition of some sort. Get the food channel to visit. Or start a dinner club to visit restaurants in the evenings. How many people can you transport in the van?"

"Depends on how many wheelchairs. Emily brought the kittens."

"Oh? Where are they?" I glanced around the reception area and lobby but saw no kittens.

"She took them to assisted living. They're awfully cute. You'll have to go see when you take a break."

I headed to my office instead. The new paint job had a wonderful impact when I walked in. I closed the door and worked my way through the budget printouts, made much clearer now by Travis' notes. When I finished, I had a good idea where we stood financially. Revenue was below projections, but if I added in the seventy thousand dollars siphoned off through bogus rentals, we were a lot closer to expectations.

Expenses were down, too, attributable in part to staff cuts. I made a list of vacant positions, including business manager, and left it for Patti to double check.

When I took it out to her, I asked, "No word from Cynthia?"

"Her door is still closed, but I can hear her talking when I walk by."

I smiled, picturing Patti making frequent trips past Cynthia's door to listen. "On the phone? Or is somebody in there with her?"

Patti rolled her eyes and gave an exaggerated shrug. "Our phone lines have been in use off and on, but I haven't listened in. She might be using her cell."

Hunter showed up mid-morning. He called up the pier cam video on my laptop and somehow, after a lot of work and a little swearing, got the recorded feed set to last Thursday.

"I got to the pier a few minutes after six." I pointed to the first few parking spaces on the circle. "We parked somewhere along here, four people in a white Subaru. One of the four was a two-year-old. Can you find us?"

It took a while, but finally there we were, on the screen. I could identify Stephanie and Barry easily, with Riley on the very edge of the screen. "I was able to move the camera around last night."

"Yeah, but that was live action. This is just a recording of what the camera transmitted that night."

I watched as an image of the four of us walked from the car to the sidewalk that ran along the bulkhead.

"Okay, now here's what I really want. A black Lexus SUV with two women, arriving about the same time, maybe an hour before or a little later than we were. There might be another person with them, maybe two. One of the women was wearing a bright green dress. The sort of woman a man would notice."

"The woman who drowned?"

"I forgot you knew her. Yes, the same woman. The *drowned* part is being questioned now. It may turn out to be a homicide."

"Really? Things like that aren't supposed to happen in Fairhope."

He checked out the cars around the rose garden and manipulated the video for several minutes. Eventually he asked, "Do you see what you want here?"

I looked and saw Lee and Jamie get out of a dark car. Lee walked off without waiting for Jamie.

We watched it a couple of times, and I asked about marking the spot so we could find it again. Hunter wrote down a frame reference and showed me where to find it.

"Okay, can you find them leaving after they had dinner?"

"How long would they spend eating, an hour? Hour and a half?" He keyed in a command or two and watched closely for a while. He located them returning to the car at the 6:55 mark.

This time, as we watched, the camera zoomed in on the two of them.

I caught my breath. "Did you see that?"

"Somebody was operating the controls," Hunter said. "It wasn't you, was it?"

"Oh no. It didn't have to be someone local, did it?"

"No, could've been from anywhere. But if she was murdered, you have to wonder who knew where they were eating. Maybe they wanted to know when to expect her back here, or wherever she went next."

Jamie and Lee didn't appear to talk, didn't look around at the scenery, just stalked to the car, with Lee's green dress showing up clearly when she walked under a streetlight. She was carrying a dark shoulder bag, probably the one I found in Jamie's car last night. They got into the car and drove away, with Jamie in the driver's seat.

The controls went back to the default position after a few seconds. We watched for a couple more minutes before I pushed my chair back and got up.

"How about that lunch," I proposed, and Hunter and I picked up Patti and went to the dining room.

Lunch on Wednesday was Mexican food, I learned, and today that meant chicken taco salads served in flat bowls on a layer of brown rice covered with little quadrants of corn, black beans, diced tomatoes and green onions. On top was a thinly sliced, baked chicken breast covered with salsa. It was colorful and quite tasty, and Carla brought Hunter a second serving.

"We don't size our portions for young people," she explained to me.

And we don't get many nice young people to cater to. I launched into my own form of pampering. "I need to pay you for this consultation. Come back to the office and Patti will help you submit an invoice."

"Oh, yes," Patti agreed.

"This is pay." He indicated the empty bowls in front of him.

I gave him the lecture about careers and resumes and how consulting would look good to a prospective employer. "Anyway, we may want you to help us with other computer stuff, so we may as well get it set up now."

"Is there a job title for Forensic Geek?"

"You might be surprised."

When we finished, I signed the lunch list and we walked out.

"I hoped we could run over and see the kittens now," Patti said. "We're almost there."

Hunter looked at me. "Kittens? You have kittens here? That's neat."

So we walked to the Assisted Living building.

The small sitting room near the entrance was full of people, some of them enjoying an after-lunch nap in recliners, others sitting on the couch or love seat. Kittens were everywhere, sleeping in laps and climbing on the furniture. I petted the one closest to me, and Patti chased down the orange one and handed it to Hunter.

"This has been the best day of my working life," Ivy said softly, suddenly appearing at my elbow. "I wish you'd been here this morning to see them. This isn't just an experiment, is it? They have to stay now."

"What about litter boxes and food?"

She shook her head. "All taken care of for the moment. They're deciding on names already. We've had visitors from the other buildings, too. We're famous for our kittens!"

Hunter and I had left my laptop on, continuing to run the video feed from last Thursday night. When we returned to the office, the time showing on the frame was nine, and night had settled in on the screen. There were fewer cars parked around the rose garden and no people in sight. I started to shut the video down, but the shimmer of the pier lights on the water was captivating.

As I looked at the night view, a single car drove onto the screen and crept slowly around the circular drive. It was bright yellow with a white top, high off the ground, with a boxy shape. I had seen it before, or one like it.

At the end of the pier, the car stopped, not in a parking space but parallel to the curb, taking up a couple of spaces. A woman got out, walked rapidly to the sidewalk and across the narrow strip of grass. With some effort, she opened the gate in the wooden fence, exposing a row of large garbage containers, the same containers the garbage truck had been emptying a few hours earlier.

"Look at this," I said, and Hunter and Patti began watching, too.

"Wow," Hunter said.

"Who is it?"

"I meant the car. A Toyota Cruiser."

"Something special about it?"

He shrugged like it was too elemental to explain. "It's awesome. Comes in primary colors, yellow or blue or red, with that white trim. Everybody I know wants one. It's cool and affordable."

Patti moved closer to the screen and squinted. "Cynthia Quarles drives a car like that and she's not young. Is that her? What's she doing?"

Hunter bent for a closer look. "Dumpster diving!"

The woman threw one of the container tops back and returned to her car.

She swung the rear door open, removed a large, bulky item and retraced her steps to the garbage corral, where she pitched the item into the open container. She glanced in quickly before lowering the lid back into position then closed the wooden gate and returned to her car. Brake lights flashed before the car moved off slowly, around the rose garden and out of sight.

"Why would someone take garbage to a restaurant garbage can? You know she's got her own container at home."

"Fish guts," Hunter said. "She didn't want them stinking up her garage."

"So everybody at the pier gets to smell it?"

"Oh, no. Of course not. Household garbage gets picked up once or twice a week, but restaurant garbage is picked up every morning. You know our little continental breakfast at the motel? It counts as a restaurant, so we get daily garbage pick-up. I'll bet you do here, too."

Interesting. "Can we watch this again?"

Chapter 15

We looked at the critical part of video a couple more times before I walked out to the lobby with my phone and called Chief Boozer.

"It was recorded Thursday night," I told him. "Lee and Jamie parked at the pier and walked away then came back to the car an hour later. Then a couple of hours after that, someone drove up and discarded a big bundle." I looked around to be sure nobody was listening. I had butterflies in my stomach, but I was trying to sound cool and not oversell it.

Chief Boozer said he'd be there in thirty minutes.

I went back to the office, told them what I'd learned and asked Hunter, "Can you stay?"

He waved empty hands, signifying an open schedule. "I'm free until six. What's this about, exactly?"

"Probably fish guts, as you said." I gave him a grin.

"I think this image can be cleaned up some, but I wouldn't want to mess it up."

"I suppose the police department has its own experts for that sort of thing. If they don't, they may need you."

"That's a real job, you think? Forensic geek? I like the sound of it. Better than desk clerk."

"Oh, Hunter." Patti rolled her eyes and bounced her curls.

Chief Boozer and Officer Montgomery must have been nearby. They made it to my office in about ten minutes.

I introduced Hunter, who explained what website we were looking at and the generalities of how he had coaxed it into revealing the past. I was sure the Chief didn't follow it, but Mary Montgomery was unpredictable.

Hunted queued up the relevant section, and the three of us moved behind the chairs to give Boozer and Montgomery the best view of the 15-inch screen.

When they'd watched it multiple times, I said, "Hunter thinks there may be some way of enhancing the image so you can see more clearly who she is and maybe see what she's discarding."

"I've seen that car," the chief said.

"Cynthia Quarles," Patti announced with certainty. "The car belonged to her son, but he's in England. It's probably parked outside right this minute." She gestured toward the parking lot.

Nobody said anything.

Patti's voice rose. "You can see in the video it's her."

I spoke up. "Hunter says the vehicle is some special model."

"A Toyota FJ Cruiser." Officer Montgomery spoke without emotion. "We have two yellow ones in town." She looked at her boss. "One belongs to that kid at the golf course, but he doesn't have the spare on the back."

The chief nodded and stood up, hitching up his gear belt. "I think it's time for a talk with Ms. Quarles."

Montgomery followed him out of the office, but they were back in a couple of minutes. "Has she been here today?" Montgomery was leaning in at the doorway.

I looked at Patti.

"She's been in her office all day with the door closed. Talking to somebody."

"I think you've been hearing a radio." Chief Boozer rested a hand high on the doorframe.

I asked, "A radio? She hasn't been in at all?"

Patti and I looked at each other, eyes wide.

"I think I should call her at home. An employee who skips work and doesn't call in? The week after we have a murder on the premises? Of course we should check on her."

Boozer shrugged laconically but didn't disagree. He came in and perched on the edge of the worktable, close enough to hear everything.

Patti showed me the phone number and Cynthia Quarles answered on the third ring. I told her who I was, as if she hadn't just seen my name on her phone.

"I wondered if you were okay, since you aren't at work today."

"Just a minute," she said.

There was a delay of a minute or more, with muffled sounds of conversation and fumbling. Then I heard a man's voice, loud and confident.

"Ms. Mack. This is Dan Vincent."

I shifted the phone to speaker so everyone could hear. Boozer and Montgomery glanced at each other and Montgomery muttered in disgust.

Dan Vincent drawled on. "I'm going to be representing Ms. Quarles in this matter. I've advised her not to talk with you or anyone else from Harbor Village. Just as a formality, of course. If you have further business to discuss with her, you'll need to call my office. I'll give you the number if you like." He pronounced the word to rhyme with the dance. Rumba.

I pulled the legal pad around and wrote down his name and the number he gave, thanked him and hung up.

Boozer sighed. "Defense attorney. The best money can buy. So she's expecting us. I'd better get with the prosecutor."

* * * *

Patti and I went to Cynthia's office after the cops left. The door was unlocked, the key box door standing open. Inside, it looked just as I remembered, keys in place, tagged in a three-color code. Someone on Boozer's team must have left the radio playing last night. I turned it off and locked up, and we went home just a little late.

* * * *

Stephanie called at bedtime to say they were in Houston. "You should see this place." She was speaking softly because Barry was asleep.

"Where are you?"

"At Lee's house. Is it Dad's now?"

I assumed she found it luxurious. "I don't know anything about it, honey. Don't jump to conclusions. It may be mortgaged to the hilt. Is your father there?"

"Somewhere. I think we're in a guest wing."

"Be nice to Travis. He's having a rough time."

"Why did you call him that?"

"Call him what? I said Travis."

"That's what I mean. You never, ever say Travis. You say 'your father,' or 'your dad.' Does it have some deep, dark significance?"

"No, no significance." Was what she said true? "I hear he has a lovely daughter. G'night, honey."

"Night, Mom."

* * * *

Thursday began like a normal workday, or the closest thing to normal since I came to Harbor Village. There were no bodies to be identified, no police cars or detectives in sight, no fire trucks and no yellow tape strung around the building. And there was also no Cynthia, no Michelle and certainly no Jamie. Even the rain seemed to be disappearing.

I left my umbrella at home and got to the office early, to make a phone call to Houston. I was hoping the offices wouldn't be closed all day for Lee's memorial service, and I got lucky. I had a long conversation with the director of HR then opened the laptop and completed a letter I had drafted while eating breakfast. I sent it to Patti with instructions for printing multiple copies.

Since she wasn't in yet, I sent Patti another quick note asking her to see if Emily could come in to help us with a special project. "And Stewart, too, if he's available for a couple of hours." It wasn't a scheduled workday for Emily, and I didn't know if she would be available on short notice. "Tell Stewart we'll need two extra passkeys," I added as an afterthought.

Patti was busy with publicity, posting last-minute notices of the political forum on Facebook sites. "I'm going to e-mail reminders to everybody. The media outlets, too."

She still had flyers on hand for residents who came to the big house. I picked up a few copies from the stack on her desk and walked over to the Assisted Living building. A dozen residents were still finishing breakfast, and others had already moved to the front sitting room. I gave the flyers to Rutie for distribution to staff and residents, waved to Ivy and stopped to watch the kittens chasing each other through a cardboard box. Someone had cut out kitten-sized doors and windows.

Ivy joined me after a few minutes and the two of us went on to the little back office that had belonged to Jamie. It had no windows and was crowded with furniture.

"We need to do something about this office." I pulled out a chair and slid into it.

I began by thanking her for the good work she had done all week, and under such difficult circumstances. I could feel her bracing up, waiting for me to say her services were no longer needed. But I inquired about her licenses and certifications instead and, when the answers were what I expected, offered her a permanent job, directing the Assisted Living program. Ivy was delighted. She didn't need time to think about it, just accepted on the spot.

"Come by the office later and we'll complete the paperwork," I said.

"I know you're still getting used to this place, but do you have suggestions for me? Ideas about what you'd like to see in this unit?"

I hadn't come with ideas already developed, but we spent a few minutes talking about possibilities. I told her about the open, inclusive management style I was employing.

"You might create some committees. Put residents on them, along with the staff. We're doing something similar for the entire facility. An activity committee, entertainment committee, meals, whatever. I'd like to get residents more involved in decisions. People seem excited about the idea."

We talked for several minutes before Ivy mentioned the kittens.

"We're going to need some money for them, I suppose. Food and litter and toys. Vet visits will be the most expensive thing. It won't be cheap with four of them."

"Why don't you ask Melba? Isn't that her name? I haven't met her."

Ivy looked puzzled. "You mean the...what is she, the activity director?"

"Right. She's got a budget and hasn't used much of it, even though the year's more than half gone. She can afford the kittens, I'm sure."

"I'm glad to know she has a budget." Her eyes narrowed. "She's been in and out awfully fast this week. I'd better leave her a message to talk with me next time she's here. I need to find out what her schedule is, so I can hold her to it."

She pulled out a writing surface on the old wooden desk and ran her finger down a list of phone numbers printed there. Melba's name was in the typed section. Ivy copied the phone number onto a sticky note.

I saw Michelle's name and phone number on the list. "Have you talked with Michelle at all?"

"Not since Tuesday," Ivy said. "I wasn't comfortable saying much while I was temporary, but I've been arranging for backups for her. I was hoping she'd show up today."

"Let me call her." I took a sticky note from the pad on the desk and wrote down the number as Ivy read it out.

"Is she going to come back?"

I shrugged. "I heard a rumor she won't. Better make plans without her and start thinking about a replacement. We'll know for certain in a couple of days. Maybe one of the part-time people wants to go full-time. And there's one other thing. Emily came in here a few days ago looking for a receipt book."

"Emily?"

"The bookkeeper. Red hair."

"Oh, yes. Nice girl. Talks like a machine gun."

"That's the one. She found what she was looking for in this desk, but I wonder if she might have overlooked anything. Mind if I check?"

"Of course not."

We went through both desks. The one in the back office was empty, except for a few pencil stubs and a bulldog clip holding a skinny, dried out joint, of the herbal variety.

"Now who would that belong to," Ivy asked, dripping sarcasm.

"I'll flush it." I took a tissue out of my trouser pocket and wrapped the joint. "You'd better come with me, so I have a witness."

Ivy led the way to a ladies' room across from the dining room. I held the little bundle under running water in the sink until it was soaked then dropped it into the toilet. Ivy flushed, and we watched it circle and disappear.

The other desk in Jamie's office contained two file folders, one fat and bound with rubber bands, one of which broke when I removed it. Inside were two receipt books like the one Emily had found. A second folder held an orderly collection of bank statements, addressed to a post office box in town. The name on the account was Ferrell & Associates.

"Just what I was looking for." It wasn't true. It never occurred to me that the bank records would be at Harbor Village. But it was a lucky find, considering Jamie and Michelle were on their way back to Fairhope and might try to clean up their trail.

I continued to search but found nothing else of interest in the desks. I took both folders and stopped at the front office to gather the staff. We went to the sitting area, where a few residents were dozing or playing with kittens.

"I'd like all of you to join me in welcoming Nurse Ivy to the permanent staff of Harbor Village."

There was a round of applause and hugs, everyone proclaiming their delight. I gave the tuxedo kitten a scratch under the chin and went back to my office.

Patti had the letter to Cynthia Quarles ready for signing. She watched with a twinkle in her eyes as I read through it, noting the power of the phrasing HR had come up with.

Cynthia wasn't fired; her relationship with Harbor Village was *terminated,* due to *complicity in or neglect of recently revealed fraudulent rental practices.* I grinned at Patti and signed four copies then turned them over to her for distribution.

"Use Registered Mail for Cynthia's copy, so she has to sign when she receives it."

"Right. I talked with Emily and Stewart. They'll be here by ten. Oh, I'd better hurry if I'm going to get back by then." A cloud crossed her face. "You do want me, too, don't you?"

"Yes. We'll wait for you."

She smiled again but hesitated. "I was wondering, are you thinking about giving the rental agent job to Emily?"

I smiled. "No, I don't think so. I've got someone else in mind."

She looked disappointed. I was ready to tell her my idea, but she asked another question. "Can you tell me what this special project is?"

"Sure. We're going to check all the rental units."

Her eyes grew large. "You know there are two hundred of them."

I nodded. "That's why we need help."

Jim Bergen came in while Patti was at the post office. "Got any coffee around here?"

"Let's go to the dining room." I led the way.

On the walk down the hall, I made a wager with myself. Either he knew something, or he thought I did. Which would it be? We got coffee, and somehow a little plate of cookies appeared on the table.

Jim pulled the plate closer and asked, "Don't you want some, too?"

"How do you know they're not for me?"

He grinned and slid the plate back where it had been. "Have you heard about Cynthia Quarles?"

"Only that she's been dismissed from her job here. What else is happening?"

"She's got two lawyers, one of them a big shot out of Mobile." He rubbed his thumb and two fingers together to indicate money, lots of it. "They're trying to work out a deal for her."

"What's the charge?"

He spoke with cookie crumbs on his chin. "What do you think? Murder."

"Oh. Not theft? Or fraud? Or embezzlement?"

He looked crestfallen. "I didn't think about that. Is that why she's fired?"

I had a lot to do, and I didn't spend much time sipping coffee and watching Jim snack. I went back to the office and wrote up an announcement welcoming Ivy to Harbor Village and sent it to Patti for distribution.

Next I got a legal pad, went to Cynthia's office, folded the door of the key box back against the wall and pulled a chair up. Using a marker, I listed, in order, each apartment in the residential buildings at Harbor Village and drew vertical lines down the pages, creating a chart where we could verify the rental status. If it had a green tab, I put a check in the first column, headed Rented. If there was a yellow tag, I put a check in the next column, marked Vacant. Units with red tags were probably rented off the official books, and I identified them with a star in the third column, to indicate that special attention was required. A wide space remained, where we could record a few words of explanation. Ready for rental, work needed, something else.

I wasn't quite finished when Patti came to say she, Emily, and Stewart were waiting in my office.

"Do we have enough water for everybody?"

She went off to check while I finished up. "

"And clipboards," I called after her.

When I got to the office five minutes later, Patti was standing at the worktable, arranging yellow and white flowers in a pair of short blue vases. Emily and Stewart sat side by side, sipping water and watching her.

"I got two bunches of flowers while I was out. Daisies and Peruvian lilies. We'll put both vases in the ballroom tonight, one on the candidates' table and one with the refreshments. Is that okay?"

"Perfect," Emily answered.

Patti added, "And we'll move them to your office and the lobby tomorrow."

"The lobby and your desk," I said. "More people will see them there."

"Oh, do you think so?"

I took a few minutes to explain to the group what we were about to do.

Stewart approved. "This is just like a store taking inventory. We should do it once a year, but it's never been done, not in the time I've been here."

"But you keep up with all the repairs and cleanups," Patti pointed out.

Stewart grinned. "A lot of things can fall through the cracks in eight years. I bet we get some surprises."

"Emily and I will take the south side of the street and you two can take the north side. We'd better tell Carla we'll be late for lunch so she can save us something. We've got one hundred two units on each side of the street, so as soon as you get the hang of things, split up. Then we might finish by noon."

I gave a quick rundown of exactly how we'd proceed. "If it barks, mark it rented and move on. If you see furniture through the windows or chairs on the patio, there's no need to go in. But if it's empty, you have to see if it's ready to rent. What else do you need to know, Stewart?"

"See if the refrigerator and carpet are clean, or if it needs painting."

"The units marked with a star require a little extra attention. We know my unit is rented, and the Ukraine students are moving out in a day or two. Probably the other starred units are rented, but we need to know for sure, and there won't be anything in our files."

I looked around. "Everybody knows what to do? Any questions?"

"What about the units in this building?" Stewart pointed upward, to floors two and three.

"Oh." I slapped my forehead. "I forgot about them."

"Stewart and I will do them after lunch." Patti twinkled at him.

"Are we ready? I have my passkey. Stewart, do you have—"

He held up two keys, and presented one to Emily, the other to Patti.

I divided the record sheets among us. "Let's go."

I finally met the chief housekeeper, Joyce, coming out of an upstairs apartment in Riley's building. I looked over her shoulder, saw furniture, and marked the apartment as rented.

"I'm sorry I haven't tracked you down before now," I said. "I kept thinking our paths would cross."

"My path is from one apartment to the next." She pushed glasses higher on her nose. "I keep asking for more help."

We chatted for a minute and then I prepared to move on. "Which way are you going, left or right?"

"Let's see." She got out a folded paper out of her pocket. "I'm going across the street next. I walk my legs off some days."

"Oh, don't you just hate that," I sympathized, making a mental note to check into the housekeeping procedures. Maybe a simple reorganization of schedules would give them more time to clean.

Emily and I finished our buildings at noon, but Patti and Stewart, when they showed up, seemed much happier than we were. We headed for the dining room, ready for sustenance.

"One nasty refrigerator." Patti made a face and circled the unit number

"I'm going to need a gas mask for that one," Stewart said. "Maybe I'll send one of the guys."

We laughed.

We had lunch, and an extra glass or two of tea before Patti and Stewart went off to inventory the units on floors two and three of the big house. Emily and I stayed at the table, and I steered the conversation to her career plans.

"Would you want a full-time job?"

Her eyes popped wide. "Here? Definitely!"

"Business manager and bookkeeper sounds like a lot of work for one person, but since we've gotten by without a business manager for a while, and since you're handling the bookkeeping in three days, maybe it would work out."

She agreed enthusiastically.

"We're all going to spend more time talking with residents, making sure they have what they need to be safe and comfortable here, and we're all going to help each other out as needed."

"I like the bookkeeping," Emily said, "but I don't like being shut off from people all the time. Combining it with different responsibilities sounds perfect for me."

We talked about salary, and she was happy with that, too. So happy that she teared up just talking about it and had to go tend to her mascara.

The candidates' forum was only a few hours away. Carla and Liz were setting out trays and cups, disposable plates and glasses, sweetener and napkins. Everything they needed to serve refreshments.

Mr. Levine had stopped in to check their progress and obviously he had a case of nerves.

"Let's start taking things down there," he told Carla, snapping his fingers unconsciously. "I want to be sure we have enough tables set up before the work crew gets away."

Lizzie was putting on a clean apron, but her hands shook so that Carla had to tie it for her. "I'm just going to keep things neat and restock the trays," she told Carla. "I'm not going to pour. I'll spill something."

"Whatever you like." Carla patted her on the back. "Don't worry. You'll do just fine."

My office still gave me a little shock every time I walked in. I sat at the desk and swiveled the chair around for the panoramic view. Had Patti watered the fig tree? I rolled back and leaned over to feel the soil. Dry, but I didn't know where to find a water container.

I rolled back to the desk and reached into my pocket to pull out a tissue to wipe my hand. Attached was a blue sticky note. Michelle, it said, with a phone number.

I brushed off my hand and reached for my phone.

A woman answered on the third ring. "Hello," she said, in sort of a bark.

"Michelle?" I knew it wasn't.

"Michelle who?"

"Uhmm," I stalled, trying to think of Michelle's last name.

"Who are you?"

Uh-oh. "Officer Montgomery? Is that you? This is Cleo Mack, at Harbor Village. I was trying to reach Michelle, in assisted living. Did I get the wrong number?"

Montgomery snorted. "Honey, this is the phone you turned in. We charged it up and just waited for somebody to call. And who should that somebody be but you! Naturally. Now tell me about this Michelle. Has she got a last name, or not?"

* * * *

Patti asked what we were going to do without a rental agent. "There are a couple of messages waiting for Cynthia already." She shuffled through the message slips. "Nothing looks urgent. Yet."

I called Vickie, Nita's realtor friend, to ask for advice. She already knew that Cynthia was off the job. "Cynthia had an assistant," I said, "but he only works weekends and I haven't met him yet."

"He's licensed," Vickie said. "May not know much but he'll learn."

I crossed my fingers and asked, "I don't suppose you'd be interested in the job, would you?"

"I don't know. What does it pay?"

I told her Cynthia's salary and she laughed. "I'm surprised she'd work for that."

"But it's regular hours. No weekends, no expenses. Good benefits."

She laughed again. "I know I complain all the time, but real estate is a gold mine for somebody like me. I don't mind a little hard work so long as I'm having fun."

"Well, then, could you recommend somebody?"

"That I can do. Give me a couple of hours. I could've warned you about Cynthia Quarles, too, if anybody had asked."

Mr. Levine needed an extra table at the last minute. He'd forgotten to tell us that representatives from the League of Women Voters would be at the meeting, to register new voters. Stewart was cool with the last-minute details. I didn't recognize him at first, with his hair all slicked back and no tool belt.

I was the League's first customer and met Marjorie Zadnichek, a darling with twinkling eyes and steel-gray hair. Even though she still worked, she was only a couple of years younger than Nita. I didn't tell her I wouldn't be voting in the municipal election. I didn't think I knew enough about the issues or the candidates or even the city, yet. But I did promise to have lunch with her at the Birdcage Lounge on Tuesday.

Guests were beginning to take seats when I looked out the window and saw Nelson Fisher feeding the koi in the fishpond. I walked out to chat with him for a few minutes. He didn't look at me but told me the names of each fish, and I admired them. I asked him about lawn mowers, and he really warmed up. I even mentioned Travis' name, but Nelson didn't seem to remember him.

The forum was standing room only, and there wasn't a cookie left at the end. Mr. Levine and his committee, as well as Carla and Lizzie, were showered with praise and appreciation, and I got to meet the mayor and all the council members and challengers. Maybe I would vote after all.

It was a successful night, but later than I expected when we finally locked the doors.

Riley Meddors was waiting outside, to walk back to the apartment with me.

"Did you notice that Dolly stayed to the very end," he asked. "The latest she's been out in years, I'll bet. Maybe she'll stay up to see us on the ten o'clock news."

"I wonder if I can stay awake to see it."

"Mexican Trains tomorrow night." He waited on the sidewalk for me to get inside and lock the door.

Tinkerbelle was waiting, meowing. I petted her and topped off her food dish, rinsed out the water dish and refilled it. Stephanie left a message while I was in the shower and called back a few minutes later.

"Mom, it was awful. There was this woman, Michelle somebody. She stayed at the house last night. The cops came in before the service started and led her out by the arm, and then Lee's sister started crying and collapsing all over the place, and Dad had to take *her* out. And Boyd and I had to stand with Debra—that's Lee's daughter, you know—and shake hands with all these people I'd never met. Guess who was there. Rick Perry! You know, the governor of Texas."

"Former governor."

Stephanie ignored me. "I still can't believe it. And you know what? The Bushes live not far away. Meanwhile, Birmingham has *no* celebrities! We're going to stay another night, did I tell you? Debra is wonderful, and we want to get to know her better. She's Lee's daughter, did I already say that? She's my age exactly and lives in New York, and she's lost both her parents now. Do you realize she's my stepsister?" She squealed, like a stepsister was the most thrilling thing in the world.

"Technically, I guess I'm probably her closest relative now, and neither of us has a real sister. Or brother. She's going back to New York tomorrow, and we decided to stay another night, too."

"That's nice of you, sweetie." Tired as I was, I could still suppress a giggle. "I'm sure your father appreciates your being there. And our political forum was a great success."

"Your what? Oh yes, I was just about to ask."

"Right. Standing room only. Well, g'night, sweetie."

"Bye, Mom. Talk to you tomorrow."

I managed to brush Tinkerbelle thoroughly while I analyzed Stephanie's gush of words. Michelle had been at the memorial service, and Jamie had collapsed when the cops escorted Michelle out. But why were the police focusing on Michelle instead of Jamie? They must know something I didn't. They wouldn't just attack the weakest link, would they?

I was asleep in no time. And I needed no Sudoku sleep aids after the day I'd just had.

Chapter 16

My first task Friday morning was to get Stewart to show me how to write up a work order so he could change all the outside locks in the office wing.

"Can you get to it today? I'd like to get it done before the weekend. And that opening between the lobby and the office area will have to be secured, too." I was talking to myself as much as to him.

"We've got some decorative iron doors that Ms. Ferrell had me take down last year. They do look kind of like a prison. She didn't like everybody calling this the big house."

"Can they be locked?"

He nodded. "I can change the locks on them, too."

"Do they look really bad?"

Stewart shrugged and nodded yes. "They could be painted. Or we could add something decorative. A cutout giraffe pecking over the top? I can do it in a nice wood."

"Okay." I knew how Barry would love a giraffe. "I don't think anything is ever locked in Assisted Living, except the drug cart. Why don't you change the lock on Ivy's back office so she can leave the cart there when she wants to? That office is going to need your decorating touch, Stewart."

He smiled and looked around my office, which he'd improved so dramatically. "I'll put it on the list, right after Patti. So, a giraffe cutout and maybe some vines or flowers for the gate, right?"

Speaking of flowers, there were arrangements on Patti's desk and in the lobby. She was busy printing and labeling photographs from the forum. My neighbor Ann and another resident were helping put names with the pictures. Ann knitted while standing, her working yarn looped out of a big pocket.

Ann saw me observing. "Why don't you take up knitting, Cleo? It's so relaxing."

"That's what I planned to do in retirement. Will you help me?"

"Of course. Did you know we're going to be on the news? Today at noon. I know they interviewed Jim Bergen, maybe some others."

Patti's head snapped around and her curls jiggled. "Can we get a TV for the lobby? People could stop by after lunch and watch local news and socialize a little."

"Sure," I laughed. "But not by noon. I like your glasses." They were round and bright yellow, the color of a school bus.

I hadn't seen Jim since the forum. I wondered what was going on in Houston and in Chief Boozer's world, but I had my own work to do and shifted my attention to it.

Emily had prepared checks refunding deposits to the Ukrainian students. I signed all eight and the students showed up soon afterward, giving out hugs and thanks. Hunter was with them. His girlfriend made a pretty speech, saying they hoped to see us again next year.

In between visitors, I was summarizing the findings from yesterday's apartment inventory, checking our list of vacancies against Cynthia's key box. It felt good to be doing ordinary, routine tasks.

The final tally corresponded with Emily's report. There were seven units to follow up on, probably all rented off the books. I listed the apartment numbers and planned to visit the residents over the weekend. They'd need to meet our requirements and sign official leases or else move out soon.

Stewart had twenty-four units that needed attention of some sort. It might be cleaning or painting or new carpet, a broken window replaced or lesser projects like batteries for beeping smoke alarms. There were two drippy sinks and one cracked fiberglass shower that would have to be replaced.

"We've been tiling them when the fiberglass breaks down," he said.

"I don't expect you to get to all these immediately." I gave him the list.

"You heard about a doorknob falling apart for Patti? I've already replaced it and told the residents I'd come back and check anything else that's not working right. Maybe we'll do that in each building. Handyman house calls. Don't you like the sound of that?"

Eighteen units were vacant and ready for immediate rental, and most of those were upstairs in the two L-shaped buildings. There must be some reason these units didn't appeal to our target market, but I wasn't sure what we could do about it.

A couple of quick calculations showed we were close to the corporate average of seventy-nine percent occupancy, counting the units rented off the books and, until now, contributing nothing to our income.

I had discovered a discrepancy in the employee count, too. The official roster included not just Nelson Fisher, who was still on the payroll even though he no longer worked, and the two people in PT, Tiko and Cassidy, who rented their space from Harbor Village but ran their own operation.

Just as Travis had suspected, HR told me Nelson Fisher's paycheck was being deposited to the Ferrell & Associates account. Riley's warning to be skeptical of the financial data was proving to be spot on.

Patti wandered in, and I dropped the vacancy problem on her. "Eighteen vacancies, and twelve are on the second floor of the two-story, L-shaped buildings. Any ideas what we do about them?"

She tilted her head left and then right, lips pursed while she thought. "How about this. Screen those second-floor walkways and furnish them like your screened porch. Wicker chairs and tables, all-weather rugs, a ceiling fan. Add wind chimes and a string of twinkle lights." She gazed upward, sweeping her hands around, as if she were actually seeing the finished project. "Get a few plants, in beautiful pots. That creates a gathering place, not just a bare walkway. And put out birdfeeders and flowers where people can see them. Maybe a bright blue ceramic birdbath and some pink-and-white cleomes, some red salvia." She snapped out of it and looked at me. "The hummingbirds are passing through right now. Get some life in this place."

"Won't that draw squirrels?"

"People love squirrels. Get one of those whirly things that holds corn. Let the squirrels ride it."

"I'm impressed, Patti. We can give residents a social setting, something they miss by being isolated at the far end of the complex. And it gives other people a reason to walk up there, to see what's going on. We could have a cookout up there some night. You have a knack for this sort of thing, you know. Why don't you close the door so we can talk a minute?"

Her natural exuberance ratcheted up a notch. She jerked a chair up to my desk, sat and almost vibrated with pent-up enthusiasm.

"What do you think your ideal job would be?"

"Rental agent," she answered immediately.

Not the answer I'd hoped for, but it reminded me again of how similar she was to Stephanie.

"So you'd like dealing with the legal aspects of leases and taking the classes and tests and continuing education to get a real estate license.

Keeping the key box secure and organized and up-to-date, keeping up with all the available units, knowing which ones are coming available and matching them up with prospective residents?"

"Cynthia didn't do all that. She never did much of anything."

"But Cynthia may be on her way to prison. You don't want to use her as your model."

Patti recoiled in shock, eyes wide. "Are you kidding me? Prison?"

I was surprised, too; I thought she knew. "You've heard of embezzlement? That's what the diversion of rental income is."

"Oh no! Prison? Cynthia?" She flopped forward and leaned on her elbows. "What if she gives the money back?"

"Maybe the judge will reduce her sentence, but it's out of our hands. Now, back to your ideal job. What part of the rental agent's duties appeals to you?"

"Prison. Oh my gosh." She swallowed hard. "Well, maybe that last part, about talking to new residents. Getting to know them and introducing them to everybody." Her sparkle began to return.

"What you're describing sounds more like the Resident Services position."

"Okay." She did a double take. "But that's you, isn't it? Don't tell me you're leaving! Oh no." She shrieked and covered her face with both hands.

"Relax. I'm thinking I may be stuck with the director's job for a while." I immediately felt guilty for implying I didn't love this job.

Patti peeked through her fingers. "Resident Services? Would I get this office?"

I laughed. "No, you'd stay right out front, accessible to all your admirers. But I think we can spruce things up a bit out there. Did you choose a paint color yet?"

"No, but I will. I love this!" She clapped her hands. "When is it going to happen? Can I tell people? I've been so afraid I'd have to go back to driving and miss all the excitement."

Travis phoned as I was about to go to lunch. "I just got out of a meeting with your detectives."

"What's going on?"

"Everything's moving back there. I'll be there tonight."

"What about Jamie and Michelle?"

"Jamie and Michelle are returning voluntarily and cooperating with law enforcement. Translation—they're trying to save their butts."

"What're we talking about? Embezzlement or murder?"

"Jamie admits to skimming off some rent money but says the idea came from the Quarles woman."

"What about Lee? Does anyone know who killed her?"

"Officer Montgomery doesn't talk, you know. One of the detectives does and tells me they're tightening the noose. You want to have a late dinner tonight?"

"Tonight? No. I've got plans. Sorry." I didn't admit they included dominoes.

Jim Bergen met me in the lobby. "Are you having lunch here? I thought I'd join you while Nita gets her hair done. We can compare notes."

"I don't know much." I slowed my gait to match his and gave him a summary of Travis's information. "Somebody from the police department went to Houston and Jamie and Michelle consented to come back here."

He knew more than I did. "That's Henry and Clark, the detectives. And Mary Montgomery flew out last night to escort the females back. I guess they'll get here today."

"Are Jamie and Michelle under arrest?"

"I'm still thinking Jamie can wiggle out of this. Street smarts, you know." He tapped his temple. Not only did he not seem to care about Michelle, he didn't acknowledge she existed. Which was one reason the world needed social workers, I supposed—to look after the little guy, even when he, or she, wasn't very loveable.

A dozen people were already in the dining room, with more coming in behind us. I stopped at the long table and talked with residents about the candidate forum.

"Who's that handsome man with you," someone joked. "I've seen him on TV."

Jim preened under all the attention.

The steam table still had food in every tray, although not a lot, and Lizzie was smiling as she put more salad into the large bowl sitting in a bed of ice. We had a choice of thin, fried fish filets or grilled shrimp, and Jim took both. I got fish, green salad with tomatoes and two squares of polenta with corn and bits of red and green peppers visible through the grill marks.

"Why do people complain about the food here," I asked Jim. "Everything I have is good."

"It's taken an upturn. Maybe Annie's helping her."

Sure enough, Ann came out of the kitchen a few seconds later.

"Nita doesn't want any talk about murder tonight," Jim warned, taking the corner booth. It offered two advantages—it was near the dessert table, and he could observe the entire room at once, even the entrance. "Some people like a little excitement, but not Nita. That's just the way she's always been."

"I see her point. I prefer a bit more boredom, myself."

He finished his shrimp before starting on the fish. "What do you call this?" He poked a fork into the polenta. "Tastes like mush but doesn't look like it."

"Polenta. It's Italian. I think Jamie and Michelle are both being charged. Isn't that why Officer Montgomery went out there?"

"That was yesterday's news. Maybe you didn't get today's report. The fingerprint data came back, and Michelle's prints are all over a wheelchair from the storage room. That girl's looking at a murder charge."

My heart sank. "What about the lampshade? Did it have any prints?"

He shook his head. "Don't know about prints, but the frame was bent, like she wrenched it off the lamp. Which is long gone, of course."

"You know about the video? Cynthia Quarles put a lamp-sized bundle in the pier dumpster Thursday night."

"Did she now?"

"I was hoping they could trace it."

"You ever been to a landfill?" He shook his head, looking like a shaggy white buffalo.

After a moment of thought, I was shaking my head, too. "I don't like it, Jim. Michelle's a nursing assistant. Of course her fingerprints are on a wheelchair. But she doesn't have enough initiative to conk anybody. She's taking the blame for somebody else. And you know who."

It was his turn to resist conclusions. "There's that phone, too. Don't forget it, the one Dolly found. It belonged to Michelle and was found in the pool area. That says she was there."

"Okay." I agreed reluctantly. I wasn't arguing with facts. Michelle must've been at the pool. Maybe I felt a little sorry for her, but I just couldn't see her as a murderer. Couldn't someone else have left her phone at the pool, either by accident or intentionally?

I asked Jim, "Any news about Cynthia Quarles?"

"Nope." He shook his head. "People like her..." He made his money sign again, rubbing thumb against fingers. "They get off. I expected Chief Boozer to meet us here. Must've got caught up in something."

"Cynthia Quarles may not be as rich as you think. She drives an inexpensive car."

"Have you seen her house?"

I had not.

I went back to the office a few minutes later and spent a lot of time calculating that each housekeeper had to clean seven units a day, not including the offices, ballroom, hallways, the lobby and whatever else they were responsible for. We needed to add another housekeeper now, before any more apartments were rented. I wrote a note and left it for Joyce.

I didn't see Chief Boozer all day, but I did leave the office a little early, just for a change of scenery. I drove down to the pier to admire the bay. It was already blue and glassy after the rain, with pelicans sitting on every post around the marina. The sky was too clear for a cathedral sunset, and there was no breeze. I took the walking trail and did a couple of slow laps then sat on a still-damp bench in the shade and watched a ship heading toward the harbor north of Mobile.

The parking space Jamie and Lee had used last Thursday was nearby, empty at the moment. I looked at it then beyond, up the bluff to the trees where the pier cam was mounted. I suspected Michelle, half of the co-dependent poster couple, had taken control of the camera Thursday night, zooming in to watch Lee and Jamie walk to their car after dinner. Maybe she wanted to see how Lee was reacting after learning about the rent scam, or maybe she just wanted to know when they'd get back to Harbor Village.

I wondered if Hunter could work some magic on the computer in the Assisted Living office and persuade it to reveal if it had been used for that purpose.

My phone buzzed. It was Stephanie, calling from the Houston airport, where she and Boyd and Barry had dropped her new stepsister. I told her where I was and how beautiful the bay looked.

"We can be there by midnight," she said, "if you want company."

"You know the answer to that."

A few minutes before six, as I crossed the boulevard, heading for Nita's and a rousing game of dominoes, a police car whipped to the curb and Chief Boozer stepped out.

"Got your lamp!" He had a big smile on his face.

I took a big step onto the sidewalk. "You're kidding! Where was it?"

"Come on, let's go in so I only have to tell it once."

He took long strides to the Bergens' door, and I hurried after him.

"We put an observer out at the landfill," he was saying a few minutes later, a tall glass of iced tea in hand and an attentive audience circled around. "They keep records about where they dump on which day, so they knew where to look. And after a few hours of digging, they spotted something."

"The lamp," Jim said, nodding like it was exactly what he'd predicted.

Boozer nodded, too. "Wrapped in a ragged old quilt. The plug's stretched out from being ripped out of the outlet, and the bulb's broken off."

"Does it have fingerprints?" Jim asked.

Dolly asked, "Was it the murder weapon?"

Riley had his own question. "Any DNA on the quilt? Can you identify it from the video?"

"The video was the key." Boozer looked at me. "I want to hang onto that young man."

"Yes. Hunter is a jewel. I wish we had a job for him."

Boozer thought there was enough evidence to convict Cynthia. "But of what, I can't say. Charges get reduced, you know."

"What about the embezzlement," I asked.

"Quarles and Barnes will be charged, for sure. And Michelle will definitely get obstruction of justice, for moving the body. She's admitting it freely."

"Anything to avoid a murder charge," Jim said. "But Jamie had nothing to do with the murder, did she, Chief? I told you."

"She didn't harm her sister. I'll give you that," Boozer answered cautiously. "Phone records show Ms. Ferrell called Cynthia Quarles from here, right after dinner. We don't know if she fired her, or threatened her with arrest, or maybe asked her to come over, but whatever was said, Ms. Quarles came here and attacked Lee, using a bronze lamp as a weapon."

Riley had been listening attentively. "That doesn't sound premeditated. Maybe it *should* be a lesser charge than murder."

Boozer didn't disagree. "Jamie and Michelle were out back in their building, with no idea Ms. Quarles was here. And Jamie persuaded Michelle to go talk to Lee, to smooth things over about the rent fraud. Michelle found her dead."

Jim was nodding again.

Boozer took a drink of tea. "Michelle thought Jamie had killed Lee and sent her to cover it up. And she decided—spur of the moment, she says—to move the body to the pool and hope it would look like an accident."

I looked at Dolly. "And Michelle put her phone down at the pool and forgot it."

"And I found it." Dolly seemed surprised.

"And called us." Boozer lifted his hands, signaling the end of the story.

"I don't think there was any love lost between those two sisters." Nita sounded sad.

Jim agreed.

"There's a lot of evidence," the chief said. "Fingerprints and biologic traces, even a video of her putting the weapon in a dumpster down at the pier. This lady is responsible for finding that." He nodded at me.

"Thanks to Hunter."

"But you knew to ask for his help. And the video told us where to look for the weapon we recovered today. But Ms. Quarles has got a good defense attorney."

Riley said, "I wonder if Michelle was in the habit of disguising deaths around here."

Dolly frowned. "Maybe they were high on something. Weren't some drugs stolen?"

Chief Boozer shrugged. "It's possible. Might explain why they didn't come forward right away."

"And why Michelle wouldn't take a drug test this week," I realized.

Nita looked at Jim, a faint smile curving her lips. "Was it, by chance, your idea for Jamie to leave town?"

He looked surprised but not totally innocent. "I hated to see her go, but it might've helped." He wasn't admitting anything.

I thought about Jamie's promotion. "Do you still think Lee died about eight o'clock? The message transferring Jamie to Charleston was sent after ten. And Travis says the terminology wasn't what Lee would've used."

Chief Boozer already knew all that. "So which one of them do you think wrote the message? Jamie or Michelle?"

I shrugged. "Lee's phone was in Jamie's car."

"But Michelle did most of their driving."

"Too bad she couldn't transfer some of her devotion to more deserving people," Nita said. "But I wonder, Chief Boozer, how that phone got into Jamie's car. Lee was using it after dinner, you said."

Boozer turned from Nita to me. "Any ideas?"

"Well, let's think it through." I shifted into my *one cell at a time* mode. "Michelle moves Lee's body to the pool, where she puts down her own phone and forgets it." I traced the movements with my hand, from big house to pool. "She has to return the wheelchair to the storage room and, after that, she goes back through the lobby. Lee's purse is there, on the couch or the floor, and Michelle takes it with her so it won't draw attention to the lobby and whatever evidence is there."

Riley spoke up. "I think that's exactly what happened. And when she got out to the parking lot, the two SUVs were parked with the driver's doors together. She had to walk between them to get into Jamie's car, but she was carrying the key fob for Lee's car, too. That explains why the lights flashed on both cars."

He gave a slight bow to me, and I nodded, finally understanding.

"I like it, Riley." Jim slapped the leather arm of his recliner.

Boozer liked it, too. "That's the first explanation that's made sense of the lights flashing."

Maybe he thought I had made it up? I resumed my analysis. "So she put Lee's purse into Jamie's car and drove around to assisted living. She must have told Jamie what she'd done—at least that she'd taken care of the problem—and when she realized Jamie hadn't killed Lee, didn't even know she was dead, she knew they needed to get away from here."

"Probably intended to throw the purse off a bridge," Jim mused.

I agreed. "But she went through it first and found Lee's phone. She must've known about the job opening in Charleston. Maybe they'd talked about it."

"Poor ol' Jamie. Believed her sister finally appreciated her." Jim shook his head gravely. "How much cash was in Ms. Ferrell's purse?"

Boozer smiled. "None when we got it."

"Yep," Jim said, "that's Michelle."

Riley spoke up again. "When we drove past the lobby about eight, the lights were on. Somebody turned them off in the next couple of minutes. Who was it?"

Boozer answered right away, revealing he'd already worked through this point. "The parrot lamp was always used as a night light, but the Quarles woman took it with her when she left. So when Michelle arrived, the lobby was dark."

We nodded, and he continued. "She might've thought Ms. Ferrell had left, but she flipped the switch for the chandelier and saw Ms. Ferrell was dead. Maybe she saw you drive past and turned the light off while she figured out what to do. And that's the moment when you walked around the building."

Jim finished the scenario. "While Michelle was coming up with the idea of a drowning."

Our little group fell silent again. Finally, Chief Boozer sighed and got to his feet. "Well, I need to move along. Thank you for the tea."

"So sad." Nita got up and took his hand.

We all thanked him for the personal report and for the opportunity to understand the drama that had played out around us. Then Nita and Jim walked the chief to the door and saw him off.

It was almost time for the sandwiches to arrive. Four of us, still subdued, moved to the table and began to set up our game of Mexican Trains. Jim stopped at the doorway, gave us all a silent salute and disappeared into the back of the apartment.

Riley flipped the last of the dominoes face down and moved the score pad into position at his side, and we each drew out our seven dominoes.

We played one quick round and were setting up for the next one when Riley asked, "Did anybody see Nelson Fisher out riding a lawn mower this afternoon? I thought that man died a year ago but there he was, back on the job, as good as ever."

When the doorbell rang, Jim was on the scene in a flash. And just as quickly, he was back.

"Look who's here."

I glanced over my shoulder to see Travis McKenzie staring at me. "I didn't mean to interrupt anything."

"Oh, you're not interrupting," Jim assured him. "I wish you'd been a little earlier."

"Chief Boozer was here," Dolly said. "He explained everything. Somebody else can tell you."

"Come on back to my office." Jim steered Travis to the back room. "Nita, get out another plate when the sandwiches get here."

I noticed that Riley was grinning at me. I raised my eyebrows. "What? What is it?"

"It's your turn."

He smiled, and I smiled back.

CPSIA information can be obtained
at www.ICGtesting.com
Printed in the USA
LVHW092148230519
618963LV00001B/64/P